Bloodline of the Eternal Ocean

Book One of The Eternal Ocean Series

Lyndall Kai

Book One of The Eternal Ocean Series
A Novel
Born of waves. Bound by blood.
The hidden bloodline connecting Atlantis,
the lost tribe of Israel, and the throne of Kings
Lyndall Kai

© 2026 Lyndall Kai. All rights reserved.
No part of this publication may be reproduced, distributed, or transmitted in any form or by any means, including photocopying, recording, or other electronic or mechanical methods, without the prior written permission of the author, except in the case of brief quotations embodied in critical reviews and certain other non-commercial uses permitted by copyright law.

ISBN: 978-1-7645543-0-5
Published by: Lyndall Kai
First published: 2026
Cover design by Lyndall Kai.

This is a work of fiction. Names, characters, places, and incidents are either the product of the author's imagination or are used fictitiously. Any resemblance to actual persons, living or dead, events, or locales is entirely coincidental.
www.lyndallkai.com[1]

---

1. http://www.lyndallkai.com/

For the swimmers who forgot they were the Ocean,
and for those who are beginning to remember
The eternal ocean of consciousness knows no boundaries,
no time, no separation—only the dance of remembering and forgetting.
— Ancient wisdom tradition

CONTENTS

A Reader's Guide to The Eternal Ocean

Introduction for New Readers

If you're holding this book, you're about to embark on a journey that weaves together history, mystery, and consciousness in ways that may challenge what you think you know about the past—and about yourself.

This story doesn't ask you to believe anything. It only asks you to imagine. What if?

A Note Before You Begin

Bloodline of the Eternal Ocean is a work of fiction. The characters, events, and organisations within it are imagined. But they are built on ground that is real.

The **Merovingian dynasty** ruled Francia from roughly 450 to 750 CE. Their origins remain genuinely debated by historians, and legends about the bloodline have persisted for centuries. The **Tribe of Asher**, one of the twelve tribes of Israel, scattered after the Assyrian conquest of 722 BCE; the question of where their descendants ended up is one history has never fully answered. The **Monastery of Hemis** in Ladakh exists. Documents purporting to describe a young Yeshua studying in the East have been claimed, debated, and dismissed by scholars since the nineteenth century.

The **Hemis manuscripts** referenced in this novel are disputed. Whether they are genuine, fabricated, or something more complicated, readers are encouraged to investigate for themselves.

Atlantis and Ancient Wisdom

The lost civilisation of Atlantis, first described by the philosopher Plato, has captured imaginations for over two millennia. Whether it was a real place, a metaphor, or a myth, the story of Atlantis represents humanity's search for a golden age of wisdom we may have lost. In this book, Atlantis serves as a symbol for knowledge that exists beyond conventional history—wisdom encoded in bloodlines, landscapes, and consciousness itself.

Consciousness as an Ocean

Throughout the book, consciousness is portrayed not as something confined to individual minds, but as a vast, shared ocean in which we all swim. This is a metaphor drawn from various mystical and philosophical traditions, suggesting that our awareness may be more interconnected than we typically imagine. You don't need to accept this as fact—simply allow it to serve as the story's guiding metaphor.

The philosophical concept at the heart of this story — consciousness as a shared ocean rather than a collection of separate minds — appears in one form or another in Buddhist, Hindu, Sufi, Christian contemplative, and various indigenous traditions. This novel asks what it might mean if those traditions were describing the same thing.

Everything else: the characters, the families, the conspiracy, the bloodline connections, the Remnant — fiction, built on the questions that real history leaves open.

[From the Archive of the Eternal Ocean — all documents, operations, and agencies within this series are entirely fictional]

▪ CLASSIFIED — EYES ONLY · UNIT 14 · SONGLINE OPERATION

▪ CLASSIFIED — EYES ONLY · UNIT 14 · SONGLINE OPERATION

SUBJECT: ROUSSEAU, Amélie D. — Academic / Field Asset (Unwitting)

FILE REF: SONGLINE / OMEGA-3 / ██████████████████

STATUS: Under active surveillance. Do NOT approach. Do NOT intercept. Do NOT alert subject.

NOTE: Subject's research document published 14 October 2024. 1,000,000+ downloads within 7 days. Containment window has closed. Subject has become a vector. ████████████████████ confirms bloodline markers present.

Grandmother (ÉLISE ROUSSEAU, deceased) was known to us.

Subject is not yet aware of operational interest.

She will find the manuscripts. She always does.

Let her find them. Then we move.

AUTHORISED BY: ████████████████ · DIRECTOR CRALE · EYES ONLY

PROLOGUE

The Inheritance

Paris, April 2024 — Six Months Earlier

The apartment still smelled of her.

Lavender water and old books and something Amélie could never name — something that had been simply Grand-mère for as long as she could remember. She stood in the doorway of the rue des Rosiers flat and could not make herself step inside. It had been three days since the funeral. She had promised the notaire she would sort through the belongings by the end of the week.

She had been standing in this doorway for twenty minutes.

Her grandmother had lived here for sixty-one years. Amélie could track her own entire life in this apartment — the small chair by the window where she'd done homework at six years old, the kitchen table where she'd cried over her first heartbreak at seventeen, the narrow corridor where Grand-mère had held her face in both hands after Amélie's mother died and said: Tu n'es pas seule. Tu n'as jamais été seule. You are not alone. You have never been alone.

She had believed her then. She was less certain now.

She finally stepped inside.

The flat was exactly as it always was. Impossibly tidy. Every book on its shelf. Every photograph in its frame. Grand-mère Élise had been ninety-three and she had not conceded a single inch to old age — not in her posture, not in her mind, not in the fierce order of her small domain. Amélie trailed her fingers along the spines of the books on the hallway shelf. French history. Medieval manuscripts. The Bible in four languages. A worn copy of the Zohar that had no business being in a Parisian flat belonging to a woman who attended Mass every Sunday.

She had always meant to ask about that.

She never had.

On the kitchen table was the box. A plain wooden box, hinged, no bigger than a shoebox, with Amélie's name written on a small card in her grandmother's handwriting. The notaire had given her a long look when she'd picked it up at the reading of the will. As if he knew something. As if he'd been waiting for this moment and was relieved it had finally arrived.

She sat at the kitchen table and looked at the box for a long time without opening it.

The handwriting on the card was still sharp and clear. Grand-mère had always had beautiful penmanship — she'd been taught by nuns, she'd said once, and they had not tolerated sloppiness in any form. Amélie could still hear her voice saying it.

Pour Amélie. Ouvre seulement quand tu es prête à voir.

For Amélie. Open only when you are ready to see.

Amélie pressed her palm flat against the wooden lid.

She was thirty-four years old. She had a doctorate from the Sorbonne. She had spent her career studying the dead and their secrets. She had held her grandmother's hand as the life left it, had watched the chest still, had done what was required in the days that followed with the efficiency of someone determined not to fall apart in public.

She was not ready.

She opened the box anyway.

The first thing she saw was a photograph she had never seen before — her mother, young, perhaps twenty, standing somewhere coastal that Amélie didn't recognise. Her mother was laughing at whoever held the camera. Her hair was loose. She looked free in a way she had never quite looked in Amélie's memory of her, which was filtered through illness and effort and the shadow of what was coming.

Amélie pressed the photograph to her chest and closed her eyes. Maman.

She allowed herself sixty seconds. She had learned, after her mother died, to measure grief in intervals — to let herself feel it fully but briefly, like going underwater and coming back up, because if she stayed under too long she wouldn't surface. Sixty seconds. Then she put the photograph carefully aside and kept reading.

The letter was at the bottom of the box, in an envelope sealed with wax — old-fashioned, deliberate, as if Grand-mère had wanted even the act of opening it to feel significant. Amélie broke the seal with her thumbnail and unfolded two pages of her grandmother's careful script.

Ma chérie,

If you're reading this, I'm gone. And you're finally ready to know the truth about what you are.

You're not just French. Not just Parisian. Not just academic. You carry something older. Something that has been passed down through the women in our family for longer than records remember.

Your great-great-grandmother had it. I had it. Your mother had it, though she died before she could teach you. And you have it. I've seen the signs since you were a child.

The knowing before you should know. The sensing of others' feelings. The dreams that come true. The ability to find things, to know things, to perceive things that others miss. You've spent your life explaining it away — intuition, good guessing, coincidence. But it's not coincidence. It's inheritance.

We come from Asher. One of the lost tribes. The ones who were never lost — just hidden. The ones who carried the gift of seeing what others cannot see. The blessing Jacob spoke of. The oil Moses promised. It's not metaphor. It's biology. It's consciousness. It's what flows through our blood.

The documents in this box will show you the evidence. But Amélie — be careful. There are others who know about the bloodlines. Who hunt for them. Who try to control them or eliminate them. The families who stole our inheritance centuries ago still search for those who carry the original markers. They want what we have. Or they want to ensure we never awaken to it.

There are two kinds of people in this story, my love. I don't mean good and evil — it has never been that simple, and anyone who tells you otherwise is selling something. I mean those who learned to give, and those who learned to take. Those who discovered they could dive into something deep and beautiful and bring back gifts for others. And those who looked at the same depth and saw only what could be owned, controlled, withheld. Both lines go back further than history. Both run through the families whose names you will find in this box.

When the shape of it begins to frighten you — and it will, my darling, I won't lie to you — remember this: the ones who take are not monsters. They are people who made a choice so long ago it became their nature. Generation after generation choosing the shore until they forgot the water existed. That does not make them less dangerous. But it means they are lost, not evil. And you were never raised to abandon the lost.

I never taught you the practices. I thought I was protecting you. Letting you live a normal life. Now I see that was a mistake. You need to know what you are so you can protect yourself. So you can choose whether to develop the gifts or let them lie dormant.

But if you choose to awaken — and I think you will, because the blood calls and you've always been too curious for your own good — find the others. The Remnant. They're scattered, hidden, but they're out there. Descendants like you. Practitioners who remember. Teachers who preserved what was almost lost.

Find them. Learn from them. And then decide what to do with this inheritance.

The world is changing. Consciousness is rising. What we carry may be needed more in your generation than it was in mine.

I love you. I'm proud of you. And I'm sorry for leaving you with this burden.

But it's also a gift. Remember that. What we carry is sacred. Don't let them make you forget.

Grand-mère

Amélie sat at the kitchen table for a long time after she finished reading.

Outside, Paris continued as it always did — the clatter of the street, a child's voice from the courtyard below, someone's radio trailing through an open window. The city had no opinion about what had just happened to her. It offered neither confirmation nor comfort. It simply went on.

She looked at the other contents of the box. Letters. Documents. A genealogical chart that went back further than should have been possible — past the Revolution, past the Renaissance, past the Middle Ages. Names she recognised from her research. Merovingian names. Royal names. Names that shouldn't have been in her family tree but were.

She did not reach for any of it yet.

She sat with the letter in her hands and thought about her mother's voice in the hospital — don't let them convince you it isn't real — and thought about the Zohar on the hallway shelf and the notaire's careful look, and thought about every time in her life she had known something she had no logical right to know and had explained it away, because explaining it away was safer.

Then she reached for the documents, and began to read.

CHAPTER ONE

The Decision

Paris, October 2024

She had not slept properly in six months.

Dr. Amélie Rousseau sat in a café in the Marais, drinKing espresso and trying not to cry. She had a doctorate in medieval history from the Sorbonne. She had published two well-received books on Merovingian France. She had been on track for tenure. Everything had been going exactly as planned.

Then her grandmother died — and left her a box that changed everything.

She had spent the months since trying to verify what the box contained. To prove the documents were forgeries, family legends, wishful genealogical thinKing. But everything checked. The names were real. The connections were documented. The trail led back exactly where her grandmother claimed.

And the more she researched, the more she found. Not just about her family. But about other families. Patterns in royal marriages. Genetic studies showing unusual markers in certain populations. Historical references to bloodlines that carried special gifts. Suppressed texts. Burned libraries. Knowledge that had been systematically erased.

She'd written it all up. Compiled it into a document. Genetic evidence, historical sources, contemporary accounts. Everything.

And then she'd been fired.

Not overtly. They couldn't fire a tenured professor for her research. But funding disappeared. Her office was reassigned. Colleagues stopped returning calls. Papers were rejected from journals that had published her before. Someone started rumours about mental illness, about obsession, about her grandmother's death unhinging her.

Within months she was out. No job. Reputation destroyed. Blacklisted from academia.

So now she sat in a café, unemployed and unemployable, staring at the document on her laptop — months of work that no journal would publish, that no institution would defend.

She had two choices.

Let it die. Let the research fade into obscurity, give up, find some other career, live a normal life with an inheritance she'd never develop.

Or publish it anyway. Put it online. Free. Open-source. Let anyone who wanted to see it. Risk everything — her reputation, her safety, possibly her life — on the chance that somewhere, someone would read it and understand. Would recognise themselves. Would remember.

Her finger hovered over the publish button.

She had not noticed the man two tables away.

He was unremarkable in the specific way that certain people are trained to be unremarkable — medium build, a coat the colour of November, a newspaper open that she had not seen him turn a page of in the forty minutes she had been sitting here. He had arrived eleven minutes after she did. She did not know this. She had not been counting.

He had been.

The inheritance her grandmother had written about — she'd felt it all her life. The knowing. The sensing. The dreams. She'd dismissed it as good intuition. Smart guessing. Academic insight. But she had read the letter now. She had sat with it for six months. And she no longer believed in coincidence.

Amélie closed her eyes. Took a breath. And in that breath, something shifted. A warmth in her chest. A presence. Not mystical, not dramatic — simply the feeling, specific and quiet, of being held. Of not being alone in this.

This is the inheritance, she thought. Not the documents. Not the bloodline. This feeling. This knowing that I'm not alone.

She opened her eyes. Looked at the screen.

And she hit publish.

The document uploaded. Spread across servers. Became available to anyone with an internet connection. Free. Ungated. Open.

"Bloodline: The Genetic and Historical Evidence for Inherited Consciousness Capacity"

By Dr. Amélie Rousseau

Within an hour, it had a hundred downloads.

Within a day, ten thousand.

Within a week, a million.

Amélie finished her coffee, paid her bill, and walked out into the October evening.

She didn't know what would happen next. Didn't know if the families her grandmother had warned about would come for her. Didn't know if anyone would care.

But she felt the warmth in her chest. The presence. The ocean-deep knowing that she'd done what she was meant to do.

The inheritance wasn't just genetic markers or historical lineage or consciousness capacity. It was this. This trust. This willingness to follow what called, even when it led into the unknown. This courage to share truth even when truth was dangerous.

This was what her grandmother had passed down. What Asher had carried. What the bloodline preserved through millennia.

Not power. Not gifts. But remembering.

She walked through Paris as night fell, and somewhere in her chest the warmth settled like a hand covering hers — warm, certain, reliably present, the way her grandmother's hands had always been.

She had spent thirty-four years explaining that feeling away.

She didn't think she would do that anymore.

The man with the newspaper folded it neatly, set it on the table, and reached for his phone.

He made a call that lasted eleven seconds.

Then he left.

CHAPTER TWO

The Mark of Kings

Paris, October 2024 — 11 PM

She had not spoken to another person in four days.

Not since Dr. Beaumont — former colleague, former friend — had hung up mid-sentence when she'd called to ask about access to a restricted archive. She'd held the phone against her ear for almost a full minute after the line went dead, listening to the silence, before setting it down.

She had made a list once, in a dark moment, of what the last six months had cost her. The list was practical — the salary, the office, the institutional email address, the access codes revoked one by one like someone methodically turning off lights. The professional relationships that had gone quiet. The invitation to the Lyon conference that had not arrived. The paper rejected without review.

The list did not include: someone to eat dinner with. Someone who knew her well enough to notice when she went quiet. The feeling of being a person who belonged somewhere.

She had not put those things on the list because they did not have a monetary equivalent. Also because writing them down would have made them real.

Her apartment, which had once felt like a sanctuary, now felt like a place where she was waiting. The walls were covered in research — maps, photographs, printed pages connected by red string — and she knew, she absolutely knew, that it looked exactly like the cliché of someone who had lost perspective. She had looked at it through a visitor's eyes once, standing in her own doorway, and thought: this is what it looks like when a person unravels.

But that was the thing. She hadn't unravelled. She felt, if anything, more focused than she had been in years. The research was not madness — it was evidence. Documented, sourced, verifiable. What she was building on her walls was not delusion; it was a case. The kind of case that would have earned her a book contract and a sabbatical if it concerned any other subject. The kind that no serious academic could dismiss — if they were willing to look.

No one was willing to look.

She made tea she wouldn't drink and stood at the window watching the rain move in sheets across the Seine. Somewhere in the building above her, someone was playing music — something old and slow and Algerian, drifting down through the ceiling. She had never met this neighbour. She knew only their music: late-night jazz sometimes, occasionally something that sounded like prayers.

She thought about her grandmother's hands. Grand-mère Élise had been a small woman — smaller each time Amélie visited, as though she were slowly returning to some essential form — but her hands had always been warm. Specifically and reliably warm, even in winter, even at ninety-three. When Amélie was a child and frightened of something she couldn't name, those hands had covered hers, and whatever the fear was had subsided.

You carry something old, her grandmother had said once. Old things know how to survive.

At eleven o'clock she put on her coat. The manuscript at the Bibliothèque nationale would not examine itself, and the custodian she'd paid expected her at midnight. She checked her bag twice — phone, camera, notepad, the USB drive with her research files. She stood at the door for a moment, looking back.

The maps on the walls. The photographs. The red string connecting everything to everything else.

She thought: if something happens to me tonight, no one will know where to start. And then: that's why you have to write it all down. That's why none of this can stay only in this room.

She opened the door and stepped into the corridor.

The rain, when she reached the street, was cold and indifferent and soaked her coat immediately. She didn't mind. There was something clarifying about being uncomfortable. It meant she was still in her body. Still here. Still doing the thing.

One foot. Then the other.

The library was waiting.

2:47 AM — Bibliothèque nationale de France

The storm had been building over Paris for three days.

Dr. Amélie Rousseau pressed her forehead against the cold window of the Bibliothèque nationale de France and watched lightning fracture the October sky. Below, the Seine churned like molten lead. At 2:47 AM she was alone in Reading Room J — or believed she was. The night custodian, Henri, had pocketed her €200 and her sworn silence before retreating to his office to sleep away his shift.

The manuscript lay open on the reading table behind her.

Chronicle of Fredegar. Seventh century. She had spent weeks comparing this copy with others, studying the variations, chasing the small divergences that most scholars dismissed as scribal error. Most copies carried the standard text about the Quinotaur and Chlodio's wife. But this copy was different. Someone, centuries ago, had added an expanded interpretation in the margins — cramped, hurried handwriting, as if the annotator feared being discovered at any moment.

She returned to the passage her eyes had traced a hundred times:

"Fertur dum Chlodeo resedisset in litore mari cum uxore sua, meridiae uxor eius ad mari ad lavandum vadens, bistea Neptuni Quinotauri similis eam appetiit. Cum ergo aut a bistea aut a viro fuisset concepta, peperit filium nomen Meroveum."

— Chronicle of Fredegar, c. 658 CE

It is said that while Chlodio was staying at the seaside with his wife, at midday his wife went to the sea to bathe, and a beast of Neptune resembling a Quinotaur encountered her. Whether she conceived by the beast or by her husband, she gave birth to a son named Merovech.

And in the margin, in that cramped fearful hand:

"Non est fabula. Vidi signum. Sanguis recordatur."

Not fable. I have seen the mark. The blood remembers.

The lights flickered.

Amélie glanced up, her heart rate spiKing. The reading room remained empty except for the distant glow of Henri's office. She'd paid him well to let her work after hours — to give her access to documents kept in the restricted archives for reasons that had nothing to do with preservation and everything to do with suppression.

Her phone buzzed against the table. A text from an unknown number:

Stop looking. They know.

She deleted it immediately, but her hands shook as she photographed the manuscript pages.

In her research she had traced the Merovingian bloodline back through centuries of carefully hidden records — past Clovis I who united the Franks, past Childeric I whose tomb had yielded treasures of gold and Byzantine coins, past Merovech himself who might never have existed except as a symbol, a code for something older. The trail led not forward into history, but backward into something that predated civilisation itself.

What she had found at the end of that trail still unsettled her.

The Merovingian birthmark — a distinctive patch of darker skin between the shoulder blades, sometimes blue-grey, sometimes brown, following the distribution of nerves across the upper back — appeared nowhere else in any European royal line. Contemporary accounts called it a mark of destiny, a sigil of Divine right. The underground genetic analysis she'd commissioned with the last of her savings told a stranger story: a mutation affecting both melanin production and neural development, creating not just the visible mark but an unusual density of pathways in the cervical spine. As if the mark were a map. As if the body were trying to point toward something the mind hadn't yet found.

Three weeks ago, a contact at the British Museum had sent her a photograph that made her sit down and not move for a very long time.

A Bronze Age tablet, recovered from a shipwreck off Santorini. Dated to approximately 1600 BCE — before the eruption that destroyed the Minoan civilisation. On its face: a cross within a circle, rendered in a style that predated any known heraldry. The same symbol she had been following for six months through medieval manuscripts and royal genealogies and suppressed genetic studies.

And beneath it, in characters that were neither Linear A nor Linear B but something older still, a single word her Phoenician specialist contact had translated with shaKing hands:

Atlantis.

Lightning struck close enough to rattle the windows.

In the flash of white light, Amélie saw movement between the stacks. A figure, tall and absolutely still, watching her.

Her blood went cold.

She swept the manuscript pages into her satchel — her notes, her phone, the USB drive with her research files — and moved toward the emergency exit, her footsteps echoing through the cavernous hall. Behind her: nothing. No pursuit. Only the oppressive silence of something that didn't need to chase.

She passed Henri's office. Through the glass she could see him slumped in his chair, head at an angle that no sleeping person's head should reach.

She stopped. One hand on the door frame. For three full seconds she stood there, and the question of whether to go in, whether to call someone, whether Henri was simply deeply asleep or something else entirely — that question pressed against her chest like a weight.

She kept moving. She would have to live with that.

The figure was waiting at the emergency exit.

He was tall, wearing a dark suit that seemed to absorb the dim light. Angular face. Ageless. Eyes that held no warmth whatsoever. In his right hand, something gleamed dully under the emergency lights.

Not a weapon.

A ring.

"Dr. Rousseau." His accent was indeterminate — cultured, European, from no specific country she could place. "You've found the thread. Now you must decide whether to pull it."

"Who are you?"

"Someone who has been watching this particular thread for a long time." He held up his hand. The ring was heavy gold, set with a stone the colour of deep ocean water. Carved into its face was the same symbol she had spent six months following. The cross within the circle. The Merovingian mark.

"There are bloodlines that never truly died," he said. "They simply learned to hide. And there are people who have spent a very long time ensuring they stay hidden."

"Are you one of them?"

Something moved in his expression — not warmth exactly, but a shift, like deep water disturbed from below.

"That," he said quietly, "is precisely the right question."

He stepped closer. Amélie's hand found the release bar behind her.

"The question you should be asking," he continued, "is why you can read the signs when others cannot. Why this research found you, rather than the reverse. Your grandmother's grandmother carried

the mark, Dr. Rousseau. Which means you carry something too —
whether you have chosen to or not."

Thunder crashed. The lights went out entirely.

She hit the release bar and burst through the emergency exit into
the rain-lashed night, the manuscript pages clutched to her chest.

His voice followed her into the storm, unhurried, carrying
through the wind as if distance meant nothing at all:

The blood always remembers. It always calls its children home.

Amélie ran.

CHAPTER THREE

The Drowning of Atlantis

Paris, October 2024 — 4:47 AM

Amélie's apartment in the Marais had never felt smaller.

She'd returned at 3:30 AM, soaked to the skin, her coat dripping onto the floorboards, her heart still running at a pace that had nothing to do with the distance she'd covered. The man with the ring. Henri slumped at that angle in his chair. The manuscript pages clutched to her chest through three streets of rain until she'd realised her hands were shaKing and had to stop under an awning to breathe.

She had not called the police about Henri. She had told herself this was tactical — the questions, the exposure, the impossibility of explaining what she had been doing in a restricted archive at 3 AM. But standing in her wet coat in her own hallway, she knew the truth was simpler and less comfortable: she had kept moving because stopping would have meant feeling it.

She changed out of her wet clothes. She made tea she wouldn't drink. She stood for a moment in the doorway of her research room — the maps, the red string, the photographs connecting everything to everything else — and felt, as she sometimes did at this hour, the vertiginous sensation of a person standing at the edge of something that could not be un-stood-at.

The man's voice followed her. Unhurried. Carrying through the rain as if distance meant nothing.

Your grandmother's grandmother carried the mark. Which means you carry something too.

She sat at the table. Opened her phone. Scrolled back through years of photographs until she found what she was looking for — a family photo from her great-grandmother's funeral wake. Amélie had been eight years old. In the photograph, someone had helped

Grand-mère Élise change into burial clothes, and for just a moment the camera had caught her back.

Amélie zoomed in, her breath catching.

There. Between the shoulder blades. A birthmark she had never noticed as a child — dismissed as shadows in the photograph, a trick of old film and poor light. But now, knowing what to look for, the shape was unmistakable.

A cross within a circle. Faded with age, barely visible against wrinkled skin. But unmistakable.

The mark she had been following through medieval manuscripts for six months. On her great-grandmother's back.

"No," she whispered to the empty room. "No, no, no—"

But even as she said it, something else was happening beneath the denial. A quiet, inexorable clicKing, the way tumblers move in a lock. Her grandmother's intuitions that had always proven correct. Her mother's hands, which seemed to ease pain when she touched someone who was hurting — not through technique, not through training, simply through presence and intention. Amélie's own uncanny ability to sense when someone was lying, to see patterns others missed, to know things she had no logical right to know.

She had spent her life calling these things intuition. Insight. Academic pattern recognition. The comfortable, professional, deniable language of a woman who had learned, very young, that there were two available verdicts on what she perceived: fantasy, or madness. She had accepted neither, and so had accepted silence instead.

Not gifts. Not madness. Genetics.

She set the phone down on the table. The photograph glowed on the screen. Her great-grandmother's narrow back. The mark between the shoulder blades that she had looked past a hundred times without seeing.

She sat in the chair for a long time.

Not reading. Not analysing. Just sitting inside what the photograph meant — inside the evidence of something Élise had carried her entire life and never named. Had never named to me, Amélie corrected herself. She had named it. She had named it in the letter and sealed it with wax and left it in a box on the kitchen table, and decided at ninety-three that her granddaughter was finally ready.

Amélie had spent six months being furious about that letter. The careful, loving, infuriating letter. She had felt, reading it for the first time, as if she had been handed the manual to a house she had lived in for thirty years — all the instructions, finally, for things she had been navigating by instinct and guesswork and sheer stubbornness for as long as she could remember.

She had wanted to say: why didn't you tell me when you could still answer questions? She had wanted to say: I would have listened. I was always listening. I just needed you to speak.

But Grand-mère was gone, and so was her mother, and Amélie was alone in an apartment at 4:47 AM with wet hair and a photograph and a slowly spreading certainty that everything she thought she knew about herself was a partial truth.

Her mother had known. She must have known.

Her mother — Claire — had died of cancer when Amélie was nineteen. Quickly, brutally, without sufficient warning or preparation. Amélie's last clear memory of her was in a hospital bed, thinner than she had any right to be, holding Amélie's hand and saying something that Amélie had always filed away as medication-induced confusion:

You can feel things, my love. Real things. Don't let them take that from you. Don't let them convince you it isn't real.

She had not thought about that sentence in fifteen years.

She thought about it now.

There were things she had always known she wasn't supposed to know. The cheating husband at her mother's friend's dinner party — she had been twelve, had no language for it, had felt it as a wrongness in the air, a sourness, like milk just beginning to turn. The colleague at the Sorbonne who was going to be diagnosed with something serious — she had known three weeks before anyone did, had felt it as a dimming, a withdrawal, like a lamp turned down. She had said nothing. She never said anything. She had learned from childhood that what you perceived without explanation was better kept quiet, because the world had no category for it that wasn't damaging.

And now here was her grandmother telling her: those are not anomalies. That is your inheritance. That is the blood remembering what the mind has been trained to forget.

Amélie pressed her fingers against her eyes.

Maman. Grand-mère. The women before them, stretching back through the centuries, carrying this — not as a burden, but as a gift. An inconvenient, disorienting, occasionally terrifying gift that each of them had learned to hide in their own way. Her grandmother behind the Catholicism of Sunday Mass. Her mother behind the language of feeling and intuition. Amélie herself behind the armour of academic methodology, the footnote and the sourced claim, the professional scepticism that kept the knowing at a manageable distance.

None of it had worked. The knowing had kept coming, quiet and persistent and entirely indifferent to whether she had professional language for it or not.

She wished, with an intensity that surprised her, that she could call someone. That there was a person in the world who knew this story, who understood what she was sitting inside of, who could say something useful or at least something human.

There was no one.

She wiped her eyes. Straightened in her chair.

She reached for the next document.

The first document was a scan from the Chronicle of Fredegar — not the Merovech passage she had been working on in the library, but Book IV, a section she had initially skimmed as tangential:

"Et dicunt quidam quod gens Francorum de tribu Israel descendit, de his qui trans mare fugerunt quando Assur cecidit..."

And some say that the Frankish people descended from the tribe of Israel, from those who fled across the sea when Assyria fell...

722 BCE. The Assyrian conquest of the Northern Kingdom of Israel. The ten so-called lost tribes, scattered, never to return. Except that perhaps they had returned — or at least, some of them had. They had simply gone so far west that no one had thought to look for them in the forests of Gaul.

She pulled up a second document — a genetic study published in 2019 in a small peer-reviewed journal, largely ignored by the academic mainstream, that had analysed Y-chromosome and mitochondrial DNA from medieval graves across France. The researchers had found unexpected markers linKing certain French populations to Levantine origins. They had theorised about Phoenician trade routes, Roman legions, the usual explanations.

They had not considered that the connection might go back further.

Much further.

She opened her laptop — the new one, bought with cash and registered to a name that was not hers, after the sixth time the previous machine had been mysteriously wiped — and opened the encrypted file she had received two days ago from a geneticist at Stanford who owed her a significant favour.

The file contained the analysis of DNA samples Amélie had obtained through channels she would not have described to her former department head. Seven samples, all from verified descendants of Merovingian bloodlines.

The results had made her sit very still for a long time.

She set the genetic report aside and reached for her physical notebook — kept in a locked drawer, because nothing that mattered lived on a screen anymore — and opened it to the section she had headed, three months ago, with a single word she had not been entirely sure she believed:

Before, she had been collecting sources. Accounts from cultures with no contact with each other, separated by ocean and century and language, all describing the same thing: a time before this one. Not a mythological golden age. Something more specific. A form of consciousness that preceded this one and operated at a different frequency of being.

The Egyptian Papyrus of Turin described the Shemsu-Hor — the Followers of Horus — as beings who had reigned for 13,420 years before the first human pharaohs. Neither fully Divine nor fully human. Bridges between two orders of existence.

The Sumerian Uruk King List documented the Apkallu — seven sages who had emerged from the primordial waters before the Flood. Part fish, part human. But the fish-form was code, she had come to understand. Not zoology. Origin. They came from the water. They came from somewhere the water had swallowed.

The Kabbalistic texts were more precise. Seth — Adam's third son, born after the Fall — was described as the first to receive the secret wisdom directly. Through his line came Enoch, who walked with God and was taken up without dying. Then Noah, who preserved life through catastrophe. Then Abraham, who rediscovered the Divine through contemplation. This lineage — what the mystics called the golden chain — transmitted its knowledge not through written texts but through direct transmission, consciousness to consciousness. The knowledge was encoded in what the ancients called "the book written in flesh and blood."

"For many generations they retained their Divine nature, living virtuously and caring little for wealth or power. But gradually, as the Divine blood was diluted through intermarriage with mortals, their nature changed. When the human portion overtook the Divine, they grew corrupt — filled with avarice and unrighteous ambition."
— *Plato, Critias*

Amélie set down her pen.

She had been reading this passage as a moral cautionary tale. The way scholars always read it — as allegory, as a warning about hubris, as Plato doing what Plato did: inventing a myth to illustrate a philosophical point.

But sitting here at 4:47 AM with the genetic report open on her laptop and her great-grandmother's birthmark glowing on her phone screen, she found herself reading it differently.

Not as allegory. As description.

There had been, before this civilisation, a form of consciousness less bound by the material. Not immaterial — not pure spirit, not the stuff of Victorian séances and wishful romanticism — but lighter. Less dense. A frequency of being in which the faculty of direct perception was simply how you experienced reality, the way eyesight is how you navigate a room. It was not supernatural. It was natural — the nature of consciousness before it became so thoroughly, so comprehensively, so irrevocably material.

Atlantis was not the first such civilisation. The Egyptian and Sumerian sources described timescales that dwarfed it, ages of consciousness preceding it, each descent into matter slightly denser than the last. But Atlantis had been the most recent, the transitional one, the civilisation poised on the boundary between what came before and what we are now. Its people had carried in their bodies the genetic memory of what they had been and the biological reality of what they were becoming.

And then she thought of something she had always known, in the way she knew things before she sourced them: when the Bible described God clothing Adam and Eve — that was not a story about modesty. The garments were bodies. The Fall was not a moral failure. It was a cosmological event: the descent of consciousness into the density of matter, the slowing of frequency from something vast and oceanic into something individual, bounded, mortal, and heavy with forgetting.

When Atlantis fell and the water came, what scattered across the ancient world was not simply refugees.

It was seeds.

Consciousness-carrying seeds. People who still had the wiring. Whose DNA still expressed — faintly, variably, but measurably, as her Stanford contact had just confirmed — the markers of a different way of being human.

The Shemsu-Hor in Egypt. The Apkallu in Sumer. The golden chain of Seth and Enoch and Abraham. The Asher bloodline — the blessed ones, the Keepers, the daughters who married into the priesthood because the priesthood needed what they carried. Anna in the Temple, an old woman from an obscure tribe, who looked at a child being presented for dedication and simply knew — not through prophecy, not through revelation, not through anything that required an intermediary — what she was looking at.

She had Seen. Capital S, the way the gift actually worked in those who still carried it cleanly, without interference from the noise of a world that had forgotten this was possible.

And then: the Assyrians. And then the Babylonians. And then Rome. And then the Church. And then the Carolingians in 751 CE, with the explicit authorisation of the papacy, cutting the long hair of the last Merovingian King and sending him to a monastery, placing on the throne the first of a dynasty that did not carry the mark, that did not carry the gift, but that understood power in the old, dense, purely material sense: who controls the land, who controls the gold, who controls what is permitted to be known.

Amélie stood and moved to her wall map.

In red: every location where credible accounts described pre-Flood civilisations, advanced ancient knowledge, claims of Divine bloodlines. They formed a crescent — Mesopotamia, the Levant, across the Mediterranean, into Western Europe. The Phoenician route. The Asher territory. The path the lost tribes would have taken fleeing the Assyrian conquest.

In green: the locations where Merovingian royal holdings had been strongest in the sixth and seventh centuries.

In blue: documented accounts of the Merovingian healing touch. The laying on of hands. The uncanny perceptions. The gift for knowing what could not be known.

The patterns overlapped almost perfectly.

She stood back and looked at what she had built. Six months of solitude and obsession. Lost friendships. Revoked access codes. Rumours of mental illness circulated in faculty lounges she was no longer invited to enter. Six months of waking at 3 AM with her heart pounding and the red string pulling at her from the walls and the creeping, terrifying, liberating certainty that she was not unwell.

She was awake.

And she had just understood something that would either change everything or cost her everything.

Possibly both.

Her phone buzzed. Unknown number.

She almost didn't answer. But something in her chest moved — the old familiar movement, the one she had spent thirty-four years explaining away — and she picked up.

"Dr. Rousseau." A woman's voice. French, but with an accent she couldn't locate — not quite Parisian, not quite anything. Precise and unhurried. "You're still awake. Good."

"Who is this?"

"Someone who was in the Bibliothèque tonight. Not with the man who stopped you at the exit — on the other side of that equation entirely."

A pause. In the silence Amélie heard the faint sound of a city at night. Traffic. A door closing somewhere distant.

"He frightened you," the woman continued. "I understand why. But he wasn't there to stop you."

Amélie's grip tightened on the phone. "Then what was he there for?"

"To see if you were ready." A pause with a quality of consideration in it. "They've been watching your research for some time. So have I."

"You're going to need to be considerably more specific."

"Not on the phone." The woman's voice was the voice of someone accustomed, over a very long time, to being careful. "You've built a map, Dr. Rousseau. Months of work. You've found the thread from the Frankish chronicles back to the Levant, back to Asher. You've had the genetic analysis done. You know what it shows."

Amélie said nothing. The apartment was very quiet.

"What you don't know yet," the woman said, "is that your grandmother's family is not the only one. There are others — not many, scattered, most of them not yet aware of what they carry. But they exist. And there are people who have spent a very long time ensuring that none of them ever find each other."

The room felt suddenly smaller. The map on the wall. The red string. The photographs of women who had known things and been silent for generations.

"Until now," Amélie said.

"Until now." Something shifted in the woman's voice — the quality of a door opening one inch. "Meet me tomorrow. Marché d'Aligre, the café on the south side, nine in the morning. Come alone. Bring nothing digital."

"You haven't told me who you are."

"No. But I will tell you one thing tonight. One thing your grandmother's documents don't."

Amélie waited.

"The mark between your shoulder blades," the woman said quietly. "The one you've been looking at in the photograph of your great-grandmother. Check your own back, Dr. Rousseau. Use two mirrors. Do it before you sleep."

The line went dead.

Amélie stood without moving for a long time.

Then she walked to the bathroom. Turned on the light. Found the angle with two mirrors that she had never, in thirty-four years, thought to look for.

She looked for a long time at what she saw.

Then she went back to the kitchen table, sat down in the lamplight with the map on the wall and the documents spread before her and the old deep hum in her chest that had always been there and always known, and she did not sleep again.

CHAPTER FOUR

The Bloodline Keepers

Paris, October 2024 — 8 AM

Marché d'Aligre, Paris — Sunday, 8 AM

She went to the market on Sunday because it was a thing that normal people did.

This was her reasoning. Entirely cynical, which made it no less true. She had noticed, somewhere in the fifth month of her isolation, that she was losing the rhythms that connected her to the world — the small, stupid, comforting rhythms of coffee at the same time and bread from the same boulangerie and the weekly noise and colour of the Marché d'Aligre. She had let them go in favour of more hours at the desk, and the desk had taken everything she gave it without giving anything back.

So: the market. Eight in the morning, one hour before the woman with the careful voice. The light low and gold and autumnal, the air sharp with October.

She bought a bunch of dahlias because they were absurd and excessive and she had no reason to. She bought a small wheel of cheese from a man who gave her a piece to taste without asking, who seemed to understand instinctively that cheese was one of the things that required no justification. She stopped at the olive stall and the vendor — old, Algerian, with a gap-toothed smile — offered her three different oils to taste, and she stood in the morning light tasting olive oil from small ceramic cups and thought: this is also real. This is also what I am.

Not only the research. Not only the mission. Not only the frightened, determined woman who had run through the rain last night clutching stolen manuscript pages, or who had sat alone until dawn with her wall of evidence and the reflection of a mark she had not known she carried.

Also this: oil on her tongue. The smell of bread from three stalls over. The dahlias wrapped in newspaper against her coat. The ordinary miraculous fact of being a body in the world on a Sunday morning in Paris.

She thought of her grandmother at the market. Grand-mère Élise had been an excellent shopper in the French sense — never hurried, touching and considering and occasionally dismissing with the quiet authority of someone with decades of expertise and no patience for poor quality. Amélie had walked these markets with her as a child, had been bored and then intrigued and then gradually, without noticing it was happening, educated. She understood now what Grand-mère had been teaching her, and it had nothing to do with cheese.

Be present. Feel what is real. Don't let the world rush you past your own life.

The vendor wrapped her oil in brown paper. She tucked it into her bag alongside the dahlias.

She had a mission. She was, apparently, part of something that mattered in ways she was only beginning to understand. But she was also a woman who could stand at an olive stall on a Sunday morning and feel the warmth in her chest — not the mysterious warmth of the Ocean her grandmother had written about, just the ordinary warmth of being alive and fed and not, for this one hour, afraid.

Whatever was waiting at the café on the south side of the market could wait nine more minutes.

She walked home through the early crowd, dahlias under her arm, and thought: I will remember this morning. Whatever comes next, I will remember this.

The café on the south side of the Marché d'Aligre was crowded at nine in the morning, the last of the market's Sunday regulars pressing in alongside the first of the neighbourhood's late risers.

Amélie sat at a corner table, an espresso in front of her, her eyes scanning every face that entered.

She'd come early, as instructed. Sat where she could see both entrances. Her laptop bag rested against her leg, containing copies of everything — the only originals were in a safety deposit box at a bank she'd never used before, registered under her mother's maiden name.

After last night, she'd learned to think like someone being hunted.

The woman who sat down across from her seemed to materialise from nowhere — one moment the chair was empty, the next it was occupied. She was perhaps sixty, elegant in that way French women managed effortlessly, with silver hair cut in a precise bob and wearing expensive but understated clothing. Her eyes, however, were anything but gentle. They were dark and intense, the eyes of someone who had seen too much and forgotten nothing.

"Dr. Rousseau," the woman said, her voice the same as from the phone. "Thank you for coming."

"I'm not sure I had a choice."

A slight smile. "There's always a choice. You could have run. Destroyed your research. Pretended ignorance. Most do, when they get close to the truth. The fact that you're here tells me you're different. The blood calls more strongly in you than most."

"Who are you?"

"My name is Marguerite Valcourt. My family has served as... archivists, I suppose you'd call us. We preserve what others try to erase. My father's mother was a Valmond. Her grandmother was a Montrose. Before that..." She shrugged. "The names change. The blood remains."

Amélie's throat went dry.

"You're saying you're —"

"Descended from the Merovingians? Yes. As are you, though more distantly. As are approximately thirty thousand people currently living in Europe, about two thousand in the Americas, and smaller populations scattered across the world. Most don't know. Most never will. But some..." She leaned forward slightly. "Some carry the gifts strongly. And you, doctor, are one of them."

"I don't have any gifts," Amélie said, but even as she spoke, she knew it was a lie.

The knowing. The sense of wrongness when someone deceived her. The way patterns leapt out at her from chaos. The dreams that sometimes came true. She had been calling them by other names her entire adult life, and the other names had never quite fitted.

Marguerite's smile was sad. "You've spent your whole life explaining them away. Coincidence. Intuition. A good education and a sharp mind. But deep down, you've always known you were different. And now that you've discovered why, you're terrified. Because if the gifts are real, then so are the responsibilities. And so are the enemies."

"The man last night —"

"Was from the Council of Guardians. A very old organisation. Nominally they exist to protect the bloodline. In reality, they've spent centuries suppressing it. Because the truth they guard isn't just about ancestry — it's about power. Real power. The kind that can't be bought or stolen. The kind that's written in DNA."

Marguerite pulled out a slim folder and slid it across the table. "Everything I'm about to tell you is documented in here. You can verify it. You should verify it. Trust nothing, not even me, until you've seen the evidence yourself."

Amélie opened the folder. Inside were photocopies of documents — some ancient, some recent. A classified genetic study from 1987. Medieval manuscript pages with margin notes in three different hands spanning centuries. A photograph of a young woman, dated 1943, Berlin. Modern brain scans with annotations in medical terminology.

"The Council has known for at least five hundred years, probably longer, that certain bloodlines carry genetic anomalies that manifest as what we'd call psychic abilities," Marguerite began, her voice low but clear. "Increased pattern recognition. Empathic sensitivity. Enhanced intuition. And in rare cases, genuine precognition — the ability to see potential futures."

She tapped the 1943 photograph.

"This was my grandmother's sister, Céleste. The Nazis were very interested in bloodlines, as you might imagine. They weren't just looking for so-called racial purity. They were looking for something else. Old families. Ancient names. People who showed evidence of the gifts. They called it the Ahnenerbe program — the ancestral heritage project. Officially it was archaeology. Unofficially..." She trailed off, her expression hardening.

"Céleste was murdered in Ravensbrück after refusing to cooperate with their breeding program. But others weren't so principled. Some of the families collaborated. And after the war, their research didn't disappear. It was acquired. By various intelligence agencies. Private institutions. BanKing families who suddenly became very interested in genetic counselling and selective marriage arrangements."

"They were looking for the Atlantean bloodline," Amélie whispered.

"Among others. They understood, better than anyone since the fall of the Merovingians, that the gifts were genetic. That they could be tracked, studied, potentially controlled. And after the war, that understanding was preserved and extended."

Marguerite pulled out the last document in the folder — a medieval manuscript page, beautifully illuminated, with text that made Amélie's blood run cold:

"Rex Pippinus, filius Caroli Martelli, duxit in uxorem Bertram, filiam Caribert, ex stirpe Merovingia. Et sic sanguis sanctus translatus est de domibus regis-sacerdotis ad domos regis-militis. Et potestas data est propter servitium, usurpata est ad dominationem."
— Carolingian court manuscript, c. 9th century CE
King Pippin, son of Charles Martel, took as wife Bertha, daughter of Charibert, of Merovingian stock. And thus the holy blood was transferred from the houses of priest-Kings to the houses of warrior-Kings. And the power given for service was usurped for domination.

"This understanding emerged in the generation after the coup," Marguerite said quietly. "Scholars in the Carolingian court recognised what had happened. That it wasn't just a throne that was stolen — it was a sacred mandate. The Carolingians claimed the bloodline through Pippin's marriage to Bertrada, kept the gifts running in their family. But they used them for conquest, not service. For wealth, not wisdom. And every dynasty since has followed the same pattern."

"The families who stole the bloodline discovered a problem," Marguerite said, leaning forward. "The gifts don't work well when wielded for selfish purposes. The empathy that makes you sensitive to others pain also makes it hard to exploit them. The ability to see truth makes it nearly impossible to sustain lies, even your own. The precognitive sense warns you away from dark paths. It's as if the gifts themselves have a moral component, a built-in mechanism. Use them for service, and they flourish. Try to use them for domination, and they turn against you.'

"So what did they do?" Amélie asked, though part of her already knew.

"They found a way to break that mechanism. To split the gift from the moral foundation. To create individuals who could use the abilities without the constraint of conscience." Marguerite's eyes held terrible knowledge. "They discovered that severe trauma, particularly in childhood, can fragment the psyche. And if you subject a child with the gifts to specific kinds of trauma, you can create personalities that have the abilities but lack the empathy. Seers without souls. Healers without compassion. Prophets without conscience."

The café seemed to recede around Amélie.

"They torture their own children?"

"Their own children. Adopted children from the bloodline. Children stolen or purchased. For centuries, doctor. They call them 'special projects.' 'Enhanced training programmes.' 'Family traditions.' But the core mechanism is always the same: systematic trauma designed to split the psyche and separate the gifts from the moral foundation that would prevent their abuse.'

Amélie thought she might be sick.

"That's... that's—"

"Evil. Yes. The purest form of it. And it's not ancient history. It's happening now, in estates across Europe, in certain private schools, in family compounds that outsiders never see. The bloodline families that have retained power — the ones who sit on boards and corporate thrones and political councils — many of them maintain the practice. Because a child who's been properly trained becomes an adult who can see market futures without moral qualms about the exploitation required to profit from them. Who can sense what people want without caring about manipulating those desires. Who can heal or harm with equal ease."

"Is that why you contacted me?" Amélie asked.

"Partly. But also because of what you represent. You found the truth on your own. You followed the evidence despite the danger. And you have the gifts — not as strong as some, but genuine. You can See, doctor. And what you see, you can teach others to see. That's what terrifies the families most. Not the bloodline itself, but the awakening. Because if enough people understand what happened, if enough descendants realise what was stolen and refuse to serve the system that stole it..."

"The whole structure collapses," Amélie finished.

"Exactly." Marguerite stood up, leaving the folder on the table. "Take this. Study it. Verify everything. And then decide what you're going to do. Because once you publish, once you make this public, there's no going back. They'll come for you. They'll try to discredit you, destroy your career, perhaps worse. But the truth will be out there. And others like you — others who carry the blood, who have the gifts — will begin to understand what they are."

She turned to leave, then paused.

"One more thing. The dreams you've been having? The ones you haven't told anyone about? They're not just dreams. They're the gift awakening, now that you've begun to understand what you carry. Pay attention to them. And trust what you See, even when it seems impossible."

Then she was gone, disappearing into the market crowd as mysteriously as she'd appeared. One moment she was there; then a gap in the flow of bodies; then only the half-empty coffee cup and the folder on the table, as if she had never existed.

Amélie sat for a few minutes without moving. Then she gathered the folder, left money for the coffee, and went out into the Boulevard de la Bastille.

The street was doing what Parisian streets did at that hour — full, moving, indifferent. She walked toward the metro and found herself doing something she had never done before: looking at faces.

Not idly. Not the abstracted metro-gaze of someone waiting for a thought to resolve. She looked at them the way she had been trained to read manuscripts — as documents with histories, as surfaces that implied depths. The man in the grey coat checKing his phone. The woman with the pushchair arguing quietly with herself. The teenage boy with headphones who moved through the crowd with the unconscious grace of someone who had grown up in cities.

Any of them could carry what she carried. Most of them would never know. Somewhere in Europe, right now, in rooms she would never see, children who carried it were being broken for the crime of carrying it. And somewhere in this city, descendants of the same bloodline were living ordinary lives, having inexplicable dreams, feeling warmth in their chests and calling it nothing, because they had no other word.

She descended into the metro.

In her coat pocket, one hand rested on the folder Marguerite had left. The weight of what it contained. The weight of what she was going to do with it.

She opened her laptop when she got home. And the first line came easily:

This is the story of a theft that changed the world, a bloodline that predates recorded history, and a gift that humanity was never meant to lose...

CHAPTER FIVE

The Theft of 751

Saint-Denis / Paris, October 2024

Amélie's research took her to places she'd never expected to go.

Three days after meeting Marguerite Valcourt, she found herself in the archives of the Abbey of Saint-Denis, north of Paris. This was where the Carolingian dynasty had buried its Kings, where the mythology of France itself had been written in stone and stained glass. But she wasn't here for the official history.

She was here for what had been erased.

The archivist, Brother Thomas, was young for a Monk—perhaps forty, with intelligent eyes behind wire-rimmed glasses. He'd been recommended by Marguerite as "sympathetic to the truth." Now, in a climate-controlled vault beneath the abbey, he spread before Amélie manuscripts she'd only heard whispered about in academic circles.

"The Annals of Metz," Brother Thomas said quietly, pointing to a ninth-century manuscript. "Written when the Carolingians were consolidating power. Notice what they say—and don't say—about Dagobert II."

The manuscript was sparse on details. Amélie read what little was there, then looked up. "It barely mentions him."

"Exactly. The Carolingian chroniclers wanted him forgotten. But earlier sources tell a different story." He pulled out another text. "The Life of Saint Wilfrid, written in the eighth century, closer to the actual events. It says Dagobert was assassinated in December 679 near Stenay—killed while hunting."

"Assassinated by whom?"

""Treacherous Dukes," the text says, "with the consent of the bishops." But look at who benefited. Brother Thomas pulled out a timeline he'd constructed. "Dagobert died in late 679. By 680, Pepin of Herstal—grandfather of Charlemagne—had become mayor of the palace in Austrasia. The very position Dagobert had been trying to limit."

"You think Pepin was involved?"

"Pepin wasn't mayor yet when Dagobert died, but he became mayor immediately after. The nobles clearly preferred Pepin's family to a King who actually wanted to rule. Whether anyone personally ordered the assassination, we'll never know. But his family certainly profited. After Dagobert's death, no Merovingian King ever held real power again."

Brother Thomas's voice grew quiet. "Dagobert had been exiled to Ireland as a boy—spent years in monasteries there. When he returned in 676, he tried to be an actual King, not just a puppet ceremonial figurehead. And three years later, he was dead. The last Merovingian who tried to truly rule. After him, it was only a matter of time before the Pippinids took the crown outright."

"The church was involved?" Amélie asked, thinKing of what she'd read about priest-Kings.

"According to the Life of Wilfrid, bishops consented to his death. Whether that's historically accurate or later Carolingian propaganda, we can't be certain. But it raises questions." Brother Thomas removed his glasses to clean them. "If the Merovingians really did claim some kind of sacred authority—not just political power but spiritual legitimacy—that would have been deeply threatening to Rome. The church had spent centuries establishing that spiritual authority rested solely with the Pope and his bishops."

He turned to another document. "Seventy years later, Pepin the Short—grandson of the man who had become mayor when Dagobert fell—controlled the Frankish Kingdom in everything but name. The Merovingian King, Childeric III, was a puppet. And Pepin wanted to make the reality official."

Brother Thomas pulled out a modern transcription of the Royal Frankish Annals. "According to the official chronicle, Pepin sent two envoys to Pope Zacharias with a single question: Is it right that those who have no royal power should be called Kings? The Pope's answer was brief: It is better that he should be King who has the royal power than he who has not."

"That's it?" Amélie asked. "One question, one answer, and an entire dynasty falls?"

"That's the official record. Notice what Pepin doesn't ask. He doesn't say: Do we have the right to take the throne? He asks about a philosophical principle. It's carefully worded—a request for a technicality."

"And the Pope gave him one," Amélie said slowly.

"Exactly. No theological argument. No discussion of Divine right or sacred lineage. Just pragmatic recognition of power. It sidesteps entirely the question of whether the Merovingians had any legitimate claim." Brother Thomas looked troubled. "The brevity of it has always bothered historians. For such a momentous decision, you'd expect more. Documentation. Debate. Instead, we get two sentences that overturn three centuries of dynastic rule."

"What do you think was really happening?"

"I think Pepin and Pope Zacharias both wanted the same thing—an alliance against the Lombards who were threatening Rome. Pepin needed papal legitimacy, and the Pope needed Frankish military protection. The Merovingians were irrelevant to that equation, except as obstacles. So they were removed, with the minimum of discussion necessary."

He spread out several documents. "But here's what's interesting. After the coup in 751, Pepin didn't just take the throne. He married strategically. His wife was Bertrada of Laon, and according to the Annals of St. Bertin—written in the ninth century—she had connections to the previous Merovingian dynasty through her father

Charibert. Some scholars believe her grandmother, Bertrada of Prüm, was descended from King Theuderic III."

"So the Carolingians preserved the bloodline," Amélie said, remembering Marguerite's documents.

"Whether intentionally or by happy accident, yes. And they emphasised it." Brother Thomas pulled out more documents. "In 754, Pope Stephen II didn't just anoint Pepin—he anointed Bertrada alongside him, and their sons Charlemagne and Carloman. This was unusual. It emphasised her role, her legitimacy."

"They needed her bloodline," Amélie said.

"That's one interpretation. After Pepin's death, Charlemagne gave Bertrada a residence at Choisy-au-Bac—a place sacred to the Merovingians, where several of their Kings were buried. Every choice suggests they understood she carried something they needed to preserve. Whether that was political legitimacy, genetic heritage, or something else..." He trailed off meaningfully.

Brother Thomas pulled out genealogical charts spanning centuries. "And if you trace the marriages through subsequent generations, you find Carolingian princes repeatedly marrying into families with claimed Merovingian connections. The pattern continues through the Capetians, the Valois, even later dynasties. Sometimes the connections are obvious. Sometimes they're obscure, buried in local chronicles."

Amélie studied the charts. Generation after generation of strategic marriages into old Frankish noble families. "They were preserving it," she whispered.

"So it appears. And there are curious details in the chronicles." He pulled out photocopied pages from Einhard's biography of Charlemagne. "Einhard writes that Charlemagne had an almost supernatural ability to inspire loyalty, to detect deception. He's described as having a penetrating gaze that could see into men's hearts. Now, this is likely hagiography—medieval biographers routinely attributed quasi-Divine abilities to powerful rulers. But the language is oddly specific."

"What if it wasn't just propaganda?" Amélie asked.

"Then we'd have to ask whether something genetic was being passed down through these strategic marriages. Something that manifested as enhanced intuition, pattern recognition, even precognitive ability in some individuals." Brother Thomas met her eyes. "Which brings us to your research. What you've found in the genetic data—the markers associated with enhanced cognition and empathy—do they correlate with these family lines?"

"Yes," Amélie said. "The correlation is statistically significant. But correlation isn't causation, and—"

"And you're a historian, so you'll frame what you can prove." He nodded. "I understand. But let me show you something else." He pulled out a folder of more recent documents. "This is from the nineteenth and twentieth centuries. Census records, genealogical research, psychiatric case studies. I've been collecting them for years."

He spread out several papers. "Look at the pattern. Descendants of these old families—families with documented connections to the Merovingian bloodlines—show up in psychiatric records at rates significantly higher than the general population. Diagnosed with everything from schizophrenia to bipolar disorder to various anxiety conditions."

"That could just mean—"

"That mental illness runs in families? Yes. Or it could mean that people with unusual cognitive abilities—the capacity to sense things others don't, to recognise patterns that seem impossible—get diagnosed as mentally ill because we have no framework to understand what they're experiencing."

Amélie thought of her own experiences. The visions she'd dismissed as stress-induced hallucinations. The knowing she had never been able to explain.

"You're saying the gifts could be mistaken for madness."

"Or that the two might be related. Enhanced perception without the context to understand it could easily manifest as something that looks like psychosis." Brother Thomas pulled out another document—a scholarly article from a psychiatric journal. "This is from 2003. A study of familial patterns in bipolar disorder found genetic clusters in old European families, particularly those with aristocratic lineages. The study was never followed up. Funding disappeared."

"Someone didn't want the research to continue."

"That's my suspicion. Because if these abilities are real, if they're genetic, if they're concentrated in specific bloodlines—then the families who carry them have a vested interest in keeping that knowledge controlled. Some might want to suppress it entirely. Others might want to exploit it."

Brother Thomas stood and walked to the window, looking out over the grounds where Kings had been buried with full honours. "Here's what we know for certain: the Merovingian dynasty ended in 751 through a carefully orchestrated political coup. The bloodline didn't end—it was absorbed into subsequent dynasties through strategic marriages. Descendants of those bloodlines continue to exist today, scattered across Europe and beyond. And some of those descendants display unusual cognitive abilities that correlate with specific genetic markers."

He turned back to Amélie. "What we don't know is whether those abilities were intentionally cultivated, whether they were suppressed or exploited, whether there's an organised effort to control them. That's speculation. But the historical pattern—the strategic marriages, the careful preservation of certain lineages, the sudden disappearances of certain individuals from the records—suggests that someone has been paying very close attention to these bloodlines for a very long time."

"The Council of Guardians," Amélie said, thinKing of the man in the library.

"The Council is... I don't know what they are, to be honest. Guardian organisation? Control mechanism? Some of both? They've existed in various forms since at least the twelfth century—I've found references to them in manuscripts from that period. They claim to protect Merovingian descendants. But protection can become control very easily."

"They know about me," Amélie said. "Someone from the Council approached me in the library. Warned me to stop my research."

Brother Thomas's expression darkened. "Then you need to be careful. Very careful. I don't know what resources they have or how far they'll go to protect their secrets. But I do know that people who've investigated these matters too publicly have had... unfortunate accidents."

"Are you saying they'd kill to keep this quiet?"

"I'm saying that power structures don't give up easily. And if what you're investigating threatens to expose something that's been hidden for twelve centuries—" He left the sentence unfinished.

Amélie felt cold. But she also felt determined. "Then I need to work faster. Get the information out where it can't be suppressed."

"Yes. But strategically. Create backups. Distribute them to people you trust. Don't keep everything in one place." Brother Thomas began gathering his documents. "And focus on what you can prove. The genetic markers, the historical patterns, the documented facts. Frame this as a historian's survey of inherited traits in European populations—something defensible, something that draws on the academic record. The larger lymplications will speak for themselves."

"Even though there's more to it than that."

"Especially because there's more to it than that. The best way to hide truth is to present it in a form people won't take seriously. Conversely, the best way to ensure people take truth seriously is to present it as dry academic research." He smiled slightly. "Work within the system to expose the system. It's slower, but it's safer."

Amélie spent the next four hours in that vault. Brother Thomas shared everything he had—genealogical charts, historical documents, census records, scholarly articles. By the time she left the abbey, the sun was setting, painting the Gothic spires in shades of blood and gold.

Her phone vibrated as she crossed the courtyard. She nearly ignored it—then tilted the screen without picKing it up, and saw that it was not a text but a call. And the number was one she recognised: Professor Delacroix, her former department head at the Sorbonne. The man who had written her letters of reference for three grant applications. The man whose office she had passed on her last day at the university without stopping.

She did not answer. She held the phone until the vibration ran its course.

When it stopped, something had changed in the quality of the remaining light. Brother Thomas was still visible through the vault window, replacing documents with methodical care. She stood in the courtyard with the sense of someone standing between two rooms—the room of who she had been, and whatever came next.

She encrypted the afternoon's photographs before she reached the station, and walked to the platform with a new understanding of what she carried—not just the research, but the weight of it. This wasn't purely academic any more. If the genetic data were correct, if the historical patterns were real, then there were potentially thirty thousand people alive today who carried these markers. Most would never know. But some would experience the gifts—the enhanced intuition, the pattern recognition, the occasional flash of genuine precognition—and think themselves mad. And if Brother Thomas was right, there were organisations that had been tracKing these bloodlines for centuries. Some to protect them. Some to control them. Some, perhaps, to exploit them.

The theft of 751 hadn't ended. It had just evolved.

On the train back to Paris, Amélie opened her laptop and began organising her research. She needed to be systematic. Careful. Scientific. Frame this as a historian's survey of inherited traits in European populations. Let the implications speak for themselves.

But in her private notes, where no one else would see, she wrote:

The coup of 751 was not a single event but the beginning of a process—the systematic appropriation of a bloodline that may carry genuine cognitive enhancements. What the Carolingians began, others continued. And what began with Kings and Popes has become something else entirely: a network of families, of guardians, of interested parties, all circling around a secret that may be among the most significant genetic discoveries in human history.

If I am right, we are not alone in the universe. We never were. The gifts in the bloodline point to something older, something that predates recorded history. And someone has been hiding that truth for over a thousand years.

She paused. Then added one more line, and encrypted the file.

If something happens to me, if this research disappears—know that it was real. All of it.

The research continues.

The ocean does not forget.

CHAPTER SIX

The Bloodline of Seth

Paris, November 2024

Three weeks after her meeting with Brother Thomas, the trail led Amélie to Jerusalem.

Not in person—she was not yet ready to move, and the surveillance she had felt closing around her since the library made travel unwise. But Dr David Dowed, a geneticist who specialised in the genetic history of the Jewish diaspora, had agreed to speak with her after she sent him a summary of her research. Not the full document. A careful distillation, enough to convey the direction without exposing everything she had.

She had expected scepticism. She got precision instead.

"Family traditions aren't genetic proof," he said, on their first call, his face clear and composed on her screen. "Many European families claimed exotic ancestry—it was prestigious to claim Eastern origins in certain periods. Without rigorous genetic testing against documented Jewish populations, you can't prove Ashérite descent specifically."

"What if I'm not trying to prove it definitively?" she said. "What if I'm asking whether it's genetically plausible?"

"Plausible? Yes. Provable? Not with current data." He paused. "But I can tell you this: there has been recent research on genetic diversity within Jewish populations. Some studies have identified subgroups with distinct genetic signatures that may correspond to ancient tribal divisions. It's controversial—many scholars think tribal identities were lost too early for genetic signals to remain distinct. But a few researchers have found patterns suggesting some families really did maintain separate lineages."

"Including Asher?"

"There are a handful of families that claim Ashérite descent based on family tradition. Whether those claims are accurate..." He shrugged. "Genetic testing has been limited. Most of these families are Orthodox, suspicious of secular science, unwilling to submit to testing. But yes, there are communities that maintain these traditions."

She sent him the markers after that call. Waited four days. Then scheduled the second call.

"Dr. Rousseau." He leaned forward, his face filling the screen. Behind him she could see shelves crammed with books and journals, and something that might have been a genealogical chart tacked to the wall. "I've reviewed the genetic markers you sent me. These are... remarkable. Where did you obtain these samples?"

"I can't reveal my sources, but they're legitimate. What can you tell me?"

Dowed hesitated, glancing at something off-screen. "Before I answer that, I need to know what you're really investigating. Because these markers—some of them—match patterns I've only seen in one other context."

"Which is?"

"The Cohen Modal Haplotype. Have you heard of it?"

Amélie pulled up her notes. "The genetic signature of the Jewish priesthood. Male descendants of Aaron."

"Exactly. The CMH is a specific pattern of markers on the Y-chromosome that appears with high frequency in men who identify as Cohanim—the priestly line. It's one of the most dramatic examples of genetic continuity over three thousand years. But what you've sent me... these aren't Y-chromosome markers. These are mitochondrial, passed through the maternal line. And they show a similar pattern of preservation—a signature that appears to have been maintained through selective breeding over an equally long period."

Amélie's heart began to race. "Maintained how?"

"That's what I can't understand. The CMH makes sense—the priesthood was patrilineal, passed from father to son, and priestly families would naturally marry within their class. But this mitochondrial pattern would require the reverse: a tradition of priestly families choosing wives from specific lineages, generation after generation, for thousands of years."

"What if I told you," Amélie said slowly, "that there's historical evidence of exactly that? Of a specific tribal lineage whose daughters were sought after by the priesthood?"

Dowed's eyes widened. "Which tribe?"

"My speculation is that it is the tribe of Asher."

There was a long silence. His expression cycled through disbelief, consideration, and finally a kind of awed understanding.

"The lost tribe," he murmured.

"One of the ten northern tribes that disappeared after the Assyrian conquest in 722 BCE. But if they weren't lost—if they survived through the maternal line..." He leaned closer to the camera. "Dr. Rousseau, what exactly are you investigating?"

"The genetic basis of prophetic gifts. And their preservation through European bloodlines."

Another silence. Then: "Are you familiar with the Sethite hypothesis?"

"The idea that there were two bloodlines after Cain killed Abel—the line of Cain and the line of Seth?"

"More than that. In the Jewish mystical tradition, the line of Seth is said to have carried something special—a spiritual inheritance from Adam and Eve before the Fall. The Zohar calls it the 'light of the first day'—the Divine spark that Adam carried before sin corrupted creation. This light was supposedly passed down through the righteous line: Seth, Enosh, Kenan, Mahalalel, Jared, Enoch, Methuselah, Lamech, and finally Noah."

Dowed shared a document on screen—a genealogical chart, starting with Adam and tracing down through the generations. Its validity had been disputed, as these documents always were. But something in it rang true to Amélie in a way that went deeper than academic verification.

"After the Flood," Dowed continued, "the line continued through Noah's sons. In Jewish tradition, the knowledge keepers—those who preserved the sacred wisdom—came from this lineage. Abraham, called out of Ur to become father of nations. Isaac. Jacob. And from Jacob came the twelve tribes, each carrying different aspects of the original inheritance."

"Different aspects?" Amélie asked.

"Think of it like genetic traits—different branches expressing different characteristics. Judah carried the Kingship, the messianic line. Levi carried the priesthood. Dan..." He paused. "Dan is complicated. Some traditions say Dan carried the prophetic gift but corrupted it, which is why Dan is omitted from certain biblical genealogies."

"And Asher?"

Dowed pulled up another document—an ancient Hebrew text with English translation below. "This is from the Testament of the Twelve Patriarchs, a second-century BCE text. The patriarchs speak one by one of their inheritance. Zebulun's testimony is instructive, because his tribe was closely connected to Asher—both sons of Zilpah, Leah's handmaid, neighbours in ancient Israel. He says:"

"And now, my children, I command you: keep the commandments of the Lord, and show mercy to your neighbours, and have compassion on all, not on people only, but also on beasts. For on account of this, the Lord blessed me, and when all my brothers were sick, I was not sick, for

the Lord knows the purposes of each. For he who shows mercy to his neighbour receives mercy from the Lord also."

"Mercy and healing," Amélie said. "Compassion as a defining characteristic."

"Exactly. And it reflects what the traditions say about Asher directly." He pulled up another passage. "Jacob's blessing of Asher in Genesis 49:20 says: Asher's food will be rich; he will provide delicacies fit for a King. On the surface, this seems to be about prosperity. But in mystical interpretation, 'food' often represents spiritual sustenance—wisdom, knowledge. 'Fit for a King' suggests service to higher authority."

"And Moses's blessing?" Amélie asked, pulling up her own notes. "Deuteronomy 33:24—25: 'Let Asher be blessed with children; let him be acceptable to his brothers, and let him dip his foot in oil. The bolts of your gates will be iron and bronze, and your strength will equal your days.'"

"Dipping his foot in oil." Dowed's voice quickened. "In ancient Jewish practice, oil represented the anointing of the Spirit—the presence of God that rested on prophets, priests, and Kings. To 'dip your foot" in oil suggests walKing in that anointing, carrying it wherever you go. And being "acceptable to his brothers" suggests a role as mediator, as bridge.'

He pulled out another document. "Now look at this—recent genetic research on Jewish populations. Some studies have found unusual patterns in certain families that claim pre-diaspora lineage. Enhanced sensory processing. The ability to perceive connections between things that normally register separately. Controversial, and the interpretation remains contested. But some researchers have proposed it could be a preserved genetic trait, selected for over thousands of years."

"Because it made you more sensitive to spiritual realities," Amélie said. "Better able to perceive patterns, to sense truth, to see what was hidden."

"That's one reading." Dowed paused. "Look at your mitochondrial markers. Compare them to these patterns."

Amélie did, and her breath caught. The overlap was striKing—not perfect, but significant. The markers she'd found in Merovingian descendants matched patterns that appeared in Jewish families claiming pre-diaspora lineage.

"I am starting to believe that the line of Asher survived," she said. "When the northern Kingdom fell, when the ten tribes were scattered, Asher preserved their lineage through the maternal line. Through strategic marriages. Through hiding in plain sight."

"And some of them went west," Dowed added. "Following the Phoenician trade routes. Intermarrying with the populations there. Eventually becoming..." He trailed off.

"The Merovingians," Amélie finished. "Or at least, possibly contributing to their bloodline. Bringing the gifts of Asher—healing, prophetic sight, compassionate service—into European populations."

Dowed sat back from his camera, running his hands through his hair. "Dr. Rousseau, if you're right about this, it changes everything. It means the genetic inheritance of the patriarchs is real—that it survived through the diaspora, that it's still present in modern populations. That the gifts mentioned in scripture weren't metaphorical or supernatural in the sense we usually mean. They were genetic. Passed through bloodlines. Preserved through careful, deliberate breeding."

"It could also mean," Amélie said quietly, "that this inheritance was stolen. Corrupted. Used for purposes opposite to its original intent."

"How so?"

She told him. About the Merovingians and the Carolingian coup of 751. About the systematic breeding programs designed to concentrate the gifts while suppressing their moral foundation. About the trauma programming that turned seers into instruments—people with the gifts but without the conscience that had always been their counterweight. About children being broken now, today, in houses that no one from outside would ever enter, to serve families who had stolen their heritage centuries ago.

By the time she finished, Dowed was pale.

"My God," he whispered. "Do you understand what you're describing? The sacred gifts—the inheritance of the patriarchs, the anointing that was meant to bless all nations—has been weaponised. Turned into a tool of oppression instead of liberation."

"Yes."

"And you have evidence?"

"I'm compiling it. Genetic data, historical documents, contemporary cases. But I need to trace the genealogy further back. I need to show a direct genetic line from the ancient priesthood to modern populations."

Dowed was quiet for a long moment. Then: "I can help you. I have access to genetic databases that you don't. And I have contacts in the Orthodox community—families that have maintained meticulous genealogical records for centuries. Some of them claim direct descent from specific tribal lines."

"Including Asher?"

"Possibly. There's a community in France, actually—descendants of Spanish Jews who fled the Inquisition. Their family traditions claim Ashérite descent. They've been suspicious of genetic testing, afraid of persecution, but if I vouch for you..." He paused. "But Dr. Rousseau, you need to understand something. If we do this, if we prove this connection, we're not just challenging historical narratives. We're maKing claims about the nature of spiritual gifts, about the reality of biblical genealogies, about genetics and theology intersecting in ways that will make both religious and secular authorities very uncomfortable."

"I understand."

"There's something else you need to know," Dowed said. "Something I haven't told you yet because I wasn't sure if I should." He took a breath. "The genetic markers you sent me—I said they matched patterns in priestly families. That's true. But they may also match something else. Something I've only seen in one other context."

"Which is?"

"In 2015, a team of researchers published a genetic study of the Shroud of Turin in a peer-reviewed journal — Scientific Reports. It caused immediate controversy and has been largely set aside by mainstream scholarship. But the findings were intriguing. They extracted DNA from dust particles vacuumed from the Shroud surface. The human genetic profiles were varied — centuries of handling by people from across the world. But among them, a haplogroup strongly associated with populations from the Levant. Israel, Jordan, Syria, Lebanon. And the overall profile was assessed as consistent with a linen of Middle Eastern origin from the first century CE."

Amélie felt cold. "Are you saying—"

"I'm saying that the Levantine profile they found — that Middle Eastern signature, first century, geographically consistent with the region your research points to — when I put it beside the markers you've found in Merovingian descendants, the ones that match Ashérite populations... the overlap is not nothing." He paused. "I want to be precise about what I'm doing right now. I am not claiming the Shroud is authentic. I am not claiming the DNA is his. What I am saying is that the geographic and temporal profile of what was found is consistent with what your research describes, and that the convergence is — statistically, at minimum — interesting." He stopped himself. "I'm not maKing theological claims. I'm a scientist. I can't prove any of this. But genetically, there could be a connection between these bloodlines and the bloodline of—"

"Yeshua," Amélie finished.

Dowed nodded. "If the Shroud findings are authentic—and that's a massive if—then yes. And it would explain something that has always puzzled scholars. Yeshua was from the tribe of Judah, traced through his legal father Joseph. But Mary's lineage is less documented. The only Gospel that mentions it says she was a relative of Elizabeth, who was from the tribe of Levi. But there are apocryphal texts that suggest Mary may have had Ashérite ancestry through her mother's line."

He pulled up another document—a second-century text not included in the biblical canon. "This text describes Mary's mother, Anna—not to be confused with Anna the Prophetess, though possibly related. It says she was from a family of temple servants, suggesting Levitical connections. But there is a tradition, recorded in some Orthodox sources, that her mother—Mary's grandmother—was from the tribe of Asher."

"Which would mean," Amélie said slowly, working through the implications, "that Yeshua carried both Judahite DNA through Joseph's legal lineage and Ashérite DNA through Mary's actual bloodline."

"Kingship and priesthood. Authority and compassion. The ability to rule and the ability to heal." Dowed's expression was awed. "In Jewish tradition, the Messiah is supposed to unite all the tribal inheritances—to carry the complete blessing of Jacob, the fullness of what was meant to flow through all twelve tribes. If Yeshua had Judahite and Ashérite genetics, that would be a literal fulfilment of that expectation."

"And Anna the Prophetess," Amélie said, the understanding coming as a warmth rather than a thought. "She was from Asher. She recognised Yeshua immediately when he was presented at the temple. Not because of faith alone, but because—"

"Because she Saw," Dowed finished. "With the prophetic sight that ran in the Ashérite bloodline. She recognised the genetic signature. The fullness of the inheritance, carried in an eight-day-old child."

They sat in silence for a moment, the weight of what they had spoken settling over them both.

"This is why the bloodline matters," Amélie said finally. "This is why it was stolen and why it's been suppressed. Because it's not just about supernatural powers or genetic advantages. It's about a sacred mandate—a purpose encoded in the DNA itself. To heal, to serve, to elevate others. And when that mandate is corrupted, when those gifts are turned against their purpose..."

"You get the world we have now," Dowed finished. "Where the descendants of seers manipulate markets instead of guiding people. Where healers harm instead of help. Where prophetic sight is used to exploit futures instead of blessing them."

"Can it be recovered?" Amélie asked. "If the bloodline is still out there, if there are still thirty thousand descendants carrying these markers—can the original purpose be restored?"

"Genetically? The markers are there. The potential exists. But genetics isn't destiny, Dr. Rousseau. Having the markers for enhanced empathy doesn't mean you'll use them compassionately. Having precognitive abilities doesn't mean you'll use them to help people. The gifts can be developed or suppressed, used for good or ill. It depends on the choices people make."

"And on whether they know what they're choosing," Amélie added. "Most descendants don't even know they carry the bloodline. They live their whole lives never understanding why they're different, why they sense things others don't. How can they choose to use the gifts properly if they don't even know they have them?"

"Which is why your research matters," Dowed said. "Why exposure matters. Because knowledge is the first step to reclaiming what was stolen." He smiled slightly. "In Jewish tradition, the Messiah doesn't come to bring new truth but to reveal truth that was always there. To help people see what they'd forgotten, understand what they'd lost. Perhaps that's your role in this, Dr. Rousseau. Not to create something new, but to help people remember something very, very old."

After the call ended, Amélie sat in her apartment surrounded by her research, and saw it all with new eyes.

The line of Seth, preserved through Noah, branching into the twelve tribes. Asher carrying the gifts of healing and prophetic sight, the oil of anointing. Scattered in 722 BCE, but surviving through the maternal line, travelling west along the Phoenician routes. Intermarrying with European populations. Eventually becoming part of the Merovingian bloodline.

And Yeshua—the fullest expression of all the tribal gifts, carrying both Judah's authority and Asher's compassion, recognised by Anna who carried the same prophetic sight.

A story written not in books but in blood. Preserved through three thousand years of history, hidden but never truly lost.

She opened her manuscript and began a new section:

To understand what was stolen in 751, we must go back much further—to the beginning of the bloodline itself, to a man named Seth who replaced his murdered brother Abel. In Jewish tradition, Seth carried the 'light of the first day'—a Divine inheritance that would pass through Noah, through Abraham, through the twelve tribes of Israel. Each tribe carried different aspects of this inheritance, different expressions of gifts meant to bless all nations. And one tribe—Asher, the blessed one—carried the gifts of healing, prophecy, and compassionate service. This is their story. And it is still being written.

52

CHAPTER SEVEN

The Council of Shadows

Paris, November 2024

The email arrived at 3:17 AM.

The alert tone jolted her awake. She lay still for a moment in the dark, then reached for her phone. The sender was listed only as A Friend. No return address. Routed through multiple servers, according to the client.

The message was brief:

You have found the bloodline. Now find the families. They meet tomorrow night. I can get you in, but you have only have one chance. If you are serious about exposing this, meet me at Pont Neuf at noon. Come alone. And Dr. Rousseau—prepare yourself. What you have learned is theory. What you are about to see is practice.

Amélie stared at the screen, her heart running fast. Every instinct told her trap. The Council knew she was investigating. The families had resources she couldn't imagine. This could be a setup to silence her permanently.

But it could also be the breakthrough she needed.

She copied the email three times, encrypted each copy, and sent them to different secure locations. Then she began to prepare.

At noon she stood on the Pont Neuf—the oldest bridge in Paris—watching the Seine move beneath her. Tourists clustered around street performers. A bateau-mouche cruised past, its guide pointing out landmarks in several languages. The ordinary world, continuing entirely oblivious to what churned beneath its surface.

"Dr. Rousseau."

She turned. The voice was familiar—Marguerite Valcourt, the woman she'd met at the Marché d'Aligre a month ago. She wore sunglasses despite the overcast sky, and a silk scarf covered most of her silver hair. She looked like any other elegant Parisian woman out for a midday walk. But her expression was grave.

"It was you who sent the email?"

"One of my associates. We've been monitoring the families" communications for some time. There's a meeting tonight—one of their quarterly gatherings. Normally they're impossible to infiltrate. But we have someone on the inside who can get you in as hired help. You'll be invisible to them, just another member of the catering staff. But you'll see everything."

"Why are you doing this?" Amélie asked.

Marguerite's expression darkened. "Because my daughter is one of them now. One of the broken ones. They took her when she was seven—I didn't even know what they were until it was too late. I thought I was marrying into a respectable business family. By the time I understood what they did to children who showed the gifts too strongly, she was already..." Her voice cracked. "Already split. Trained. She's twenty-eight now. Sits on corporate boards. Makes decisions that affect millions of lives. And she feels nothing. No empathy. No conscience. Just the gifts, operating in service to profit."

"I'm sorry," Amélie said softly.

"Don't be sorry. Help me stop it. Help me make sure no other mother loses her child to these people." Marguerite handed her a small package. "Inside is a uniform, credentials, and an earpiece. The meeting is at Château Montable. You'll be serving a private dinner. Keep your head down, serve the food, and observe. The earpiece will record everything." She gripped Amélie's arm. "But Dr. Rousseau—don't react. Don't let them see that you understand what you're hearing. These people are experts at reading faces, sensing reactions. If they realise you're not actually staff, you won't leave that château."

The Château Montable was a nineteenth-century mansion that looked like it had been lifted from a fairy tale—towers and turrets, manicured gardens, ancient forests pressing in from all sides. Built by the Robert family; now used for private events and, apparently, for gatherings of the kind that did not appear in anyone's diary.

Amélie arrived with the other catering staff at six o'clock. They were processed through security: metal detectors, bag searches, a cursory background check. Her false credentials, provided by Marguerite's contacts, held up.

The head of catering—a severe woman named Claudette—distributed assignments. Amélie was placed in the main dining room. She suspected Marguerite had arranged it.

"Remember," Claudette said to the assembled staff. "You are to be invisible. Do not speak unless spoken to. Do not make eye contact. Do not react to anything you might overhear. The guests value their privacy absolutely. Anyone who violates this discretion will be dismissed immediately and will never work in this city again. Am I understood?"

A chorus of Oui, madame.

Amélie took her position in the serving line, holding a tray of champagne flutes, and tried to look like she'd done this a thousand times before.

Then the guests began to arrive.

She recognised some of them immediately from her research. Wilhelm Eisen, chairman of Eisen Financial Group. Marie-Claire Valan, head of one of the oldest banKing families in Europe. Sir Malcolm Ashford, whose family had controlled significant portions of British finance since the eighteenth century. Others she didn't recognise, but their bearing, their manner, the way other people arranged themselves around them—these were people for whom power was not something they had acquired. It was something they had always had.

And there, near the back, looking impossibly young for such company—a woman about thirty, with flat eyes and a cold smile. The woman from the photograph Marguerite had shown her weeks ago. The one who sat on three boards and predicted currency movements with uncanny accuracy.

Marguerite's daughter.

Amélie kept her face blank and circulated with champagne. The guests took glasses without acknowledging her existence.

She was furniture. Background. Exactly what she needed to be.

"Shall we begin?" Wilhelm Eisen said, and the conversation around the room died. The guests moved to the dining table. Amélie and the other servers took their positions along the walls.

Eisen remained standing. "Thank you all for coming. There are matters that require our collective attention." He gestured to a young man—perhaps twenty-five—sitting near the head of the table. "Some of you have already met my grandson, Friedrich. He's recently completed his training and will be joining the board of our primary holding company. Friedrich has shown particular aptitude in pattern recognition. His assessments of the Asian markets have proven... remarkably accurate. We're very pleased with his progress."

Amélie studied Friedrich. He had his grandfather's aristocratic features, but there was something missing behind his eyes—a flatness, as if the machinery of expression were operating without the person who should have been driving it. He smiled at the appropriate times, said the appropriate things.

Another broken child, raised up to serve the family business.

The dinner began. Seven courses, each more elaborate than the last. And between courses, conversation that made the blood run cold.

"—the merger should go through by Q3. My sources indicate the regulatory committee is sympathetic. A few strategic donations never hurt—"

"—the Bradshaw girl. Such potential, but her empathy levels were too high. Had to implement an advanced protocol. She"ll need another year before she's ready—'

"—the Deutsche situation is well in hand. There will be some complications for the middle class, of course, but that"s unavoidable—'

They spoke of human suffering the way others might discuss a change in the weather. Policies that would destroy thousands of lives, debated over foie gras and vintage wine. And threaded through it all, the other conversation: children with gifts. Children being "trained." Children who were "resistant" or "receptive" to the protocols.

Children being broken.

Amélie kept her face blank, her movements mechanical, while the rage burned in her chest like something she was not allowed to touch.

"There is one other matter," Marie-Claire Valan said during the fifth course. She was perhaps sixty, impeccably dressed, with sharp eyes that missed nothing. "We've become aware of certain research. An academic in Paris, investigating the bloodlines. She's made some concerning connections."

Amélie's heart stopped.

"How concerning?" Eisen asked.

"She's traced the genetic markers. Connected the Merovingian bloodline to the ancient tribal lines. She's spoken with geneticists, historians, church archivists. And she's compiling evidence for publication."

"Can she be dissuaded?" This from Sir Malcolm.

"We're exploring options. The Council is monitoring the situation. But she's been careful—distributed her research, created backups, contacted colleagues. Simply eliminating her would draw attention."

"Then we discredit her," a German banker said. "Academic misconduct. Mental instability. The usual protocols."

"That's being arranged," Valan confirmed. "But it may not be sufficient. This one is... persistent. And she appears to have allies we haven't fully identified."

"What about recruitment?" This from a younger member, perhaps forty. "If she has the gifts, if she's from the bloodline—could she be trained?"

Valan's smile was cold. "She's thirty-four. Far too old for the protocols to work properly. Adult personalities are too integrated. The fracturing is much more difficult and often fails. No, if she can't be silenced or discredited..." She left the implication hanging.

Amélie forced herself to keep breathing. To continue serving food as if she hadn't just heard her potential death sentence discussed over braised lamb.

"I leave it in your capable hands, Marie-Claire," Eisen said. "But I want this resolved before the autumn meetings. We can't have someone publishing genetic research that could expose our connections. Bad enough that DNA testing has become popular with the masses—we don't need academics explaining what the markers mean."

The conversation moved on to other topics—upcoming elections, policy recommendations for various governments, investment strategies. But Amélie had heard enough.

During the seventh course, she noticed Marguerite's daughter watching her. Those flat eyes fixed with sudden interest.

"You," the young woman said.

Amélie's throat went dry. "Madame?"

"You've been very attentive. Very focused on our conversation." The woman's smile was predatory. "Almost as if you were listening rather than merely serving."

The table went quiet. Every eye turned to Amélie.

"I apologise if I've been intrusive, madame," Amélie said, keeping her voice steady, her eyes down. "I was simply trying to anticipate when your glass might need refilling."

"Really." The woman stood and walked around the table toward her. "Because I'm sensing something. A resonance." She stopped directly in front of Amélie, studying her face. "Tell me your name."

"Claire Dubois, madame. With the catering service."

"Look at me."

Amélie raised her eyes, meeting that flat gaze. And felt something—a subtle pressure, a careful, systematic attention, like being read by someone who had been doing it all their life.

She did the only thing she could think of. She thought about champagne. About needing to refill glasses, about hoping she wasn't about to be dismissed, about whether the kitchen was running behind on the coffee service. Surface thoughts. Mundane thoughts. Hiding everything deeper behind the most ordinary fears she could manufacture.

The pressure intensified. Then, after what felt like a very long time, the woman laughed. "Apologies. I thought I sensed something, but I see I was mistaken. You're exactly what you appear to be—ordinary help, worried about doing her job properly." She returned to her seat. "My gifts sometimes give false positives when I'm tired."

The conversation resumed.

But Amélie noticed Wilhelm Eisen studying her with narrowed eyes. He had not been fooled as easily as his granddaughter's colleague. He suspected something.

Time to leave.

During the clearing of the seventh course, Amélie slipped into the kitchen, then out through a service door. She stripped off her uniform in the garden, stuffed it in a bin, and walked quickly toward the tree line.

"Dr. Rousseau."

She spun. A man stepped from the shadows—the same one from the library, the angular face, the ring bearing the Merovingian symbol.

"You shouldn't have come here," he said. His tone was more weary than threatening. "Now they know you're not just theorising. You've seen them. And they will act."

"Then why aren't you stopping me?"

"Because the Council is divided. Some believe in maintaining the old agreements, protecting the families regardless of what they do. Others..." He touched the ring. "Others believe the theft has gone on long enough. That it's time for the bloodline to be reclaimed by those who would use it properly."

"Which side are you on?"

"The side of truth. Which is why I'm going to help you get out of here." He handed her a key. "My car is in the west lot, space seventeen. Drive to Paris. Don't go home—they'll be watching. Go to the address on this card." He pressed a card into her hand. "You'll be safe there. And you'll find others—people who carry the bloodline and want to reclaim its purpose."

"Why should I trust you?"

His smile was sad. "Because we're family, doctor. Distant cousins, separated by centuries and circumstance. But family nonetheless." He stepped back toward the dark between the trees. "The blood recognises its own. Now go. Before they realise you're gone."

Amélie ran.

She was halfway back to Paris, heart still running, when her phone buzzed. A text from an unknown number:

You saw what they are. Now help us stop them.

There are more of us than you know—descendants who have awakened, who have rejected the families and their corruption. We are building something new. Something that honours what the bloodline was meant to be.

Join us. Or publish and let them destroy you.

Your choice. But choose quickly.

—The Remnant.

Amélie pulled over. Sat with her hands on the wheel.

Thirty thousand descendants, scattered across the world. Most would never know what they carried. But some did. And some were organising. Building something in the space where the old inheritance had been taken from them.

She opened her laptop, connected to her phone's hotspot, and began transferring files to her secure backup sites. Every document, every interview, every piece of genetic data. The complete story of the bloodline, from Seth to the present day.

Then she opened a new email to her editor at the academic journal that had expressed interest in her work:

Attached is my complete manuscript. If anything happens to me, publish everything. The families mentioned in these documents are powerful, but the truth is more powerful. It is time for the theft to end.

—Dr. Amélie Rousseau

She hit send.

Then, following the address the man had given her, she drove toward whatever came next. Toward others who carried the gifts, who remembered the purpose, who were ready to reclaim what had been stolen.

The blood Remembers

And it was time to come home.

CHAPTER EIGHT

The Safe House

Paris / The Pyrenees, October—November 2024

The safe house was an unassuming apartment in the eleventh arrondissement, above a bakery whose morning smells of fresh bread seemed almost obscenely normal given what Amélie had just witnessed.

The man from the château — he'd finally introduced himself as Marcus Valis — led her up three flights of narrow stairs to a door with no number, just a small symbol etched into the wood: a circle within a wave.

Inside, six people waited. They looked nothing like what Amélie had expected. No occult robes, no mystical paraphernalia. Just ordinary people in their twenties to sixties, sitting in a modest living room with mismatched furniture and a tea service laid out on a coffee table. But their eyes — every single one of them had that quality she'd begun to recognise. A depth. An awareness. The look of people who saw more than most.

A woman in her forties stood to greet her — tall, with dark hair streaked with silver, moving with a grace that suggested either dance training or something more martial. "Dr. Rousseau. Thank you for coming. My name is Sophia Castellane." The others introduced themselves in turn: Daniel, perhaps thirty, with intense dark eyes; Elena, perhaps sixty, white-haired, with the weathered face of someone who had spent a great deal of time outdoors and a faint Eastern European accent; Rachel, perhaps twenty-five, soft-voiced, watchful. Priya, who sat slightly apart near the window with the particular stillness of someone who had long since stopped needing to fill silence with words. And Isabelle, dark and lean, positioned so she could see both the door and the window without appearing to watch either.

"Who are you people?" Amélie asked.

"The Remnant, as we said in our message." Sophia poured tea and handed Amélie a cup. "Descendants of the bloodline who've awakened to what we carry. Most of us discovered it accidentally — gifts we couldn't explain, abilities that made us different. Some of us were targeted by the families for recruitment. We escaped. Others simply refused to serve the system once we understood what it was."

Daniel spoke briefly. He had been taken at twelve, three weeks in the program, the attempt to fragment him. "But when they were trying to break me," he said, his hands steady now around his cup, "I went somewhere else. Not just psychologically — I went somewhere vast and alive, made of consciousness itself. And in that place I felt connected. To everyone who had ever carried this gift. Past, present, future." He looked at Amélie. "They couldn't follow me there."

"You've felt it too," Sophia said, watching her face. "Haven't you? The sense that there's something beneath everything. An ocean of awareness that most people never perceive but that we can't help but feel."

"I thought I was going mad," Amélie whispered.

"You're not." Elena leaned forward. "The Ocean — that's what Daniel found, what all of us have found — it isn't mysticism. It's the consciousness that underlies everything. Those of us who carry the bloodline feel it more easily than most. Not because we're special. Because the genetics kept the access open, even when everything around us was designed to close it."

She said it simply, as a statement of fact. And Amélie understood — intellectually, the way she had been understanding things for six months. Tracing evidence, building cases, connecting what could be sourced and cited to what could only be sensed.

The problem was that she wanted to believe it.

That was the dangerous thing. Not the scepticism — she was comfortable with scepticism, it was professional equipment, she had sharpened it for years. The dangerous thing was the wanting. The part of her that sat across from Sophia and felt the pull of everything she was saying like a tide.

She had been a historian long enough to know what happened when people wanted something to be true. They found the evidence that confirmed it and quietly set aside the evidence that didn't. They built elegant structures of logic that looked like towers and were actually houses of cards. They convinced themselves and then others and sometimes — in the worst cases, in the cases that filled history with blood and catastrophe — they convinced nations.

She did not want to be that kind of person.

And yet.

And yet she had felt the warmth in the café. She had felt it again in the library, just before the lights went out. She felt it now, sitting here, inexplicable and inconvenient and completely real. Not imagination — she knew the texture of imagination, had spent enough time alone with her thoughts to know the difference between what she manufactured and what arrived. This arrived.

"You're fighting with yourself," Sophia said.

"I'm a medieval historian," Amélie said. "Fighting with the evidence is my job."

"The evidence isn't the problem. You've accepted the evidence. You've been building a case on the evidence for six months." Sophia's voice was patient, with the quality of someone who had had this exact conversation many times and was not tired of it. "The problem is what the evidence means about you. Personally."

Amélie said nothing.

It was not a comfortable silence.

Here was the thing she had not told anyone, had barely admitted to herself: she was afraid of being wrong. She had been wrong before — every academic was wrong regularly, it was part of the method — but those times she had been wrong about things at a safe professional distance. Wrong about a date. Wrong about a source. Wrong in ways that could be corrected with a footnote and a revised edition.

This was different. If she was wrong about this — about the bloodline, about the consciousness, about all of it — then she had destroyed her career for nothing. She had stood in the Parisian rain for nothing. She had spent six months isolated and frightened and she had perhaps been, as the rumours said, simply unhinged by grief.

But if she was right. If she was right, and she followed it, and she let herself believe — then she would become someone she didn't yet recognise. Someone who had access to things she had spent thirty-four years refusing to name. Someone who dived, as Sophia said, into an ocean that had been there all along, that she had always felt at the edges of her life and ignored.

Her mother's voice: *You can feel things, my love. Real things. Don't let them take that from you.*

"My mother knew," Amélie said quietly. "She tried to tell me, near the end. I thought she was confused."

Sophia waited.

"She wasn't confused, was she."

"No," Sophia said simply. "She wasn't."

Amélie looked at her hands. The same hands that had sorted through her The same hands that had sorted through her Grand-mere's box. The same hands that had photographed manuscripts in the dark. The hands she had used to press publish on a document that had changed everything and nothing.

"Show me," she said. "Whatever this is. Show me properly."

The warmth in her chest moved, and for the first time she let herself feel it fully — not as an anomaly to be explained, but as something that had been waiting a very long time for her to stop looking away.

Elena taught her over the following days. Not formal meditation, not visualisation or mantras. Just sitting. Breathing. And learning to feel the warmth in her chest.

"Attention on the heart," Elena said. "Not the physical heart — the energetic centre in your chest. When thoughts come, let them pass like clouds. Keep returning to the warmth."

The first day was frustration. The second day brought a flicker — five seconds of something quiet and real before the excitement of noticing it pulled her back to the surface. The third day she stayed down for minutes at a time. And in those minutes she understood: not mystical, not supernatural. Simply quieter. Deeper. Like diving below the surface of a turbulent ocean and discovering the calm that existed beneath the waves. Her awareness was still there. Her thoughts still happened. But they were happening on the surface, and she was watching from below, from a place that was not disturbed by them.

On the third evening, Elena handed her a phone before they settled for the night. "One call," she said. "Someone who has been waiting to speak with you." The man who answered had a Tibetan accent and a voice that carried the same quality she was learning to recognise in the Remnant — unhurried, rooted, clear as water. His name was Rinpoche Tenzi. He had worked with Elena for twenty years, he said. He would join them at the monastery when the time was right. Until then: practice what Elena taught. Stay in the breath. Stay in the Ocean. He would know when she was ready. The call lasted perhaps four minutes. She had not known what to make of him, except that in those four minutes she had felt steadier than she had in six months.

It was that same evening that Elena sat with her after the others had gone to bed.

"When we reach the monastery," Elena said, "there will be children there. Ones we've rescued from the programs." She paused, choosing her words with the care of someone who had carried this knowledge for a long time and had never found it easier to pass on. "Some of them are severely traumatised. The programming is designed to fracture consciousness — to split the personality so the gifts can be accessed without the child's knowledge or consent." Her eyes, in the lamplight, were ancient and very sad. "Healing them requires someone who can go deep and hold that space steadily while the child works out whether it's safe to surface. I've been watching you this week. You have that capacity."

"I've only been diving for three days."

"I know. But this isn't about expertise. It's about presence. About being the Ocean while someone else remembers how to trust it." Elena's voice was steady and certain. "These children are what the families create when they take the bloodline and use it for control rather than service. They are the living evidence of everything we're fighting against. And they are also," she added quietly, "the reason we don't stop."

Amélie sat with that for a long time after Elena left the room.

She thought about her grandmother's letter. About the inheritance — not the history of it, not the genetics, but the living weight of it. What it meant to carry something this old and still be responsible for how you used it.

She pressed her palm flat against her sternum. Felt the warmth there, steady and unmistakeable. She had spent thirty-four years explaining it away. She did not think she would do that anymore. In her chest, the warmth pulsed steadily. Not anxious. Not afraid. Just present.

CHAPTER NINE

The Germanic Traditions

Paris, November 2024

It was their third morning above the bakery.

Marcus had been awake since before five, spreading his materials across the kitchen table while Elena slept in the next room. Photographs, photocopies of illuminated manuscripts, his own dense handwritten annotations. The flat was quiet except for the radiator's hiss and, somewhere outside, the particular Paris silence of the hours before the city woke.

"The Merovingian bloodline wasn't a single line," he said, keeping his voice low, when Amélie appeared in the doorway with coffee. "It was a convergence. Two streams meeting. Elena described Argotta's Asher inheritance — the Phoenician-descent practices, the breathwork, the healing. But Chlodio's side is the part most people miss."

He laid a photocopy in front of her — a page from a nineteenth-century scholarly text, dense with Germanic script. "The völvas. The Germanic seeresses. They called what we're calling the Ocean the well of wyrd — the stream of fate and possibility where past, present, and future flow together. And the seidr tradition was how they accessed it." He tapped the page. "Not prayer. Not ritual sacrifice. Deep trance states, altered consciousness, journeying in. The same practice. Different cultural container."

Sophia had been listening from the doorway, arms folded. "Or a superficial similarity that people want to read as the same thing."

Marcus looked at her.

"I'm serious," she said, coming into the room. "Every culture has shamans and visionaries. That doesn't mean they're all accessing the same mechanism. That could just be what human consciousness does when it turns inward — generates similar imagery. We could be pattern-matching across traditions and calling it proof."

"I'm not saying it's proof," Marcus said evenly. "I'm saying the documented capacities are identical. Diagnosis of illness from a distance. Predictive vision. The ability to perceive things hidden from ordinary sight. The same practitioner profile appearing in cultures that had no contact with each other."

"Similar outcomes can have different causes."

"Sophia."

Amélie said it quietly, and something in her tone brought both of them around. "Something's happening."

She was looking at her own hands.

She hadn't meant to touch the photocopy. It had been an idle gesture — fingertips resting on the edge of the page while they talked. But the moment she made contact, something had shifted at the back of her skull: a brief, clean pressure, like the moment before a sound you can't quite hear.

"I'm getting something," she said. "From this."

Marcus went very still. "What kind of something?"

"Images. Not — it's not like seeing. It's more like..." She searched for the word. 'Knowing. Information with texture." She pressed her palm flat on the page, feeling faintly ridiculous, and the pressure behind her eyes sharpened into something almost geographical: a sense of place, of cold water and flat grey sky, of a trading settlement on a river. "The Rhine frontier. I can feel it."

Sophia uncrossed her arms.

"Don't wake Elena," Amélie said. "She needs to sleep. Just — give me a moment."

She closed her eyes. She had learned, in these first days of practice, that the Ocean didn't require effort — that the harder she tried to dive, the further she got from depth. She let the page under her palm be a kind of anchor and released her grip on everything else.

The kitchen table. The radiator's hiss. The particular weight of the last forty-eight hours.

What she received wasn't a vision. It wasn't Elena's vivid, cinematic narration from inside another person's experience. It was quieter than that — closer to the feeling of reading a passage you've somehow always known, recognising something you never consciously learned.

Argotta. A young woman, eighteen, with the compact practical energy of someone who had grown up at the intersection of trade routes, who knew how to read weather and livestock and the shifting politics of river settlements. Her Asher practices were bone-deep by then — learned from her grandmother in the ordinary privacy of early mornings, mixed into the Germanic wise-woman traditions she'd absorbed from the region without separating them out, because to her they weren't separate. Presence and journey. Healing and vision. Two ways of entering the same water.

And Chlodio, who had dreamed of battles before they happened since childhood, whose mother had been a völva — who had grown up, therefore, knowing what it meant to carry something ordinary people couldn't see, and learning, through long practice, to keep it out of his face.

When they met at a trading gathering, neither of them performed anything. They simply saw each other.

Amélie became aware that she had spoken this last part aloud. The kitchen was completely quiet. Marcus had sat down. Sophia was standing with one hand on the back of a chair, leaning forward slightly, her scepticism not gone but for the moment held in suspension.

"Keep going," Marcus said softly.

She didn't know if what came next was from the Ocean or from Elena's earlier accounts settling into her own understanding — it didn't feel like a distinction that mattered. The information simply had presence:

Their wedding was conducted with two officiants. Argotta's grandmother, who brought the Asher practices — the breathwork, the particular quality of opening presence that could enter another person's suffering without being lost in it. And one of the local Germanic wise women, who brought the seidr journey work — the tradition of deliberate descent, of navigating the wyrd with intention.

At midnight, Argotta waded alone into a spring near the settlement. Three days fasted. Cold water to her chest. The breathing technique her grandmother had given her, slow and counted, sinKing her through the surface of ordinary awareness into what lay beneath — not the physical cold of the water, but the vast, depthless field she had learned to call the Waters Beneath the Waters. She went deep. Deeper than she'd gone before, because the intention she brought this time wasn't personal — it was genealogical. A calling forward. Let what was scattered concentrate. Let the swimmer be born who can carry both currents.

Chlodio entered the water. He had journeyed that night through the threads of the wyrd and chosen, consciously, the thread that led forward. Not because it was destined — because he had chosen it. What happened between them in the water wasn't only physical. They were both so deep in the Ocean that their consciousness merged with the field itself, and conception in that moment carried something forward that neither of them could have named: the amplification of what both lineages carried, concentrated and combined. The wise women on the bank later said they had seen light in the water.

Amélie lifted her hand from the page.

She felt — not drained, as Elena always did. Something else. Slightly lit, if that was a feeling. Like a muscle she hadn't known she possessed, having been used for the first time.

"The merger wasn't just genetic," she said. "The seidr tradition emphasised journey and vision — the ability to descend deliberately and navigate. The Asher tradition emphasised presence and healing

— the ability to stay, to hold, to feel what another person feels without being swept away. Together, they created something neither lineage had produced alone. That's the Merovingian gift. Not just depth. Range."

She paused. "That's why they were so threatening. They could dive and they could stay. Both at once."

Marcus nodded slowly. "And every generation after that, the marriages were strategic. Not for territory or alliance — for concentration. Clovis was the culmination: by his generation, the gifts manifested in almost every direct descendant."

"Sorcerer Kings," Sophia said. She had sat down somewhere in the last few minutes without Amélie noticing. Her voice had changed — not convinced, exactly. But something in it had opened. "They weren't doing magic. They were doing naturally what other people had to try to induce with ritual."

"Which made them impossible to control through the usual means," Marcus said. "You can't frighten someone who can feel whether you're telling the truth. You can't manipulate someone who perceives your intentions in the Ocean before you've said a word." He began gathering his papers. "Which is why they had to be systematically destroyed. Not suppressed — destroyed. The line exterminated, the practices forgotten, the very framework that made the gifts comprehensible eliminated from the historical record."

Amélie's phone buzzed.

She checked it and felt the particular cold that had become familiar over these past weeks — the cold of the net drawing tighter. A news alert. An academic fraud investigation launched in her name. Her former department at the Sorbonne had issued a statement questioning her research integrity. And beneath that: a psychiatric hold request filed with a Paris clinic, citing her as a risk to herself, requesting immediate voluntary hospitalisation.

"They've found us," she said. "Or found this location."

Marcus was already standing. "How long have we been here?"

"Three days"

"Three days too long." He was moving toward the corridor, keeping his voice level in the way Amélie had come to recognise as the particular calm of someone who had run before. "Wake Elena gently. We need to move in twenty minutes."

"Where?" Sophia asked.

"The Pyrenees. Daniel's monastery. The abbot has been holding sanctuary for people like us." Marcus paused at the doorway. "And he has something else. Documents from Tibet. The real Hemis manuscripts." He looked at Amélie. "The next piece of the history. The part that explains why all of this — the bloodline, the gifts, the suppression — leads to a single man two thousand years ago, and what the families have been so desperately trying to make the world forget about him."

Isabelle appeared from the hallway, already dressed. "I heard," she said simply. "I'll wake Elena."

In the twenty minutes before they scattered into the Paris dawn, Amélie stood at the table and looked at the photocopied page with her handprint still warm on it, and thought about Argotta wading into cold water at midnight with an intention so clear it had apparently lit up the Ocean itself.

She had felt it. Not through Elena. Through herself.

She took the page, folded it carefully, and put it in her coat.

CHAPTER TEN

The Descent

Paris, November 2024

The plan had been simple. Take different routes. Switch vehicles By dawn they were already fragments — six people dissolving into the grey arteries of Paris, moving in the opposite direction from everyone else, ordinary commuters flowing into the city as they flowed out. Amélie walked quickly with her head down, Elena's journal pressed against her ribs under her coat, her own bag heavy with the copied research. The weight of it felt different than it had an hour ago, when she'd made the promise in the warmth of Elena's flat. Out here on the pavement, in the cold, with the first blue light coming up over the rooftops, the weight felt like what it was. Evidence that could get her killed. Marcus had been specific. Don't take the Metro. Too many cameras, too many entry points they can cover. Take the bus to Juvisy, then a hire car south. Pay cash. Don't use your phone after the first hour. Don't contact anyone who isn't already in the network.

She was three streets from the bus stop when she felt it. Not a sound. Not a sight. Just a shift in the texture of the world around her — the particular quality of attention directed at the back of her neck that she'd learned, these past months, to read as reliably as weather. Somebody was watching her. And not idly. She didn't turn. She kept walKing and dropped carefully, into the first layer of the Ocean — just enough to extend her awareness behind her without breaKing stride. Elena had passed this information on from Rinpoche, quoting him almost word for word. "Your eyes give you away," she'd said. "The Ocean doesn't." What came back wasn't sight. It was weight and intention — the felt shape of two presences, both male, both carrying the particular density of people who are working. One of them moved with a deliberate, unhurried tread she felt through the pavement as much as heard: tactical training, or something like it. The other was lighter, faster, positioned — she sensed rather than saw — to cut off, a right turn. They knew where she was going.

The bus stop was ahead. Useless now — she'd be cornered waiting. She turned left instead, into a narrow residential street she didn't know, and let herself move faster. She had, in total, perhaps four minutes of calm left. She used them trying to reach Marcus. One text — already moving, two on me, diverting — and then she turned off her phone as he'd instructed and pushed the device into her coat pocket. Paris was waking around her, unhelpfully: shutters being raised, a baker rolling his cart, a woman walKing a small dog who watched Amélie with intelligent eyes as she passed. None of them saw the two men thirty metres behind her. None of them would. She turned right into an alley she'd identified from the Ocean rather than from any map — a felt sense of opening space ahead, a narrowing behind — and found herself in a courtyard. Stone walls on three sides. A locked service gate on the fourth. Morning light just beginning to pool in the far corner. Of course. She turned to face the alley's entrance. The younger man appeared first, stopping when he saw her waiting. She felt his surprise — a flicker of recalculation — and then a kind of satisfaction. He stepped aside to let the other one through. The one with the trained walk. He was perhaps fifty, broad shouldered, with the unhurried manner of someone who had done this many times and found it straightforward. "Dr. Rousseau." Not a question. "You've made this much more complicated than it needed to be. We only want the material you're carrying."

"And me?" A pause. Small enough to be telling.

She pressed her back against the gate. Her heart was slamming. She could feel it in her throat, in her wrists, in a high thin ringing at the back of her skull. This was nothing like the training scenarios Rinpoche had run, where the shouting and the startling were exercises with a known endpoint. This was a courtyard in Paris in the early morning and there was nowhere to go, and the weight of Elena's journal against her ribs suddenly felt like the most fragile and necessary thing in the world. Stay in your breath. Stay in your heart. Stay in the Ocean. So precise in her memory it was almost as if someone was beside her, speaKing to her. But this was different. The depth she had reached before was from the stillness of the practice room, from the cushion, from the particular quality of quiet that Priya and Elena had cultivated around her training as carefully as a greenhouse around a tender seedling. Now she faced a real threat. She was alone, no one to question this time. There was no exit door here. She breathed in. Filling the belly, not the chest — and she let herself fall. Not outward. Not upward. Down. She expected it to be harder. Beneath the fear, beneath the slamming heart and the cold stone against her back and the two men stepping into the courtyard light, she had braced herself for the Ocean to be unreachable — some locked and distant thing requiring the particular conditions of safety and stillness she'd always had before. However, instead, the Ocean rose to meet her.

Not gently. Not in the soft, gradual deepening she knew from practice. It came up from below like water through a breaKing hull — sudden, total, flooding everything — and for one moment of genuine terror she thought this was what drowning felt like, this was the thing Elena had warned about, consciousness untethering from the body, the Asher gift becoming the Asher undoing. She thought of the prophets that Elena had described who had gone too far and never came back, who had touched the infinite and been swallowed by it, who had lost the thread of their own names in the deep. Then something steadied. Not her. The Ocean itself. As if, sensing her fear of it, it simply waited — vast and patient as it had always been — and let her find the floor. She found it. The bottom of herself. The place that could not be more afraid because it had descended below the reach of fear. The place they had called the Ocean and her grandmother's letter had hinted at it as being something older. The place that was not French, not academic, not thirty-four years old, not pressed against a locked gate in a Paris courtyard. The place that had been present for all of that and would be present after all of that and was not — had never been — at any genuine risk from two men stepping into the early morning light. Time did something strange. The men were still moving. She could see them, could track the older one's unhurried approach at the same measured pace, could register the younger one shifting to cover the alley entrance. All of this was happening at normal speed. But in the Ocean, she had what felt like as much time as she needed, which was exactly as much time as there was. She felt them. This was the part she hadn't expected. Hadn't practised. She hadn't anticipated that in a genuine, open dive, the Ocean would give her everything that swam in it. Including them.

The older man first. He moved through the courtyard with his particular professional calm and she felt it — not sympathy, not imagination, but actual felt contact with his consciousness in the Ocean, the way she had learned to feel the traumatised children or read the dinner party guests from behind a champagne glass. And what she felt was not the cold blankness of cruelty. What she felt was the particular exhaustion of someone who had been doing this for a very long time and had long since stopped asking whether it was right. He was tired. Not of this morning's work. Of all of it. Decades of it. The younger one was different. She reached him and felt something she hadn't expected: uncertainty. He was not certain about this. He knew what the older man was likely prepared to do and some part of him, some unmistakably human part that training had not yet reached, was not prepared to watch it. He had followed because following was what you did. But the version of himself that was still capable of doubt was awake this morning, attentive and unhappy in a way he had no language for.

The Ocean doesn't judge. Doesn't distinguish. Everyone is welcome. Elena had said this. Amélie had understood it intellectually. She understood it now in a completely different way. Both of these men were in the Ocean too. Swimming in it whether they knew it or not. Disconnected from its depths by everything they'd been trained to be — by forty years of professional numbness in one case, by the ongoing education in numbness in the other — but still in it. Still held by it. Still, at some level that their training hadn't reached, capable of the thing the Ocean was made of. She knew what to do.

She didn't move away from the gate. She stayed very still, and she looked at the older man directly — not the defiant stare of someone performing bravery, but the open, steady regard she had learned to hold with the children. The look that said: I see you. Not what you're doing. You. He stopped. He hadn't expected that. She felt the small disruption in him — the professional recalculation of a man confronted with something that didn't fit the template. She kept looking. Kept the Ocean open between them. Kept feeling his exhaustion, his length of service, the decades of following instructions from people he worked for but did not love.

"You've been doing this a long time," she said. Her voice came out steadier than she had any right to expect. "And you've never once been told what it's actually for. What you're actually protecting." A silence. Long enough to mean something.

"Give me the bag," he said. But the instruction had lost some of its certainty.

"The bag doesn't matter," Amélie said. "What matters is already published. What matters is already in the world. You can take the bag and your employer can read the research they've spent decades trying to suppress, and it won't change anything. Because the Ocean doesn't work like that. You can't put it back."

She felt the younger man behind him shift his weight. "There's a woman in Paris right now," she said, "who spent thirty years as a tool for the same people who sent you here. Forty years old before she cried for the first time. And she chose differently. Last month." She wasn't performing this. She wasn't calculating it. She was simply telling the truth — the way you could only tell truth from the Ocean, where truth and feeling and fact were the same thing. "You can choose differently too. Both of you." Another silence. The morning light had reached the far wall now, golden and improbable.

The older man looked at her for what felt like a very long moment. She felt something moving in him — some slow, tidal thing that had been waiting for a long time for something she couldn't name. Then he stepped aside. Turned his face toward the alley wall. And she understood: he was not stopping her. He was not helping her. He was simply, deliberately, not seeing her. The younger man had already moved out of the alley entrance. She walked. She didn't run until she was two streets clear. Then she ran. Not from panic — panic had been replaced by something else, something with no clean name that was part relief and part awe and part the particular bodily trembling that comes after surviving something that was genuinely close. She ran because her body needed to, because it was full of the adrenaline that the Ocean had held beneath the surface and which now needed somewhere to go. She ran until she got to the bus. In the back seat, heading south on roads that gradually traded stone and glass for the first pale hints of countryside, she sat with her hands flat on her knees and breathed. In through the belly. Out slow. The October sky was clear. France was happening at speed outside the window. The journal was still pressed against her ribs. She thought about what had just happened and found she couldn't think about it the way she normally thought about things — analytically, historically, from the careful critical distance her training had given her. It wouldn't hold still at that distance. It kept resolving into the felt experience of it instead: the Ocean flooding in uninvited, the two consciousnesses she had touched without meaning to, the terrible exhausted tiredness in the older man, the flicker of something unformed and salvageable in the younger one. The way the truth had simply come out of her without strategy. The way it had been enough.

She hadn't understood what Elena meant by *The thriller is the doorway. The philosophy is the room you enter once you walk through it* when she'd first heard it. She understood now. She had walked through the door. She had taken a dive that no practice session could have prepared her for, and she had found — not the carefully managed Ocean of the cushion and the practice room, but the thing underneath that, the actual thing, wild and immediate and nothing like a metaphor. She had found that it was real. She had found that it worked. And she had found — this was the part that would take the rest of the drive to the Pyrenees to begin to process, the part she would still be thinKing about when the monastery appeared on the mountainside and the van pulled to a stop and the others came out to meet her — she had found that it was not a gift she had been given. It was a gift she had always had. The inheritance, her grandmother had called it. The knowing before you should know. The sensing of others' feelings. She had always explained it away. Intuition. Good guessing. Coincidence. She pressed her hand against the journal, felt its weight, and looked out at the French countryside moving past in the morning light.

She had never known, afterwards, exactly how she had left the courtyard. The older man had let her go — a calculation, she thought, a moment of something she had not expected from him. She had walked out of the alley and kept walKing. Found a bus and jumped in and had planned to call Luc from a public phone near the Juvisy interchange but found him already there, engine running, not asking questions.

At the Monastery the others had arrived in ones and twos over the following two hours. No one had been followed. By the time they cleared the city limits and the mountains began to show as a dark line on the horizon, she had stopped shaKing.

Not coincidence.

CHAPTER ELEVEN

The Recognition

The Pyrenees, November 2024

She smelled it before she saw it. Pine resin and cold stone and something older — the particular stillness that accumulates in places where people have been praying for a very long time. The van came around the final bend and the monastery appeared on the mountainside, and Amélie pressed her forehead against the glass and felt something release in her chest that she hadn't known she was holding. They had made it. Marcus pulled to a stop in the shadow of the trees. They didn't speak for a moment. They had left Paris in the dark, separated and regrouped and driven through the dawn watching their mirrors. Between them all they carried enough evidence to change the world — or to get themselves killed.

They sat and breathed. Then Luc said, very quietly: "I'd like to get out of this van." A small sound moved. Not quite laughter. The kind of sound that comes when relief is too large to hold and the body finds whatever opening it can. They got out.

The mountain air hit Amélie like cold water — clean and indifferent and wonderful. She stood in the pine-shadowed car park and looked up at the ancient stone walls and thought: we are still here. Whatever comes next, we arrived.

Two figures appeared in the doorway. One was a small, wiry man in his seventies. He looked at each of them in turn — a long, unhurried look — and said nothing. Just nodded. The nod of someone who had been expecting them. The nod of someone who understood what it meant to arrive. They were escorted inside in silence. They would need food, sleep, time to decompress. The work would wait until they had rested.

The mountain had its own patience. It had been waiting for centuries. It could wait one more night.

The monastery of Sant Anna de les Abadesses had stood on that Pyrenean mountainside for eight centuries — all stone and silence, surrounded by forests that carried their own kind of memory.

In the days that followed their arrival, Amélie came to understand why the Remnant had chosen it. Not only for its remoteness, or for Father Matteu's long-held sympathies, but for something less definable: the way the mountains absorbed urgency. The way the silence here was not empty but full — accumulated from generations of people who had come to this place carrying the unbearable and had, slowly, found it possible to set down.

They were careful, even so. Marcus ran security checks each morning. They used no phones that hadn't been stripped and rebuilt. They moved through the monastery's routines — prayer times, shared meals, the particular stillness of compline — like guests learning the grammar of a foreign language, fitting themselves around the rhythms of a place that had been here long before them and would remain long after.

The abbot, Father Matteu, was in his seventies with eyes that held the same depth Amélie had learned to recognise. A swimmer. He greeted each arrival quietly, offering sanctuary without questions. On the third day, when he was certain they were secure, he invited Amélie to his private study. The room was lined with books and manuscripts, many clearly very old. But what caught Amélie's attention were the tangkas hanging on the walls—Tibetan Buddhist paintings depicting enlightened beings surrounded by intricate symbolic imagery.

One in particular showed a figure seated in meditation, surrounded by what looked like waves or currents of energy. "The Ocean of Consciousness," Matteu said, following her gaze. "The Tibetans call it Dharmakaya—the truth body, the fundamental ground of being from which all phenomena arise. It's the same thing Elena describes. The same thing your ancestors from Asher would have called the Waters Beneath the Waters."

He gestured for her to sit, then carefully prepared tea in the Tibetan style he had learned decades ago — butter tea, rich and strange to Western palates but comforting in its warmth. He crossed to his desk and produced a small carved wooden box, setting it on the table between them. "There are things I can show you, when you are ready," he said. "Documents from Hemis Monastery in Ladakh. I photographed them myself in 1976. But first you need the context." He settled into his chair with a sigh that spoke of old bones and older memories. "I need to tell you about my time in Tibet," he said. "Because what I learned there changed everything I understood about Yeshua, about the bloodlines, about the nature of spiritual gifts themselves."

The Journey East: 1971

"I arrived in Dharamsala in 1971," Matteu began, his eyes growing distant with memory. "I was forty years old, a Jesuit missionary sent to study comparative religion and, officially, to explore possibilities for Catholic-Buddhist dialogue. But truthfully, I was running. Running from doubts I couldn't voice in the Church. Questions about the nature of Christ's divinity, about whether the institutional Church bore any resemblance to what Yeshua had actually taught." He sipped his tea. "The first lama I met was Geshe Rinpoche. He was elderly even then, maybe ninety, though he moved like a man half his age. When I was brought to him for the customary introduction, he looked at me for perhaps three seconds, then laughed. Not mocKingly—with delight. He said something in Tibetan to his translator, who seemed embarrassed to translate it." "What did he say?" Amélie asked. "He said: "Tell the swimming priest that he doesn't need to pretend to drown anymore. We can see he already knows how to dive." Matteu smiled at the memory. "I had no idea what he meant. I protested that I was just a simple priest, that I'd come to learn. And he laughed again and said, "Yes, you will learn. But first you must remember what you already know." Matteu stood and went to his cabinet, pulling out the wooden box Amélie had seen before, but this time removing a different set of items—prayer beads, a small bronze statue, and several journals filled with his own handwriting.

"Geshe Rinpoche took me as a student. For three years, I lived at his monastery, practicing meditation, studying texts, learning the Tibetan language. But more than that, he was teaching me to See. That's what he called it—Seeing with a capital S. The ability to perceive the Ocean of consciousness directly, to recognise patterns and currents that most humans miss entirely."

He opened one of his journals, showing Amélie pages covered in diagrams and notes. "The Tibetan system for recognising tulkus—reincarnated lamas —it's not mystical guesswork. It's a sophisticated technology for reading consciousness patterns. When a high lama dies, his senior students go into deep meditation. They're not just remembering their teacher or hoping for signs. They're diving into the Ocean itself, feeling for the specific current, the unique pattern of consciousness that was their teacher."

"Like a signature," Amélie said. "A consciousness fingerprint."

"Exactly. And they can follow that current to wherever it's manifesting again—usually in a child born shortly after the lama's death. They test the child, not just with objects the lama owned, but by observing how the child's consciousness moves. Does it carry the same depth? The same quality of awareness? The same capacity to dive?"

Matteu pulled out a photograph—himself, much younger, standing with several Tibetan Monks near a young boy who couldn't have been more than four years old. "This is the recognition ceremony for the 17th Karmapa, in 1992. I was privileged to witness it. Geshe Rinpoche had taught me enough by then that I could feel what the senior lamas were feeling— the unmistakable presence of a consciousness that had been diving for many lifetimes. The boy was four years old, but when you Saw him, really Saw him, you could perceive centuries of accumulated practice, of refinement, of deepening."

"But how does this connect to Asher?" Amélie asked. "To the genetic inheritance we've been documenting?"

Matteu's expression grew intense. "That's what I spent twenty years trying to understand. Because the lamas, when they were teaching me to See, kept talKing about what they called 'the Old Swimmers.' They said that some consciousness patterns carried genetic memory going back not just lifetimes, but millennia. That certain bloodlines maintained a capacity for diving that was passed down not just through training but through the body itself."

He pulled out another document—this one a Tibetan text with his own translation beneath: "This is from a teaching manual at the Monastery. Listen: "There are those who come to the practice already knowing how to swim, though they may have forgotten they know. These are recognised by certain signs: their consciousness moves easily between surface and depth; they perceive patterns that others miss; they feel the suffering of others as if it were their own; they know things before they happen. These marks indicate the Old Blood— consciousness patterns that have been refined through countless generations, encoded in the very flesh so that even when the mind forgets, the body remembers."

"The Old Blood," Amélie whispered. "They knew about the genetic inheritance." "They'd been observing it for thousands of years. The Tibetan Buddhist system is ancient—it didn't begin with the historical Buddha. It traces back to earlier traditions, older practices, mystery schools that existed before Buddhism formalised. The lamas told me their deepest practices came from what they called 'the Realm Before'—a civilisation that had mastered consciousness technology before falling in a great catastrophe."

"Atlantis," Amélie said.

"They preserved knowledge from Atlantis." "Under different names, but yes. And they said that after the fall, the survivors scattered. Some went east and became the founders of the wisdom traditions in India and Tibet. Others went west and became the priesthoods of the Mediterranean. But all carried fragments of the same knowledge—how to dive into the Ocean of consciousness, how to navigate its currents, how to maintain the genetic capacity for this navigation across generations."

CHAPTER TWELVE

Advanced Training

Sant Anna de les Abadesses, December 2024

Rinpoche Tenzi arrived at the monastery in the second week of December, at Priya's arrangement. She knew his voice the moment he spoke — the same unhurried clarity from that single call the night they had left Paris. In person he was smaller than she had imagined.

He was perhaps seventy, small and compact, with eyes that held both infinite compassion and infinite clarity. He walked with a slight limp — legacy of torture in a Chinese prison decades ago — but moved with a grace that seemed to defy age. Priya had arranged his visit and now watched from the doorway of the practice room as he took his seat in the centre and said nothing.

He sat. The group gathered. Waited.

After ten minutes of silence, he spoke: "Show me your diving."

They meditated. Twenty minutes. Everyone dropping into their practised depths.

When they emerged, Rinpoche nodded. "Good foundation. You can all reach the Ocean. But you're still treating it as somewhere you go. Somewhere separate from daily life. Now I'll teach you to live there. To make the Ocean your permanent home."

He spent the first day dismantling the framework they'd been working from. He picked up a cup of water. "What is this?"

"Water," someone said.

"No. This is Ocean. Everything is Ocean. The cup is Ocean taking the form of cup. The water is Ocean taking the form of water. Your body is Ocean taking the form of body. There is no surface. There is only Ocean, temporarily appearing as waves." He took a sip. "When you think you're separate from the Ocean, that's just Ocean pretending to be separate. Playing a game with itself."

"So why practise diving?" Amélie asked. "If we're already Ocean?"

"Because you forget. You identify with the wave and think you're only the wave. Diving practice reminds you that you're the water. But ultimately, there is no diving, because there is nowhere to dive to. You're already there. You always have been." He smiled. "Once this clicks, everything changes. Because you stop trying to achieve the Ocean state. You recognise you never left it."

Amélie sat with this. She thought of Peter, three weeks ago in the Belgian compound, carrying her across a dark lawn. She thought of the child who had said I always could. That's why they wanted me. If the Ocean had never left any of them — if it was simply what everything was — then the families weren't stealing something from outside the children. They were breaKing something that had always been inside. The distinction felt important in ways she couldn't yet name.

Functioning from depth

"Most people think diving means peaceful meditation on a cushion," Rinpoche said on the second day. "Very still. Very quiet. Very serene. Good for practice. But life is not a meditation cushion. Life is messy. Painful. Challenging. So how do you dive while life happens?"

He stood up. "Sophia, come here."

Sophia approached.

"Hit me," Rinpoche said. "On the face. Hard as you can."

Sophia hesitated. He nodded, and she struck him across the cheek. The sound was sharp in the quiet room.

Rinpoche didn't flinch. Didn't react. Just stood there, that same slight smile on his face.

"Did you see?" he asked the group.

"You didn't react," Marcus said.

"No. I felt. I felt the sting. I felt the shock. But I felt it from the Ocean. The sensation arose in the Ocean, moved through the Ocean, dissolved back into the Ocean. No problem. Just experience."

He rubbed his cheek. "This is functioning from depth. Not suppressing feeling. Not being stoic. But experiencing everything from a place so vast that nothing disturbs it. Waves on the surface, calm in the depths."

He looked at Amélie. "You work with traumatised children. They tell you terrible things. You feel their pain. This doesn't stop when you learn to dive deeper. The feeling intensifies. But your capacity to hold it increases infinitely. The Ocean can hold all suffering without being damaged by it."

Elena admitted, quietly, that she struggled with limits. Wanted to help every child they found. Was often exhausted by it.

"Of course," Rinpoche said. "Because you're still approaching it from the surface. From I must save everyone. But the Ocean doesn't save anyone. The Ocean holds space. Creates conditions. Invites. But doesn't force. Doesn't exhaust itself. You cannot pour from an empty cup." He looked around the circle. "By staying in the Ocean, you sense naturally where your energy should go. When to act and when to wait. The exhaustion comes from maKing these decisions from the surface — from guilt, obligation, should. From the Ocean, it's just clear. Natural. Effortless."

The practice of doing nothing

On the third day, Rinpoche gave them an unusual assignment.

"Today, we practise doing nothing. For six hours, you will sit in this room. You can sit, stand, lie down. You can move slowly if you need. But you will do nothing. No reading. No talKing. No eating. No sleeping. Just being. For six hours."

"That's it?" someone asked.

"That's it. Sounds easy. It's not. Your mind will rebel. Will tell you this is a waste of time. Will make you anxious, bored, restless.

Will try every trick to get you to do something. But you will do nothing. You will discover how difficult it is to simply be."

They tried. After twenty minutes, Amélie was crawling with restlessness. After an hour, she was nearly frantic. Her mind screamed that this was pointless, that she should be helping someone, doing something, anything but sitting here in this empty morning with the children just down the corridor and the families somewhere beyond the mountains looking for all of them.

But she stayed. Watched the restlessness. Watched the anxiety. Watched all the stories her mind told about why this was wrong.

And slowly, after three hours, something shifted. The restlessness faded. A deep quiet emerged. Not because she had achieved anything. But because she had stopped trying to achieve. Stopped trying to be anywhere other than where she was.

When the six hours ended, Rinpoche rang a bell.

"Now you know," he said. "The hardest practice is not meditation, not diving, not facing trauma. The hardest practice is simply being. Doing nothing. Achieving nothing. Just existing."

"Why?" Amélie asked.

"Because everything in your conditioning tells you that your worth comes from doing. From achieving. From being productive. And until you can simply be — without needing to do, to become, to improve — you're still operating from the surface. Still driven by anxiety. The Ocean doesn't do anything. The Ocean simply is. And from that being, all wise action flows naturally."

That night, the group dispersed quietly to their cells. The monastery was still — the particular stillness of a building that had held six centuries of prayers — and Amélie lay in the dark with the day settling through her.

At three in the morning, a helicopter passed over the village.

Not unusual, in theory. Mountain rescue. A police patrol. Any number of explanations. But everyone in the monastery was awake within two minutes, and no one pretended otherwise. They gathered in the central corridor in whatever they had been sleeping in, Marcus with his phone already showing a tracKing application, Sophia counting seconds between the sound's appearance and its fading.

It passed. Continued south. Did not circle.

Isabelle was shaKing. Barely, but Amélie saw it. She moved to stand beside her without touching, simply present, and Isabelle drew one long slow breath.

"I've felt that specific consciousness before," Isabelle said quietly. "On the night of the château." She didn't explain further. She didn't need to.

They stayed in the corridor another ten minutes. Then, without discussion, went back to what they had been doing.

The work continued. It always continued. But the monastery felt different now — not less sacred, but less removed. The world had not stopped while they learned to dive. It had simply been waiting.

After two weeks with Rinpoche, something fundamental had shifted in Amélie. She still dove daily. Still practised. But now there was an ease to it. A sense that she wasn't trying to reach somewhere else. She was simply recognising what was always already true.

She walked through the monastery differently. Saw the other members of the Remnant differently — not as fellow survivors managing the same unusual burden, but as the Ocean appearing in different forms, each one carrying something the whole needed. The former banker. The nurse. The archivist. The broken child who had become, slowly and improbably, a teacher.

She worked with the children differently too. Before, there had been a subtle trying — trying to heal them, trying to help them integrate. Now there was just presence. Being the Ocean with them.

Letting their own healing unfold in its own time. Not pushing. Not pulling. Just holding space.

And the children felt it. They relaxed more around her. Opened more. Healed faster.

CHAPTER THIRTEEN

Reading the Waters

Sant Anna de les Abadesses, December 2024

On the fourth evening, after supper had been cleared and the bell had rung for compline, Elena spread her maps across the library table.

Not the research maps — the hand-drawn ones: ancient trade routes, tribal territories, genealogical connections marked in different coloured inks. Father Matteu looked at them with the recognition of someone who had spent decades following the same threads. He glanced at Amélie, then back at Elena. "Show her," he said simply. "The way I showed you."

Elena looked at Amélie. "You've touched the Ocean. You already understand something of what it holds. Now let me show you what I've spent thirty years learning to read there."

"Can you show me the connection between Asher and the Merovingians?" Amélie leaned forward. "The actual path the bloodline took from the Levant to France?"

Elena exchanged glances with the others. Sophia nodded. "It would help her understand. And we need her to understand completely if she's going to write the true history."

"Very well." Elena stood and moved to clear a space in the centre of the room. "But you must all anchor me. When I go that deep, that far back, I need tethers to return to the present. Hold the intention of bringing me back."

They formed a circle — Elena in the centre, the others around her. Amélie watched as the older woman's breathing deepened, her body becoming very still. The air in the room seemed to change, to thicken slightly, as if the stone walls had moved a few inches closer.

Elena's voice, when she spoke, was distant, layered, as if she were speaKing from inside a much larger space:

722 BCE. Samaria falls to Assyria. The northern Kingdom shatters. But Asher—blessed Asher—they had known this was coming. The prophets had warned them. Some had already begun to move, to scatter, preserving the lineage as they'd been taught to do since the time of Judges.

I see families travelling north, into the territories that would become Syria. Others moving west, to the Phoenician cities of Tyre and Sidon. These were not strangers to them—Asher's territory had always bordered Phoenicia. Intermarriage was common. Trade was constant. They spoke each other's languages, worshipped in ways that... overlapped.

The Phoenicians called them something else. Not Asher. In their tongue—those who carry the blessing. They knew. The Phoenician priest-Kings understood that these refugees carried something precious. Not gold. Not jewels. Knowledge. Practices. The genetic inheritance that made them sensitive to the currents. What we call the Ocean.

I can see a woman now. Her name sounds like Ashira. A daughter of Asher, married to a Phoenician merchant-prince in Tyre. She carries the mark—not visible like the Merovingian cross, but present in the blood. She teaches her daughters the old prayers, the meditation practices, how to dive beneath the surface of the mind to touch the deep waters where all consciousness flows together.

Her granddaughter marries into a family that trades with Tartessos—the Phoenician colonies in southern Spain. The bloodline moves west with the trade routes. They establish themselves in the Iberian peninsula, in southern Gaul, along the Mediterranean coast. I am following the thread forward now... through centuries... The families preserve the practices quietly. They appear as merchants, as healers, as wise women whom others seek out. They marry carefully—not just for wealth or status, but to preserve the gifts. They recognise each other, these carriers. Something in the eyes. Something in the presence. They know how to swim, and they recognise other swimmers.

Forward... forward... The centuries pass. The bloodline moves, and marries, and moves again—east to west, tribe to tribe. The gifts concentrate with each convergence. Until...

Their grandson... Merovech. Yes. There he is. Born around 411 CE. The legends will say he had two fathers—one of flesh, one of the sea. The "beast of Neptune." But I can see what really happened.

His mother, during her pregnancy, went to the sea. There was a ritual—an old practice preserved from the Phoenician priestesses, ultimately from older traditions still. She entered the water at dawn, and she... opened herself to the Ocean. Not the physical ocean. The Ocean of consciousness. She let herself become a vessel, a channel. And something moved through her. The accumulated wisdom, the genetic memory, the concentrated inheritance of all who'd carried the gift before.

The child born from that ritual carried something unprecedented. The full activation of the dormant capacities. Enhanced intuition. Healing abilities. A kind of knowing that seemed supernatural but was simply... expanded perception. Connection to the deep currents of consciousness that most humans had learned to ignore.

Amélie became aware that she was holding her breath. Beside her, Daniel's eyes were closed, his face tilted slightly upward, as if listening to something just beyond the room.

Moving forward... past Childeric... to Clovis. Born 466 CE. And here—here is where something shifts. Something the histories do not tell you.

I see Clovis meeting with a Bishop. Not Remigius, the one credited with his conversion. An older bishop, whose name has been erased from the records. This Bishop is also of the bloodline—a carrier who has risen within the Church. He recognises what Clovis is. He tells him:

You carry the inheritance of the priest-Kings. Not just the Kingship of Judah, but the priesthood of Melchizedek. The ancient line that preceded Abraham. You are meant to unite temporal and spiritual authority.

Clovis understands. His baptism in 496 is not just conversion—it's claiming a dual mandate. King and Priest. The Merovingian priest-Kings, they called themselves. And the Church, initially, accepted this. Because there were still those within the Church who remembered the old ways, who understood that some bloodlines carried sacred purposes.

But the farther forward I move... the more resistance I see. Rome is consolidating power. The Pope wants spiritual authority to rest with him alone. The idea of Kings who claim direct access to the Divine, who need no priestly mediation... it threatens everything.

I see Dagobert II, the one who tried to reclaim the full Priest-King authority. Who travelled to Ireland, to the monasteries there, and learned... something. The Irish Monks preserved knowledge that Rome had tried to suppress.

I am seeing... a library. Manuscripts. The Irish Monks had been trading with the East for centuries. There are documents here that came from... Hemis Monastery. In Ladakh. In the Himalayas.

Elena's breathing changed. Her voice became strained, reaching.

The Monks in Hemis had records. They claim a young man came to them in the early first century. A Jewish scholar from the West. He studied with them for years—learning the meditation practices, the techniques for accessing what they called Buddha consciousness but what we would call the Ocean. He was trying to understand his own abilities, his own inheritance.

The young man's name was... Yeshua. Yeshua. During the lost years the Gospels do not record.

The records say he already had the gifts when he arrived—the healing, the sight, the ability to read hearts. But he didn't fully understand them. He was from the line of Judah through Joseph, but his mother... Mary. Her ancestry included Asher. Through her grandmother, Anna, whose name echoes the prophetess Anna who would later recognise him in the temple.

He went east to understand what he carried. The Buddhist masters recognised him immediately—another swimmer, like them, but with gifts they'd never seen so concentrated. They taught him to dive deeper, to access the Ocean consciously, deliberately. To heal not through technique but through direct perception of the consciousness patterns that underlie physical form.

He studied the ancient texts they preserved there—texts that predated Buddhism itself, that spoke of an even older tradition. A civilisation that had understood consciousness as fundamental. That had learned to navigate the Ocean of being with full awareness. They called it by different names, but the Monks believed he was from that lineage. A carrier of that ancient knowledge.

When Yeshua returned to Judea, he was... different. Fully awakened. Able to dive to depths others couldn't reach. To heal with a touch because he could perceive and shift the energetic patterns directly. To know hearts because he swam in the Ocean where all consciousness was connected.

Still in the current, still reading what the trance showed her, Elena's voice shifted lower:

The Vatican knows this. They have documents from Hemis—copies obtained during the nineteenth century. Stored in the private archives. Section forbidden to all but the highest cardinals. They know Yeshua trained in the East. They know the gifts were genetic, enhanced through practice. They know the early Church understood this, before the councils codified everything into theology and suppressed the original teachings.

And Dagobert... Dagobert found Irish manuscripts that hinted at this. He understood that the Merovingian gifts weren't just family inheritance—they were part of the same lineage Yeshua had carried. The line of Asher, the line of the priest-Kings, the line that stretched back to the survivors of Atlantis who'd maintained the knowledge of consciousness navigation.

That's why they killed him. 679 CE. In the forest. Because he was going to reveal it. Going to reclaim the Priest-King authority with full understanding of what it meant. Going to establish a Kingdom where the gifts were openly taught, where the practices of Ocean-diving were preserved and passed on.

The assassination wasn't just political. It was epistemic. It was preventing the revelation that would have changed everything. That Yeshua, the Merovingians, the ancient priesthoods—all were expressions of the same genetic and spiritual inheritance. All swimmers in the same Ocean, accessing the same source.

Still deep in the trance, she perceived: after Dagobert's murder, the documents were seized. The Irish connections were severed. And the knowledge was suppressed for another thirteen centuries. The Vatican locked it away. The families that eventually stole the bloodline never learned the full truth—they got the genetics but lost the context. They have the ability to swim but forgot they're in an Ocean.

But the records survive. In Hemis, there are texts. And the vision showed her this too, that they are in the Vatican's private archives—documents about Yeshua's travels, about the genetic nature of the gifts, about the true history of the priest-Kings. And in certain Orthodox monasteries, in Ethiopia and Armenia, there are copies of letters from the early Church fathers discussing those who carry the blessing of Asher and debating whether they should be allowed into the Priesthood.

All of it hidden. All of it suppressed. Because if people knew—if they understood that the gifts were genetic, that they could be activated through practice, that we are all swimming in an Ocean of consciousness that connects everything—the entire power structure collapses. Both religious and secular. Because you don't need priests or politicians or bankers to mediate your connection to the source. You can dive yourself. Anyone can learn to swim.

This is what the vision showed her. This is what she would later write in her journal as the understanding that came through: that the real secret, what was really stolen in 751 and what she believed continued to be suppressed today, Not just a bloodline or a throne, but the knowledge that we are all from the Ocean, we all carry the potential, we all can awaken.

The Merovingians were just the ones who remembered. The tribe of Asher was the one who maintained the practices. But the Ocean is available to everyone. Always has been. Always will be.

I am coming back now... releasing the thread... returning...

Elena gasped. Her body shuddered as she came back to full awareness. Sophia and Marcus caught her as she swayed, guiding her back to her chair. Her face was pale, her hands shaKing.

"Water," she whispered. Rachel quickly brought her a glass.

They sat in silence for several minutes while Elena recovered. Finally, she looked up at Amélie with exhausted but fierce eyes.

"Did you feel it?" she asked. "The truth of it flowing through the current?"

Amélie nodded, unable to speak. She had felt it—as Elena spoke, she had sensed the truth of the narrative, had felt herself almost diving alongside the older woman into those distant memories.

"The vision showed that the documents may exist," Elena said, her voice growing stronger. "The Vatican's Secret Archives—they're partially open now, renamed the Apostolic Archives, but there's still a restricted section. Researchers have suspected for years that there are documents about Yeshua's life between ages twelve and thirty. About his travels. About the genetic nature of certain spiritual gifts."

Marcus pulled up his notes. "Nicholas Notovitch, 1887. A Russian journalist who claimed to find manuscripts at Hemis Monastery describing 'Saint Issa'"—Yeshua—"travelling to India during the lost years. The story caused a sensation when he published it in 1894.'

"And?" Amélie asked.

"And it was immediately challenged. The philologist Max Müller investigated and concluded it was either a hoax or Notovitch was the victim of a practical joke. The head Lama at Hemis denied ever meeting Notovitch or possessing such manuscripts."

"But others claimed to see them," Sophia interjected. "Nicholas Roerich in 1925, Swami Abhedananda in 1922."

"All after Notovitch's bestselling book was published," Marcus countered. "The modern scholarly consensus is clear—Notovitch invented the story. Bart Ehrman, one of the world's leading New Testament scholars, states that there is not a single recognised scholar who has any doubts about the matter."

Elena leaned forward. "But what if the story Notovitch told was false, but the truth behind it was real? What if he heard rumours, legends, oral traditions—and rather than present them as such, he fabricated a manuscript to give them authority?"

"You mean the manuscripts are fake but the tradition might be authentic?" Amélie asked.

"Consider it. The Hemis Monastery dates to before the eleventh century. Ladakh was on the Silk Road. Travellers, merchants, Monks passed through. Oral traditions persist for centuries. What if there was a tradition about a Jewish teacher travelling east, and Notovitch simply... wrote it down in the wrong way?"

She pulled out a folder of articles, photocopies, research notes. "Some researchers, like Fida Hassnain, have argued for the authenticity of such records, though his work is not accepted by mainstream biblical scholars. He connected the accounts to genetic research showing unusual DNA markers in certain Jewish populations—markers that also appeared in Kashmiri and Tibetan populations. Of course, much of this may rest on forgeries. So much history has been either hidden or destroyed. But the memories stored in the Ocean confirm something was there, even if we cannot verify its precise shape through documents alone."

"The manuscripts themselves may be inventions," Elena continued. "But the underlying tradition? It may have roots in something real. When I dive into the Ocean, when I access the memories stored there, I sense a resonance. Not proof—but the feeling that some part of this story, however distorted through time, touches on truth."

Not proof. But the feeling that some part of this story touches on truth.

"So there is genetic evidence of the migration," Amélie breathed.

"Yes. The tribe of Asher travelling the Silk Road, intermarrying with Eastern populations, bringing their practices and their genetics into Buddhist communities. It's why certain meditation techniques are so similar to Jewish mystical practices—they came from the same source. The Ocean-swimming techniques, adapted to different cultures and different languages, but ultimately the same knowledge."

"And the Vatican documents? How do we access them?" Marcus asked.

Elena's smile was grim. "We don't. At least not officially. But I have a contact — a cardinal who carries the bloodline himself, though he doesn't advertise it. Not Matteu — the cardinal moves in entirely different circles, higher and more dangerous. He has been quietly photographing documents for years. Building a case for full disclosure. He's terrified, understandably. If the Church knew he was leaKing information about Yeshua's Eastern training, about the genetic basis of spiritual gifts..."

"He'd end up like Dagobert," Sophia finished.

"Exactly. But he's willing to share what he has with Dr. Rousseau. For publication. If she's willing to protect his identity and accept the consequences."

Amélie's mind was racing. This was bigger than she'd imagined. Not just the Merovingian bloodline, not just the tribe of Asher, but a complete rewriting of religious history. Evidence that Yeshua had studied in the East. That spiritual gifts were genetic and could be activated through practice.

"I'll incorporate all of this," she said. "Make it part of what's already in motion. The genetic research, the historical connections, the photographed documents, the Himalayan records. All of it. Let people decide for themselves what it means."

"They'll call you a heretic," Elena warned. "Both religious authorities and scientific ones. You're threatening too many established narratives."

"Good," Amélie said. "Those narratives were built on suppression and theft. It's time for people to know they can swim. That they don't need permission from priests or scientists or the groups that stole the bloodline. The Ocean is available to everyone."

Elena reached across the table and squeezed her hand. "Then let me tell you about the documents my contact has copied. About what the early Church fathers really wrote regarding the gifts. About the correspondence between Clement of Alexandria and certain Jewish scholars regarding the blessing of Asher and how it manifests in those called to serve. About the records from the Council of Nicaea that were never included in the official canons—the debates about whether Yeshua's abilities were unique or whether they represented an awakening available to all humans who carried certain genetic markers and underwent proper training."

She pulled out more documents. "This is going to take hours to go through. But if you're serious about the complete truth..."

"I am," Amélie said.
And they began to work.

CHAPTER FOURTEEN

The Issa Manuscripts

Sant Anna de les Abadesses, December 2024

Matteu opened the wooden box fully now, revealing what Amélie had seen before—photographs of ancient manuscripts, but many more than he'd shown her initially. "In 1976, Geshe Rinpoche told me he wanted to show me something that would help me understand my own doubts about Christ. He arranged for me to visit Hemis Monastery in Ladakh. It's remote, difficult to reach, and the Monks there are extremely protective of their texts. But Geshe Rinpoche's letter of introduction opened doors that would have remained closed to any Western scholar." Hemis Monastery: The Recognition of Issa "The head librarian was an old Monk named Lobsang. He was maybe eighty, and he'd been the librarian for fifty years. He spoke a little English, learned from British traveler's. When I told him why I'd come—that I was struggling with questions about Yeshua's nature, about whether the institutional Church's teachings aligned with Christ's actual life—he nodded as if he'd been expecting me."

Matteu pulled out a photograph of an ancient manuscript, its pages darkened with age, script flowing in elegant Pali characters. "He brought out a text the monastery had preserved for centuries. He said it had been brought to the Monastery by merchants in the second century CE, copied from oral accounts that had been carefully maintained. It was called 'The Life of Saint Issa'— Issa being the Tibetan rendering of Yeshua, Yeshua."

"I'd read about Notovitch's claims," Amélie said. "But most scholars think he fabricated it."

And Lobsang spent three weeks helping me translate it, not just the words but the context, the meaning behind the meaning."

"Because the alternative is too threatening," Matteu said. "But I held the manuscript in my hands. I photographed it—these photos.

"He spread out more photographs, showing page after page of the text. "The manuscript doesn't just describe Yeshua's travels—it describes how the Monks recognised him. And this is the crucial part, Amélie. This is what changed everything for me." He pulled out his translation of the copy of a key passage: "In the fourteenth year of Issa's life, he came to Sindh with merchants travelling the silk routes. His family had sent him away, fearing the attention of the priests and the suspicion of the Romans, for the boy showed signs that disturbed those in authority."

"When Issa arrived in the lands of the Aryans, certain holy men took notice of him. They saw not with eyes of flesh but with the inner seeing, and they perceived that this youth carried patterns of consciousness that were ancient beyond measure. A master named Udraka came from the mountains when he heard that one of the Old Swimmers had arrived. He went into meditation to perceive the truth of what others claimed, and in the Ocean of consciousness he Saw the boy clearly: his pattern was like a river that had been flowing for uncounted ages, gathering tributaries from many sources, growing deeper and stronger with each confluence". Udraka said: "This one carries the concentrated blessing of the Western lineages. I perceive in him the mark of those who came from the Blessed Land after its drowning, who scattered east and west, who preserved the ancient practices through their very blood. But more—this one is a confluence point. Multiple streams meet in him. He is both priest and King, Healer and Prophet, carrying inheritances that were meant to remain separate but have somehow merged. The other masters tested the boy. They did not test his knowledge of scripture or his ability to recite teachings. Instead, they observed how his consciousness moved. They watched him enter meditation and saw that he could dive to great depths naturally, without instruction."

They observed him among people and saw that he felt their sufferings and joys as if they were his own. They presented him with puzzles of perception and saw that he could See patterns invisible to others. One master said: 'He needs no awakening—he is already awake. But he does not know that he is awake. He has the capacity but not the control. He is like a bird that can fly but has not yet learned to navigate the winds. We must teach him to consciously use what he already naturally possesses.'"

Amélie felt chills running down her spine. "They recognised the gifts. The DNA inheritance. They could See it in the Ocean."

"More than that," Matteu said, his voice intense. "Listen to what Lobsang told me when we discussed this passage. He said the ability to recognise consciousness patterns in the Ocean—to See someone's lineage, their accumulated practice, their genetic inheritance—this is an advanced skill that takes most practitioners decades to develop.

But the manuscript says Udraka Saw Yeshua's pattern immediately, from a great distance, before even meeting him physically."

"Why is that significant?" "Because it means Yeshua's pattern in the Ocean was extraordinarily bright, extraordinarily distinct. Like a beacon.

The text describes other passages where Yeshua meets various teachers, and every single one recognises him immediately. Not because of reputation—he was just a teenager, unknown—but because of what he was. What he carried."

Matteu showed her another passage: "The Lamas of the mountain monasteries said that Issa carried the mark they had been taught to watch for."

Their oldest texts spoke of a coming together, a confluence of the scattered lineages that would produce one who could demonstrate the fullness of human potential. They said: "The tribes of the Blessed People were twelve, each carrying different aspects of the whole.

They were scattered when the Kingdoms fell, but the patterns remain in the Ocean, waiting to reconverge. This one shows signs of multiple tribal inheritances meeting in a single vessel."

They questioned him about his ancestry. Issa told them his grandmother was of the tribe called Asher in his language, the Blessed Ones, known for their healing gifts and sight. His legal father was of the tribe of Judah, the Kings. But his true father, he said, was the Ocean itself—for his mother had undergone a ritual of opening before his conception, calling upon the accumulated wisdom of all the ancient swimmers to concentrate in her child.

The lamas understood. They had similar practices in their own tradition—ways of preparing consciousness for incarnation, of calling forth particular patterns from the Ocean. They said: "Your mother was a priestess, whether the priests of your land acknowledged her or not. She knew the old ways that predate the temples of stone. She dove deep and called you forth from the depths where all consciousness dwells in potential. That is why you are both ancient and new, why you carry so much accumulated wisdom yet arrive in a young body."

"Mary as a priestess," Amélie said. "This is interesting. Memories passed down from mother to daughter. Trained in the old practices."

"Exactly. And think about what we know from the New Testament. Mary's relative Elizabeth was married to Zechariah, a priest. Mary spent three months with Elizabeth during Elizabeth's pregnancy with John the Baptist. What if those three months weren't just a family visit? What if Elizabeth was teaching Mary the old practices that ran in their family line—the Asher practices that had been preserved through the priesthood?"

Matteu pulled out another document—this one a genealogical chart he'd constructed himself over years of research. "Look at this. The Gospel of Luke says Elizabeth was 'of the daughters of Aaron'—the priestly line. But there's a tradition in certain Orthodox texts that her mother was from Asher. And Anna the Prophetess, who recognised infant Yeshua in the temple—she's explicitly identified as being from Asher. There's a pattern here. The priestly families of Judea were intermarrying with families that carried the Asher bloodline, concentrating the gifts."

"And Yeshua was the ultimate concentration point," Amélie said, understanding dawning. "Judah through Joseph's legal lineage, giving him the claim to Kingship. Asher through Mary's actual bloodline, giving him the healing and prophetic gifts. And the ritual his mother performed—calling forth the fullest expression of those gifts from the Ocean itself."

"Yes. And the Tibetan lamas recognised this instantly because they'd been watching for it. Not specifically watching for Yeshua—they didn't know his name or his destiny. But their oldest texts spoke of periodic convergences, times when the scattered lineages would reconverge in individuals who carried the potential for full awakening. They called such individuals Bodhisattvas—enlightened ones who return to help others awaken."

Matteu showed her another passage from the Hemis manuscript and Amélie wondered if this was a forgery as some had said or was it a copy of a true document.

The masters said to Issa: "You are a Bodhisattva of ancient standing. We can See in the Ocean that this is not your first time swimming these depths. Your consciousness pattern shows refinement across many lifetimes, many bodies. But in this life, you have been given something rare—a body prepared specifically to hold the full capacity. Your genetic inheritance, the concentration of the Old Blood, the ritual your mother performed—all have created a vessel capable of expressing abilities that usually remain dormant or partial.' Issa asked: 'But why me? Why this particular body, this particular life?' And the eldest lama replied: 'Because the Ocean itself moves toward awakening. It seeks to remember itself fully through its expressions in form. When the time is right, when conditions align, the Ocean concentrates its knowing in particular waves that can help other waves remember they are Ocean. You are such a wave. Your purpose is not to be worshiped as different from others, but to demonstrate what all humans can become when they remember their nature as Ocean."

Amélie felt tears running down her face. "That's what the have said the Church suppressed. Not that Yeshua was Divine—but that his divinity was meant to show us our own potential divinity. That we're all Ocean, we've all been swimming forever, we've just forgotten."

"Precisely," Matteu said. "And the Tibetan lamas understood this perfectly. That's why they were willing to teach Yeshua—because he wasn't claiming to be separate from humanity. He was trying to wake humanity up to what it actually is."

The Training —Diving with Full Consciousness

Matteu opened another section of his journals, filled with detailed notes and diagrams. "The manuscript describes three years of training. Not learning new abilities—Yeshua already had those genetically. But learning to control them, to dive consciously rather than being pulled by currents, to manifest abilities at will rather than having them emerge spontaneously." He showed Amélie a passage: "The first year, the Lamas taught Issa to still the surface mind. They said: 'You already dive naturally, but you dive without knowing you dive. You must learn to remain conscious during the descent, to observe your own consciousness as it moves through different layers of the Ocean. They taught him practices of breath and attention. To count his breaths while diving deeper, so that consciousness remained aware even as it entered states that usually bring sleep or unconsciousness. They taught him to notice the currents—to feel when his consciousness was being pulled by patterns of fear, desire, old conditioning—and to navigate by choice rather than being swept along. Issa learned quickly. The lamas said this was because his body already knew how to do these things—the genetic patterns in his flesh held memory of countless ancestors who had practiced these same techniques. His cells remembered what his conscious mind was only now learning to direct.

The second year, they taught him to perceive the patterns beneath surface phenomena. 'All physical reality,' they said, 'is condensed consciousness. Matter is frozen Ocean. When you dive deep enough, you perceive this directly—you See that bodies are patterns of light, that diseases are disruptions in pattern, that emotions are currents in the shared Ocean that all minds swim within.' They taught him to perceive the subtle bodies—the layers of consciousness that underlie the physical form. To See the energetic patterns that would become disease before the disease manifested. To feel the blockages in another person's consciousness stream, the places where the current no longer flowed freely. And most importantly, to recognise that these patterns could be influenced, shifted, healed through conscious attention.

Issa excelled at this. The Lamas said: "Your blood line inheritance shows itself here. Your ancestors were healers because they could naturally perceive these patterns and influence them. But you carry this gift more strongly than any we have encountered. You do not just perceive the patterns—you can reshape them with a thought, with a touch. As if the Ocean itself moves through your intention with unusual fluidity."

The third year was the most difficult and most dangerous. The Lamas taught Issa to consciously manifest in the physical realm. "Everything you see," they said, "emerges from consciousness before it appears in matter. If you dive deep enough, to the place where possibilities have not yet collapsed into form, you can influence what manifests. Not by forcing, but by aligning with the currents of the

Ocean that are always trying to flow toward healing, toward balance, toward love."

This required learning to hold two states simultaneously—remaining deeply submerged in the Ocean while maintaining full connection with the physical body.

Most practitioners could do one or the other, but not both at once. But Issa, because of his genetic inheritance and the preparation of his body before birth, could hold both states naturally. He could be fully in the Ocean and fully in form simultaneously.

The lamas said: "This is what was meant by the prophecy of the one who would unite heaven and earth. Not a metaphor. A literal description of consciousness that can be fully transcendent and fully immanent at the same time. This is the mark of the truest Bodhisattva —to be so deep in the Ocean that you remember you are Ocean, while still swimming in such a way that other waves can perceive you and learn from your movement."

Matteu looked up from the text. "Do you understand what they're describing? Yeshua's 'miracles' weren't supernatural interventions. They were the natural result of a consciousness that could remain in the depths of the Ocean while simultaneously operating in physical form. He could influence physical reality directly because he perceived and operated from the level where physical reality is still fluid, still responsive to consciousness."

"The healing," Amélie said. "He could perceive the energetic patterns that were creating disease and shift them before they fully manifested in the body."

"Yes. And the multiplication of food—he could perceive matter at the level of condensed consciousness and influence how it manifested. And the calming of storms—he could feel the energetic patterns creating the weather and help them shift toward calm. And reading hearts—he was literally perceiving people's consciousness in the shared Ocean where all minds meet."

"And this wasn't unique to Yeshua," Amélie said, understanding fully now. "The Lamas had seen others do similar things. Maybe not to the same degree, but the abilities themselves were known, documented, teachable."

"Exactly. The Hemis manuscript makes this clear. Listen to what the lamas told Yeshua when his training was complete: 'You have mastered what we can teach. But remember—these abilities are not yours alone. They are the natural inheritance of all humans who carry the capacity in their bodies and develop it through practice. You are extraordinary in degree, but not in kind. Your purpose is not to demonstrate that you are different, but to show others what they can become. You are a full expression of human potential, not a god pretending to be human.' Issa asked: 'Then what should I teach when I return to my people?' And the eldest lama replied: 'Teach them to dive. Teach them that the Kingdom of Heaven is not a place they go to after death, but a depth of consciousness available in every moment. Teach them that they are not separate from the Divine—they are expressions of the Divine temporarily forgetting its nature. Teach them that healing, knowing, manifesting—all are possible when they remember they are Ocean. And most importantly, teach them that they need no mediator, no priest, no temple. The Ocean is available to anyone who chooses to dive."

Matteu closed the manuscript gently. "And that's exactly what Yeshua did teach. But the Church—the institution that formed after his death—took those teachings and inverted them. Made Yeshua the mediator instead of the teacher. Made his abilities unique instead of exemplary. Changed the perception of Yeshua from one who taught about love and kindness in the simplest form to one who was separate from his fellow man. This was not what He taught. Yeshua was showing the way, being an example, not as someone separate, but as a guide on how to live day to day."

"Because if people knew they could dive themselves," Amélie said, "they wouldn't need the Church's mediation."

"Exactly. And that's why these manuscripts have been suppressed. Why they have been kept hidden. Why they've spent over a century denouncing them as frauds. Because if people read Yeshua's actual story—studied in the East, learned consciousness technology, demonstrated abilities that are genetic and developable —the entire theological structure collapses and they losem control of the masses."

He pulled out one final document from the box—this one clearly modern, a photocopy of something typed. "This is from some internal archives. A memo from 1962 when I obtained a copy during my time as a missionary, before I fully understood what I was looking at."

He handed it to Amélie. She read: "Regarding the Hemis manuscripts and similar documents: While we cannot prevent scholars from discussing these texts, we must maintain that they are either fraudulent or, if authentic, represent misunderstandings of Christ's nature by non-Christian observers. To acknowledge that Christ studied meditation techniques would undermine the doctrine of his unique Divine nature. To suggest his abilities were genetic or developable would eliminate the distinction between Christ and humanity that is essential to our soteriology. Recommendation: Continue to deny authenticity of such documents and prevent Catholic scholars from engaging seriously with these claims. The faithful must believe Christ's divinity was unique and his abilities unreplicable, or the Church's claim to exclusive mediation of salvation becomes untenable."

Amélie felt fury and grief warring in her chest. "It seems they knew. They've always known. And they chose suppression over truth."

"Because truth threatens power," Matteu said quietly. "And they've had the power for two thousand years. But now—now that we're publishing these documents, now that genetic research is confirming the bloodlines, now that people everywhere are beginning to remember they can dive—that power is ending."

He gathered the photographs and documents carefully. "This is what I'm giving you, Amélie. Not just manuscripts and translations, but testimony. I'll go on record. I'll tell the world what I learned in Tibet, what information has been hidden, why the true story of Christ has been suppressed or centuries. And yes, they'll excommunicate me. They'll destroy my reputation. But the truth will be out there. The knowledge will be free. And people will finally understand that Yeshua wasn't a god to worship—he was a brother teaching us how to swim."

A knock at the door interrupted them. Daniel entered, his face urgent. "We have a problem. Father Matteu's contact in Barcelona just called. The bloodlines are mobilising. They know we're in the Pyrenees— they don't know exactly where, but they're systematically checKing monasteries, religious communities, anywhere we might hide. They're offering huge rewards for information, and they're using their political connections to get cooperation from local authorities."

"How much time do we have?" Amélie asked.

"Maybe forty-eight hours before they find us. Less if someone talks." Amélie made a decision. "Then we publish now. This second document — the testimony, the financial trails, the network mapping. Not the same paper as before: this one names names, follows the money, connects the compounds to the families directly.

I'll upload to multiple servers simultaneously — academic journals, public websites, media outlets. Make it impossible to suppress."

"It's not finished," Daniel protested. "You haven't written the full synthesis yet—"

"Then I'll publish what I have and add updates later. The important thing is getting the core evidence into the open where it can't be destroyed." She looked at Matteu. "Can I include these photographs? Your translations of the Hemis manuscripts? Your testimonies that have been hidden?"

The old Monk's face was grave. "If you do, the Church will know I'm the source. I'll be excommunicated. Possibly prosecuted for theft of Church property, since I copied documents from the archives."

"I can protect your identity—"

"No." Matteu's voice was firm. "I'm seventy-three years old. I've spent fifty years in the Church, and most of that time keeping secrets I knew should be revealed. If excommunication is the price of truth, I'll pay it gladly. Yeshua himself was excommunicated by the religious authorities of his time for teaching what I'm teaching now—that people can access the Divine directly, that they don't need institutional mediators, that the Ocean is available to everyone who chooses to dive." He smiled, and in that smile Amélie saw something of the young missionary who'd traveled to Tibet searching for truth, and something of the ancient lamas who'd recognised in him a fellow swimmer.

"Include everything," Matteu said. "Use my name. Tell my story. And let the Church defend why they've been hiding this for two thousand years. Let them explain why they suppressed Yeshua's actual teachings in favour of a theology that makes people dependent on institutional salvation. Let them justify turning a Rabbi who taught people to dive into a god who supposedly requires Priestly mediation." He placed his hand on the box of documents. "This is the real Good News—not that one person two thousand years ago was uniquely Divine, but that divinity has always been our nature. We are Ocean. We have always been swimming. We have only forgotten. And now— finally—it's time to remember. If we survive long enough to publish it.

CHAPTER FIFTEEN

The Enemy's Face

Sant Anna de les Abadesses, December 2024

The monastery's refectory was empty at the hour before Vespers — a particular silence that Amélie had learned to recognise, the kind that gathered in old stone buildings like standing water. Father Matteu had gone to pray. The others were in the courtyard. She was alone with her laptop and three hundred pages of material she still had no idea how to protect once it left her hands.

Sophia appeared in the doorway. Her expression was not alarm exactly, but close to it. "Someone is at the gate," she said. " She says her name is Marie-Claire Valan." Amelie went very still. She knew the name. Knew the face that went with it — the precise architecture of it, the way it had looked across a candlelit dinner table in the Château Montable as the woman suggested, with the measured politeness of someone ordering wine, that Amélie's situation should be "resolved."

" Alone? "Amélie asked.

"Alone. No vehicle. On foot from the village, apparently."

Sophia's voice was careful, calibrated. " Marcus has eyes on the road. There's no one else."

"What does she want?" "She said to give you this." Sophia crossed the room and placed a folded piece of paper on the table in front of Amélie. Inside, written in a clean, controlled hand: I have documentation. I have testimony. I want to know if there is a path back from what I have done. I will understand if the answer is no.

Amélie read it twice. Then she closed her laptop, pushed back her chair, and stood. "Bring her in," she said.

Marie-Claire Valan looked nothing like what Amélie expected. At the château dinner she had been immaculate — every detail controlled, from the single strand of pearls to the perfect half-smile that never quite reached her eyes. The woman who sat down across from her in the monastery refectory still held herself upright, still wore the same quality of clothing, but something in the architecture had cracked. She was tired in the way that sleep could not fix. Around her eyes, in the set of her jaw, was the particular exhaustion of someone who had been fighting themselves for a long time.

Sophia sat at Amélie's shoulder. Marcus stood near the door, arms folded, saying nothing. Elena was not yet in the room. For a moment no one spoke.

"You were the one who gave the order," Amélie said finally. "At the château. To have me 'resolved.'"

"Yes." No hesitation. No deflection. "I did."

"And before that. The children's programme."

A pause this time. Longer.

"Yes. I oversaw two of the recruitment facilities. For eleven years." She held Amélie's gaze, which cost her something visible. "I knew what was done to them. I approved the methods. I believed they were necessary. I believed a great many things I no longer believe."

"What changed?" Sophia asked.

Marie-Claire was quiet for a moment. When she spoke, the control in her voice was not the smooth control of the château but something rougher — the effort of someone choosing precision over the simpler options of collapse or performance. "My daughter. She's nineteen. She came up through the same programmes — not as a subject, she was never subjected to the conditioning, she was always family-side. But she was trained, groomed, shaped to take a position within the structure. She's brilliant. Genuinely brilliant. And she's growing colder every year." She laid her hands flat on the table. "I look at her and I see what they made of me. What I helped make of myself. And I understand now what we're doing. We're cutting people off from the very thing that makes them human. From the depth. From the warmth." Her voice dropped. "I can't feel it myself. Whatever you call it. The Ocean. I've tried. I've been trying for six months, since I first found Dr. Rousseau's initial publication. Nothing comes. Just more surface. But in other people—" she stopped herself. "In my daughter, I can see its absence. I know what absence looks like now. I've looked at it in the mirror long enough."

Amélie said nothing. She felt Marcus shift almost imperceptibly behind her — not in threat, but in attention. Felt Sophia's careful stillness beside her. "You said you have documentation." "Three years of internal communications. Programme reports. Financial flows connecting eleven family foundations across four countries. Procurement records for a compound referred to internally as Compound Veil — a neural-suppressive agent introduced into specific urban water treatment systems beginning in the early 1960s under the classification of a standard additive. Correspondence between the Council and two senior officials at the IPHA. And—" she paused, as if deciding something, then continued, "statements. Testimony. From people who were in the programmes and could not come forward themselves. I gathered it over two years. I didn't know why, at first. I told myself it was insurance."

"And now?" "Now I know I was gathering it because I already knew this moment was coming. Because some part of me had already made the decision, even before I had the courage to make it consciously." She looked at Amélie directly. "I want it published. All of it. Under my real name. I understand the consequences. I understand what the families will do. I have no illusions about that."

A silence gathered in the stone room.

"You understand," Marcus said from the doorway, "that we can't verify any of this tonight. That we'll need time. That we won't publish anything without being certain it's genuine."

"Of course."

"And that we'll need to understand why now. Why this monastery. How you found us."

"Father Matteu left breadcrumbs, I think. Deliberately." The corner of her mouth moved, something that wasn't quite a smile. "He published a monograph two years ago — on contemplative communities in the Pyrenees. An obscure journal. The kind of thing that would interest no one unless they were already looking. But for someone following the threads he'd woven through it — the references, the footnotes, a particular monastery cited in a discussion of pre-Carolingian religious practice — it was a map. I think he's been leaving those kinds of trails for years. For people who might, eventually, need to find their way somewhere." She paused. "Or perhaps he knew about me specifically. His networks are older and deeper than most people realise."

She unclasped the bag at her feet and lifted out a worn leather folder, setting it on the table. "I was given three months to present my daughter for advanced conditioning. Her eighteenth birthday came and went and I asked for more time. I have been asking for more time for a year. They've stopped granting it."

The silence this time was different. "They would condition your own daughter," Sophia said quietly. "She shows the markers. Strong ones. They've been patient with me because of my position and my record of service. But patience has a limit." Her voice was absolutely steady, which made it worse. "So. There it is. I'm not purely altruistic. I'm also a mother. But everything I've told you is true."

Amélie looked at the leather folder on the table between them. Looked at Marie-Claire Valan's face — the exhaustion, the terrible composure, the specific courage it took to say: here is what I have done, here is what I am, and I am asking anyway. She thought of Peter. Eight years old in a Belgian compound. Of Daniel, who had been taken at twelve. Of all the children whose names she would never know. She reached forward and opened the folder. "All right," she said. "Let's start at the beginning. Tell me everything."

Elena arrived twenty minutes later and took her seat without comment, as if she had known this moment was coming for a long time. Perhaps she had. Perhaps the Ocean had already shown her the shape of it. They worked through the night.

CHAPTER SIXTEEN

Learning to Hold Depths

Sant Anna de les Abadesses, February 2025

Three months after Amélie committed to the Remnant, she sat across from a child who wouldn't speak.

His name was Peter. Eight years old. Rescued from a compound in Belgium two weeks ago. He'd been in the program for three years—identified at five, conditioning begun immediately. Now he sat in the therapy room, staring at nothing, occasionally rocKing slightly, completely non-responsive.

Sophia sat beside Amélie, teaching her how to work with traumatised children.

"Don't try to make him talk," Sophia said quietly. "Don't try to fix him. Don't even try to comfort him. Just be present. Just dive and hold the space. Let him feel that presence. That's all you can do right now."

"For how long?"

"As long as it takes. Could be hours. Could be weeks. But your presence—your capacity to stay in the Ocean while sitting with his pain—that's what will eventually let him trust enough to emerge."

Amélie closed her eyes. Dropped into her heart. Let her consciousness sink through her body, through the floor, down into the depths. Found the Ocean. Rested there.

And from that place, she simply sat. Present. Not trying to do anything. Just being the Ocean while this broken child sat in his silence.

Twenty minutes passed. Forty. An hour.

Peter's rocKing slowed. Then stopped. He turned his head slightly—the first movement that seemed conscious and directed, rather than automatic.

"Don't respond yet," Sophia whispered. "Just stay present."

Another ten minutes. Peter turned his head more, looking at Amélie without quite meeting her eyes.

Then, barely audible: "Are you like them?"

First words he'd spoken since arriving.

Amélie kept her eyes closed, stayed in the Ocean. Spoke from that depth: "No. I'm not like them. I'm here to help you be safe."

"They said that too. At first."

"I know. And I can't prove I'm different. Not with words. Only with time. With staying. With never hurting you. You'll have to decide if you can trust me. But I'll wait as long as you need."

Silence again. Five minutes. Ten.

Then Peter did something remarkable. He slid off his chair. Walked across the small space. And sat next to Amélie. Not touching. Just near.

"Can you feel it?" he asked. "The big thing. The ocean thing."

Amélie opened her eyes. Looked at him. "You can feel it?"

"I always could. That's why they wanted me. Because I can go to the ocean place. But they tried to make me go there and then do bad things. Use it to hurt people. I wouldn't. So they hurt me until I would."

"You don't have to do that anymore."

"I know. I can feel that you go to the ocean place but you don't hurt from there. You help from there. How do you do that?"

And Amélie realised: she was being asked to teach.

"The ocean place—we call it diving," Amélie said. "And you're right: it's where the gifts come from. But the ocean itself is love. It's only when we use the gifts from the surface—from fear or greed or the need to control—that they become dangerous. If you stay in the ocean while using them, they can only help. Never hurt."

She held her hand out, palm up. Not asking for anything. Just offering.

Peter looked at it for a long moment. Then he placed his small hand in hers.

"Close your eyes," she said. "Drop into your heart. You already know the way. You've been going there your whole life."

A silence. The morning light in the therapy room. The distant sound of the monastery bell.

And then Peter made a small sound—not pain, not fear. The sound of someone arriving somewhere they had been trying to reach for a very long time.

He kept his eyes closed. But his face had changed. The tightness gone. The held-breath quality gone. He looked, for the first time since he had arrived, like a child.

"Can you feel it?" he asked. Not asking Amélie. asking the air. asking the Ocean.

He sat there holding Amélie's hand and showing her, without knowing he was doing it, how the water felt when you were eight years old and someone had tried to steal it from you and you had kept it anyway. Had held on to it in the dark, in the worst of it, and brought it here intact.

That was the miracle. Not Amélie's teaching. His surviving.

They stayed like that for a long time. The monastery bell rang once, marKing the hour. Neither of them moved.

Eventually Peter opened his eyes. He didn't let go of her hand.

"They're going to come looking for me," he said. Not frightened. Just matter-of-fact, the way children state things that adults spend years learning to say out loud. "I can feel them. In the ocean place. Like something dark moving far away. Getting closer."

Amélie felt the hairs rise on her forearms. She kept her voice even. "How far away?"

He scrunched his eyes shut, concentrating. "Not today. Maybe not this week. But they're looking. They always look." He opened his eyes and looked at her directly for the first time—really looked, as if he had decided she was worth the risk of it. "That's what they trained me to do. Find people who were hiding. They'd show me a photograph and I'd go to the ocean place and follow the thread. I was very good at it."

"I know," Amélie said quietly.

"Other people like me are still doing it. Right now. looking for the ones who escaped." He paused. "looking for this place."

Sophia had gone very still in the doorway.

Amélie took a slow breath and stayed in the Ocean. Let the fear move through her without taking hold. Waves on the surface. Calm in the depths. "Can you feel how many?"

Peter closed his eyes. A long silence—long enough that Amélie almost spoke.

"Three," he said. "Maybe four. They're not together. They're searching in different directions." He opened his eyes. Something had shifted in his expression—not fear exactly, but its shadow. The knowledge of what those other children were being made to do. What he had once been made to do. "They won't stop. The people who control them make it so you can't stop. You just keep looking because if you stop, the bad thing happens."

"We're going to stop them," Amélie said. "The people who control them. That's what we're working on."

"I know." He looked down at their still-joined hands. "I could feel that in you. When I was sitting across the room. You're trying to find them." A pause. "I can help. If you teach me properly — the way you use it, not the way they did — I could follow the threads back. Not to find the people hiding. To find the children still inside." He looked up at her. "I know where two of the other places are. I remember them from when they made me search. I remember the feeling of those places in the Ocean. The way they taste."

The air in the room changed.

Sophia moved quietly to the small desk in the corner and picked up her pen.

"Tell me," Amélie said. "Take your time. Tell me everything you remember."

And Peter—eight years old, three years broken, two weeks free—began to talk.

Outside, the monastery went about its ancient rhythms. The bell. The smell of bread from the refectory. The particular silence of stone that has held a thousand prayers.

Inside, the work was already changing shape.

CHAPTER SEVENTEEN

The First Operation

The Pyrenees / Europe, March 2025

One evening, three months after Rinpoche's visit, Marie-Claire Valan asked to address the full group.

She had been at the monastery since December — working with Sophia, healing slowly, handing over intelligence piece by piece as trust was established on both sides. Amélie had watched the process with something between caution and reluctant admiration. She had not expected this woman to stay. She had not expected her to weep, either, or to spend hours in the refectory with Peter and the other children, just sitting, saying nothing, as though proximity to what she had helped create was its own form of penance.

The group gathered after Vespers. Marie-Claire stood at the end of the table, impeccably dressed as always, but three months of Sophia's work had done something to the precise architecture of her — loosened it, made it less a wall and more a frame. She placed her hands flat on the table.

"I'm ready," she said. "My group has seventeen children in the programme right now. I have access. Locations. Schedules. Security protocols. I can help you get them out."

The room was quiet. Not the silence of doubt — they had had three months to take the measure of her — but the silence of people understanding that something had just shifted.

"When?" Marcus asked.

"As soon as we're ready. But it needs to be simultaneous. If one facility goes dark, the others lock down within minutes."

The group conferred silently, that wordless communication that happened when people swam together. Agreement formed. "Then we plan," Priya said. "All of it. Together."

They worked late into the night, maps spread across the dining table, Marie-Claire walking them through layouts and guard rotations and the particular arrogance of people who had never genuinely been threatened. It was close to two in the morning when Amélie finally pushed back her chair.

The method

Some knowledge costs the person who carries it. Issy paid that cost at four years old. What follows is her account, given in her own words, to the woman she trusted to tell it.

The next morning, Amélie woke on Elena's couch to find the monastery buzzing with quiet activity. More people had arrived overnight—members of the Remnant from across Europe, summoned by urgent messages about the need to document everything before Amélie published. Among them was a young woman who couldn't have been more than twenty-two. She sat apart from the others, hands wrapped around a cup of tea, her eyes holding that particular emptiness Amélie had learned to recognise—the look of someone who'd been broken and was slowly, painfully, reassembling themselves.

"That's Issy," Sophia said quietly, sitting beside Amélie. "She escaped from one of the families eight months ago. She's agreed to tell you her story. To help you understand what the programming actually entails. But please, be gentle. She's still healing."

Amélie approached slowly, sitting across from Issy without crowding her. "Thank you for being willing to talk to me. I know this must be difficult."

Issy's voice, when she spoke, was surprisingly steady. "It needs to be told. People need to know what they do to us. What they're still doing to children right now." She set down her tea. "My family—my birth family—they're descendants of one of the old families. They'd tracked the bloodline carefully through marriages, genetic testing, genealogical research. When I was born, they did genetic screening. Found I carried the markers strongly. Enhanced empathy. Precognitive sensitivity. Pattern recognition off the charts."

"How old were you when they started?" Amélie asked gently. "Four. That's the optimal age, apparently. Old enough to have formed basic personality, young enough that the psyche is still plastic. They start with isolation." Issy's eyes grew distant, but her voice remained clinical, as if she were describing something that happened to someone else. "They separate you from anyone who loves you unconditionally. Your mother, if she's not complicit, is told you're going to special boarding school. You're taken to a family estate—mine was in the country—where the only people you see are trainers."

"Trainers," Amélie repeated, feeling sick. "That's what they call themselves. Usually psychologists or psychiatrists who've been recruited by the families. Some are true believers who think they're creating the next evolution of human consciousness. Others just do it for money. They're paid extremely well to keep quiet."

Issy took a sip of tea, her hands steady now, as if telling the story actually helped. "The first phase is disorientation. They scramble your sense of time, keep you awake for irregular periods, feed you at random intervals. No windows, no clocks, no way to anchor yourself. Within a week, you've lost all sense of where you are. Your only reality is the room, the trainers, the protocols."

"What are the protocols?" Amélie asked, though she wasn't sure she wanted to know. "They vary depending on which gifts they're trying to isolate. For empaths, they make you feel things—intense emotions, fear, pain, joy —then suddenly cut off the source. Over and over. Condition you to feel without responding, to sense others' emotions without letting them affect you. It teaches you to access the empathic gift without the compassion that would normally come with it."

Sophia had joined them, sitting beside Issy in silent support. "For precognitive abilities," she added, "they use sensory deprivation and psychoactive compounds. Keep the child in a state where the boundaries between present and future blur. Then they reward correct predictions and punish incorrect ones. Eventually, the child learns to access future probability streams, but only in service to the questions the trainers ask. They lose the ability to use the gift freely —it becomes triggered only by external demands."

"And pattern recognition?" Amélie asked.

"Puzzles," Issy said. "Endless, impossible puzzles. Mathematical, visual, linguistic. Keep the child in a state of constant problem-solving until pattern recognition becomes automatic, unconscious. But they make sure the patterns are always about systems of control—financial markets, social manipulation, power dynamics. They shape what kinds of patterns you're able to see."

"How long did this last for you?" "Three years. From age four to seven. By the end, I was... fractured. I could read people's emotions and intentions with perfect accuracy but felt nothing about what I read. I could predict outcomes but only cared about being correct, not about whether the outcomes were good or harmful. I could solve complex problems but only ones framed by authority figures. I was the perfect tool."

"What happened at seven?" Issy's expression hardened. "They sent me back to my family. To live a 'normal' life, go to 'normal' school. But I was supposed to report everything I observed—which classmates showed signs of the gifts, which teachers were sympathetic to certain ideas, which families might be useful contacts. I was a spy in my own life. And I did it. Perfectly. For eleven years."

"What changed?" "I met someone." Issy's voice softened for the first time. "Another descendant. She didn't know what she carried—her family line had been hidden for generations. But I could sense it immediately. The gifts, dormant but present. And something in me... broke. Or healed. I don't know which." She looked up at Amélie. "She was kind. Genuinely kind. And when I was near her, I started to feel things again. Not just sensing others' emotions but actually feeling my own. It was excruciating at first—eleven years of suppressed feeling all flooding back. But also... it reminded me that I used to be human. That beneath the programming, there was still someone real." "She helped me escape. Contacted the Remnant through networks I didn't know existed. They extracted me eight months ago, the same night my family was going to send me to begin 'advanced training' at one of the family compounds. If I'd gone there..." She shuddered. "The children who go through advanced training—they never come back. Not really. They're too far gone, too deeply fractured."

Amélie felt tears running down her face. "How many children are in advanced training right now?"

"We estimate about fifteen or more across Europe and North America. We've been trying to extract them, but the security is..." Isabelle trailed off. "These compounds aren't just guarded estates. They're fortresses. Private security, surveillance, and the groups have political connections that make legal intervention impossible. We've tried going to authorities. But how do you prove what's happening when the children themselves have been programmed to deny it? When the families have psychiatric evaluations declaring the children happy and thriving?"

The Rescue

Two months after Marie-Claire's announcement, she was ready.

The healing had not been quiet. Sophia had said little about the sessions, but what filtered through was enough — that Marie-Claire had cried daily, sometimes for hours. That she had raged. That she had grieved the childhood stolen from her, the decades of numbness, the harm she had overseen and approved and told herself was necessary. The woman who had sat at the château table suggesting Amélie be *resolved* with the composure of someone ordering wine had, piece by piece, been taken apart. What was reassembling itself was something rawer and, Amélie suspected, more real. But she was healing. And now she was ready to help extract seventeen children from her groups compounds.

The operation was planned in the small hours of night, around the dining table that had become the Remnant's command centre. "Three facilities," Marie-Claire said, spreading maps across the table. "One in Switzerland—Alpine estate, remote. One in Belgium—converted monastery, ironically. One in southern France—old château. Seventeen children total, ranging from age six to fourteen. Various stages of conditioning."

"Security?" Marcus asked. He'd done this before. Knew what they were up against.

"Heavy. Guards, surveillance, controlled access. But I have codes, schedules, weak points. The families are arrogant. They've never been seriously threatened. Their security is designed to keep children in, not to repel sophisticated extraction."

"Timing?" "Simultaneously. Next new moon—twelve days from now. If we hit one facility, the others will go into lockdown. We need to extract all seventeen in one night."

"That's three teams," Gabriel said. He'd brought Council resources—funds, vehicles, safe houses, forged documents.

"I can provide logistics. Vehicles, accommodation, escape routes. But the actual extraction—that requires people who can handle violence if necessary and maintain consciousness under pressure. Divers who can fight." He looked around the table. "How many do we have who qualify?"

Marcus raised his hand. "I've done this before. Twice." Elena: "I'll go. These were my torturers too. I know what the children are experiencing." Ahmed: "I'm trained in martial arts. And I can maintain presence under stress." Keiko: "I'm small but fast. And I can sense layouts intuitively— the diving helps me navigate spaces."

Four more volunteered. Eleven people total who could dive deeply and handle the tactical demands of the operation.

"Not enough," Marcus said. "We need at least five per facility— two to extract children, three to handle security and covering fire if needed."

"I'll go," Amélie heard herself say. Everyone looked at her.

"You've never done tactical work," Marcus said gently. "This is dangerous. These are not the families at a polite dinner party. This is their children. Their future assets. They will use lethal force to protect them."

"I know. But I can dive under pressure now. Rinpoche taught me. And I can connect with traumatised children quickly—Lucas proved that. I should be on one of the extraction teams."

Priya studied her. Then nodded. "She's right. She's developed quickly. And her presence with children is remarkable. She goes."

Marcus sighed but didn't argue. "Fine. But you're paired with me. And you follow my lead exactly. Understood?"

"Understood." Twelve days of intensive preparation. Physical training— learning to move quietly, to handle children who might fight or freeze, to navigate in darkness. Tactical training—escape and evasion, basic self-defence, how to respond if caught. But also diving training. This was what separated them from typical rescue operations. They weren't just extracting children. They were doing it while maintaining Ocean consciousness. Staying present. Connected. Clear. "The moment you lose presence," Rinpoche taught them, "you become dangerous. To yourself, to children, to mission. Fear makes mistakes. Anger makes mistakes. Only Ocean can navigate complexity in real time."

They practiced scenarios. Mock facilities. Pretend children (other Remnant members role-playing). Running through the extraction over and over until it became almost choreographed. They practiced diving under stress. Rinpoche would ring bells suddenly, shout at them, create chaos—and they had to drop into Ocean immediately. Had to maintain presence while the surface churned. Amélie discovered she could do it. The months of training had built capacity she didn't know she had. When Rinpoche shouted in her face, her body startled but her consciousness stayed anchored in the Ocean. Aware of the fear. Holding it. Not controlled by it.

"Good," Rinpoche said. "You're ready. But remember: practice is practice. Real operation will be more intense. Stay with your breath. Stay with your heart. Stay in the Ocean. No matter what happens."

The Night New moon. Three teams. Three targets. Team Alpha (Switzerland): Marcus, Amélie, Ahmed, Keiko, and a Council operative named Klaus who knew the terrain. Team Beta (Belgium): Elena, Gabriel, Thomas, and two others. Team Gamma (France): Remaining members led by an experienced operative from the Council. They'd synchronised watches. 2:47 AM—the exact time Amélie had been working in the library when this journey began. Marie-Claire's suggestion. She believed in signs.

Amélie rode in the van heading toward Switzerland, wearing dark clothes, tactical gear, a comm unit in her ear. Surreal. Eight months ago, she'd been an academic. Now she was part of a team about to raid a facility containing traumatised children and armed guards.

"You scared?" Marcus asked quietly.

"Terrified," Amélie admitted.

"Good. Fear keeps you sharp. Just don't let it make decisions for you. When we go in, you're not thinKing. You're flowing. Trust your training. Trust the Ocean. And follow my lead."

They arrived at the extraction point—two miles from the facility, deep in the forest. Darkness absolute. They moved on foot, night-vision equipment, completely silent.

Amélie dropped into the Ocean as she walked. Felt her consciousness expand beyond her body. Sensed the terrain. Sensed the team moving together. Sensed, faintly, the facility ahead—a concentration of suffering. The children.

"Two guards at the gate," Klaus whispered into comm. "One roving patrol. Cameras on corners."

"I can loop the cameras," Ahmed said. He had laptop, Council-provided tools. "Give me two minutes."

They waited.

Amélie breathed. In the darkness, in the cold, in the fear, she found the Ocean. Vast. Calm. Holding everything.

"Cameras looped," Ahmed confirmed. "We have fifteen minutes before they notice."

"Moving," Marcus said. They flowed forward. Up to the gate. Klaus used codes Marie-Claire had provided. Gate opened silently—she'd even arranged for hinges to be oiled during her last visit.

Inside the perimeter. Across the lawn. To the main building. Another code. Another door opening. Inside the facility looked like a school from the outside. Inside, it was prison. Bare halls. Heavy doors. The smell of antiseptic and fear.

"Children are on second floor, east wing," Marie-Claire had told them. "Four rooms. Four or five children per room. Doors lock from outside. Guards in the central station."

They moved up stairs. Silent. Fast. At the top, Amélie felt it—presences ahead. Two guards. One in the central station watching monitors. One patrolling the hall.

Marcus signalled. Ahmed and Keiko peeled off to handle guards. Marcus and Amélie continued to the children's rooms.

First door. Marcus tried the code. It didn't work. "They changed it," he breathed into comm.

"Backup plan," Klaus said. And produced a small tool—some kind of electronic lock pick. Ten seconds. Twenty. The door opened. Inside: five children. Sleeping in sparse beds. Amélie felt her heart break. So small. So vulnerable.

"Wake them gently," Marcus instructed. "We're here to help. We're taking you somewhere safe."

Amélie approached the nearest bed. A girl, perhaps eight. Touched her shoulder softly. "Hey. Wake up. Don't be scared. We're here to help you." The girl's eyes opened. Immediate terror. Amélie dropped into the Ocean, let her presence communicate what words couldn't: safe, friendly, here to help.

The girl stared. Then: "Are you like the bad people or the good people?"

"Good people. We're taking you away from here. Away from the people who hurt you."

"Really?"

"Really. But we have to go now. Very quietly."

The other children were waking. Some crying. Some frozen. Marcus and Amélie moved between them, comforting, explaining, getting them dressed in warm clothes that Klaus had brought.

"Team Beta checKing in," Elena's voice in the comm. "Seven children extracted. Moving to vehicles."

"Team Gamma in progress," another voice. "Three children out, two still inside."

"We have five," Marcus reported. "Second room now."

They moved to the next room. Four children here. Older—ten to thirteen. Harder. More conditioned. More distrustful.

"Why should we believe you?" one boy demanded. "This could be another test."

Amélie knelt to his level. "I can't prove we're different. Not with words. But feel me. Use your gift. Sense what I am. Sense if I'm lying."

The boy stared into her eyes. She let him in. Let him sense her presence. Let him feel the Ocean that flowed through her. His expression cracked. "You're like us. You have the gift. But you're not broken."

"No. I'm not broken. And you don't have to be either. Come with us. We can help you heal."

He nodded. Stood. "Okay."

The other three followed his lead. Nine children now. Moving back toward the stairs. Then: alarms. Blaring. Lights flooding on. Doors slamming shut automatically.

"They know," Klaus said. "Guards alerted. We have maybe two minutes before backup arrives from the main compound."

"Move!" Marcus ordered.

They ran. Children stumbling, frightened. Amélie scooped up the smallest girl, carried her. Down the stairs. Toward the exit. Guards ahead. Two of them, armed. Ahmed stepped forward. Amélie had seen him practice but never in real situation. He moved like water—fluid, impossibly fast. The guards didn't even get their weapons up before Ahmed had disarmed them, rendered them unconscious.

"Go!" he shouted.

Out the door. Across the lawn. Children crying now, terrified by the alarms and lights and running.

"Stay with me," Amélie told the girl she was carrying. "I've got you. You're safe."

More guards. From the gate. Three of them. Armed. Shouting. Keiko appeared from somewhere—from the shadows, from above—Amélie didn't see how. Just suddenly there, engaging them with a ferocity that seemed impossible from her small frame.

"Through the gate!" Marcus commanded. They made it. Into the forest. Into darkness beyond the lights. Running.

"Team Alpha extracted," Marcus reported between breaths. "Nine children. Moving to vehicle."

"Team Beta clear," Elena confirmed. "Seven children safe."

"Team Gamma—" The voice cut off. Gunfire audible over the comm. Then silence.

"Team Gamma, report!" Gabriel's voice, urgent. More silence. Then:

"We're clear. All five children. But one of ours is hit. Need medical."

"Extraction point," Gabriel said. "Medical team standing by."

They reached the vans. The children now free. Rescued from their various rooms in the facility. All wrapped in blankets. Still crying, but safe and the same with the other teams. Elena with her seven. Team Gamma with their five and one operative bleeding from shoulder wound. Seventeen children. All extracted. One injury. No child harmed.

The vans pulled away from their various stations as sirens echoed in the distance. Police. Or the group security. Coming too late.

The Aftermath

They all drove through the night to a safe house in northern Italy— a villa the Council owned through layers of shell companies. Medical team waiting. Beds prepared. Food. Warmth.

The children were assessed. Physically healthy, all of them. Psychologically damaged to varying degrees. But safe. Out of the program. Beginning the long journey toward healing.

Amélie worked through the morning, helping settle them. Sitting with those too frightened to sleep. Reassuring. Being present. When she finally collapsed at noon, she slept for fourteen hours straight. When she woke, Marcus was sitting beside her bed.

"You did good," he said. "Better than good. You stayed present throughout. Didn't panic. Didn't freeze. You flowed."

"I was terrified."

"I know. We all were. But you held it. That's what matters. Terror on the surface. Ocean in the depths. That's how we function under pressure."

"The operative who was shot—how is he?"

"He'll recover. Bullet through shoulder. Clean. He's done this before. Says it's not the first time and probably won't be the last."

"And the children?" "Adjusting. Sophia's with them. They'll need months, some of them years. But they're out. They're safe. And that's because of what we did last night."

Amélie felt tears coming. Relief. Exhaustion. Gratitude. Horror at what those children had endured. Joy that they were free. "Seventeen," she said. "We got seventeen."

"Yes. But Marie-Claire says there are hundreds more. In facilities around the world. This was one operation. There will need to be many more."

"Then we do more." Marcus smiled. "That's the spirit. But not today. Today you rest. Recover. Process. This kind of operation takes a toll even when you're diving. Maybe especially when you're diving, because you feel everything more deeply. So rest. We'll plan the next one when everyone's ready."

❖ ❖ ❖

The Children's Stories

Over the following weeks, as the children began to open up, their stories emerged. And each one broke Amélie's heart.

Lucas—the boy who'd challenged her at the facility, the one who'd sensed she was "like them but not broken"—told her about his training. "They'd put me in a room with three cards face down. I was supposed to guess which one was the ace of spades. If I got it right, I got food. If I got it wrong, they'd hurt me. Not a lot at first. Just a slap. But each time I was wrong, the punishment got worse. Until I learned to dive—to go to the ocean place—and from there, I could sense the cards. Could feel which one was right. They were pleased when I learned. Said I was progressing well." "But then they wanted me to use it for other things. To sense what people were thinKing. To predict what they would do. And each time, they'd hurt someone else if I was wrong. Made me responsible. Made me understand that my gift wasn't for me. It was for them. And people would suffer if I didn't use it right."

Amélie held him as he cried. Ten years old. Carrying guilt for things that were never his fault. "You're not responsible," she told him. "You were a child. They were adults who should have protected you. Everything they did was wrong. Every hurt was their fault, not yours."

"But I did it. I used the gift for them."

"Because you had no choice. That's not the same as willing participation. You survived. That's all you could do. And now you're free. And you can learn to use the gift the way it was meant to be used. For good. For helping. On your own terms."

Slowly, over months, Lucas began to believe her. Began to integrate. To heal.

A girl named Jill was twelve. She'd been in the program since age six. Had developed abilities to sense emotional states with extreme accuracy—could read a room, sense what people wanted, predict how they'd respond to different stimuli.

"They used me at parties," she said. "Fancy events where my father did business. I'd stand near people, sense what they were feeling, report back. He'd know who was anxious, who was confident, who was lying. Gave him advantage in negotiations. And I thought I was helping him. Thought that's what families did. Help each other."

"When did you realise it was wrong?" "When I was nine. I sensed that my father was using the information to hurt people. To manipulate them into bad deals. To exploit their vulnerabilities. And when I asked him why he was doing that, he got angry. Said I wasn't supposed to judge. Just sense and report. That my job was to be a tool, not to have opinions."

"I stopped cooperating. So they brought in trainers. People who specialised in maKing children compliant. And they..." She couldn't continue. Started crying.

Amélie didn't push. Just held space. Let Jill feel what she needed to feel. Let the Ocean hold both of them while the pain moved through.

These were the stories that fuelled the Remnant's work. Every child they rescued was a universe of suffering that might now become a universe of healing.

Every operation was worth the risk. And there were more operations. Over the following months, four more. Thirty-three additional children extracted. Two more operatives injured. One child who didn't survive—died during extraction, combination of pre-existing health issues and stress of the rescue. That death nearly broke the team. Sophia especially. Elena. Marcus. All of them who'd worked so hard to save her.

"Her name was Janine," Elena said at the memorial service they held. "She was seven. She'd been in the program for two years. And she died free. She died knowing people cared enough to try to save her. That's not enough. That's not fair. She should have lived. Should have grown up and healed and become whatever she was meant to become. But at least she didn't die in that facility. At least she didn't die thinKing no one cared."

They buried her in a natural cemetery in the mountains. No name on the grave—too dangerous, families might find it. Just a small stone with a hand-carved symbol: the Merovingian cross-circle. And the words: "Beloved child of the Ocean. Gone home."

Forty-nine children saved. One lost. Hundreds more still in the programs.

The work continued.

Evidence

Daniel spoke up from across the room. "That's why full documentation matters. Why testimony matters. If Dr. Rousseau publishes evidence—genetic research showing the gifts are real, testimony from survivors like us, financial trails connecting the families to each other—it creates a framework people can't dismiss. Even if they can't immediately rescue every child, they can start watching. asking questions. MaKing it harder for the families to operate

And so the work continued — building the case that would one day make it impossible to look away.

Three weeks later, they moved to Paris. Not Elena's flat — that address was burned, watched now by people who had been watching it since the paper went viral.

Marcus had arranged a borrowed apartment in the eleventh arrondissement, two rooms and a kitchen belonging to a friend of the network who had gone to Montréal for the season. Matteu had insisted on maKing the journey with them. 'Old men have their uses,' he'd said, when Sophia suggested he'd be safer in the mountains. 'I know people in Paris. I am not staying at the monastery while the work happens in the city.'

No one had argued with him.

CHAPTER EIGHTEEN

The Calcification

Paris, April 2025

They pressed upload at 3:47 in the morning. For the first thirty seconds, nothing happened. The file sat on the server, a 300-page document accumulating its first handful of views from whatever insomniacs happened to be looking at the right corners of the internet at the right moment.

Amélie watched the counter and thought, absurdly, of a stone dropped into still water — the pause before the rings begin. Then the rings began. Within ten minutes, the first responses appeared in the monitoring feeds. Some were what she'd expected: people writing finally and this explains everything and I've been dreaming about dark water for years, I thought I was going mad.

A genetic researcher in New Zealand who had apparently been staring at the Merovingian markers in her own dataset for two years without knowing what they meant.

A man in São Paulo who described his grandmother's ability to know when someone was lying, which she had simply called the knowing, which she said ran in the women of her family.

The counter climbed through a thousand, then five thousand. Then the other responses began.

"They're moving fast," Daniel said, monitoring the pushback feeds with the expression of someone recognising a pattern they'd hoped not to see.

"Look at the timestamps." The first fact-check flags appeared seventeen minutes after upload. Not from individual users — from organisations. Corporate accounts with blue verification marks and logos she recognised from the media landscape: the kind of entities that presented themselves as neutral arbiters of information and which she now, staring at their ownership structures on Elena's tablet, could trace through three layers of holding companies to the same names she'd seen on the boards at Château Montable. The same groups.

"They had a protocol ready," Marcus said. He wasn't looking at the responses. He was looking at Amélie. "This wasn't improvised. They anticipated this kind of exposure. Someone on their side has been watching our networks."

The counter climbed through ten thousand. Alongside it, a new counter she hadn't wanted to track: platforms adding warning labels. An official statement from the Sorbonne, formally questioning her research integrity, released at 4:12 AM — which meant someone had been waiting to send it.

An Interpol notice, at 4:38. Her name. Wanted for questioning. "That's the shift from soft power to hard power," Marcus said. "The narrative control failed — the document spread too fast. So now it's legal persecution."

Amélie set down her phone. She looked at her hands on the table. And she noticed something she hadn't expected. She couldn't dive. Not completely. She dropped toward the Ocean the way she had been doing instinctively for weeks — letting her attention settle, feeling for the quiet beneath the surface — and found it there, but distant. Slightly muffled. Like trying to hear something through a closed door that had been open before. She had dived in a courtyard in Paris under genuine threat and the Ocean had flooded in immediately. She had dived in Rinpoche's monastery with ease, with increasing depth each time, with the sense of something opening as naturally as breathing. Here, in this borrowed kitchen, with her phone vibrating and her name on an international arrest notice and 10,000 people reading what she'd published, the Ocean was present but — she groped for the word — clouded.

"Marcus," she said. "Something's wrong with me." He looked up. "The Ocean. I can feel it but I can't reach it properly. Something is — there's interference."

He was quiet for a moment. Then he pushed his laptop aside and placed both hands flat on the table. "Tell me exactly what it feels like." "Like trying to dive through something slightly opaque. Like the signal is being disrupted." He looked at Elena, who nodded once — a small nod that carried the weight of confirmation.

"It's not you," Marcus said. "It's the environment. And I need to show you something that I've been trying to figure out how to tell you for the last three weeks." He had the documents arranged in a particular order, she noticed — not the dramatic scatter of a revelation, but the careful sequence of a man who had thought hard about how to present something he knew would be resisted.

"I want to be precise about what I can demonstrate and what I can only observe," he said, and the qualification itself made Sophia look up. "Sophia — I want you to push back on anything that seems like a leap."

"Already planning on it," she said. He pulled up brain imaging on his laptop. Two scans, side by side: one showing a large, clear pineal gland with distinct edges; the other showing something smaller, denser, its edges blurring into surrounding tissue. "The pineal gland," he said. "What indigenous and ancient traditions called the third eye. What Descartes — a man not given to mysticism — called the seat of the soul. What modern neuroscience has established produces DMT naturally: the same compound used in shamanic consciousness practices for millennia. The biological correlate, as far as we can establish, of what we're calling the capacity to dive."

"That's contested," Sophia said. "The DMT production is established. The consciousness implications are contested. Yes."

He pointed to the second scan. "This is calcification. Calcium deposits accumulating in the gland tissue, reducing its function. This happens to some degree in most adults. What's anomalous is the degree and the rate." He brought up a third image — a population study. "Pre-industrial skulls, examined archaeologically. Medieval populations. Tribal societies that still exist today without industrialised food and water systems. Calcification rates significantly lower. Occurring significantly later in life. The calcification we see in modern adults — severe, present by age thirty — is not the natural aging pattern. It's environmental."

"Environmental means it could be many things," Sophia said. "Yes. That's exactly what it means."

He looked at her directly. "I'm not going to tell you it's deliberate. I'm going to show you what the environment contains and let you draw your own conclusions about whether it matters how it got there."

He pulled up a series of studies — peer-reviewed, mainstream, the kind that appeared in environmental health journals without any attached controversy. The micronutrient depletion in industrial food systems. The particular affinity of certain common compounds for pineal tissue. The electromagnetic sensitivity of the gland — its role in detecting and responding to magnetic fields, its function as part of the system that regulated sleep, circadian rhythm, and the neurochemical conditions under which contemplative states were most accessible.

"Modern diets are demonstrably lower in the micronutrients associated with neurological health than diets a hundred years ago," he said. "Not because of a single decision. Because of how industrial food production works — the soil depletes, the processing strips what remains, the shelf-life requirements remove most of the rest. Nobody designed this to suppress consciousness. But the measurable effect on pineal function is this." He tapped the scan. "That." "Water systems. Not a conspiracy — just the accumulated reality of treating water as a delivery mechanism for a standardised safe fluid rather than as something that interacts with biology in complex ways. Whether the standard fully accounts for neurological effects across a lifetime of exposure..." He left it there.

"The electromagnetic environment we now live inside twenty-four hours a day is something no human nervous system evolved in. We don't know the long-term effects. Nobody does. The research is genuinely contested. What we know is that the pineal gland is electromagnetically sensitive and that we have saturated our environment with artificial fields and then observed declining rates of the neurological states those fields may interfere with. That could be coincidence. It could be causation. I genuinely cannot tell you which."

Sophia had stopped interjecting. She was watching him with an expression Amélie couldn't quite read.

"And then there's the texture of modern life," Marcus continued. "Not chemicals. Not frequencies. Just — the design of existence. Work structures that leave no interior silence. Entertainment systems engineered for compulsive surface engagement so precisely that sustained contemplative practice becomes functionally impossible for most people. Sleep deprivation normalised as productivity. Urban environments with almost no access to the natural world. Social isolation framed as independence." He spread his hands. "Take all of that together and you have a comprehensive description of an environment hostile to Ocean access. Whether it was designed to be hostile, or whether it simply evolved because it was optimised for economic productivity and no one asked what it was doing to consciousness — that is a question I cannot answer definitively."

"But someone profits from it," Sophia said. It wasn't a question.

"Someone always does. That's what makes the pattern so difficult. You don't need a conspiracy when you have an incentive structure. The families don't need to have sat in a room in 1950 and decided to calcify everyone's pineal glands. They just need to have built systems that produce that outcome and then defended those systems from disruption because the systems made them rich." He paused. "Whether that's malice or just capitalism is, philosophically, a genuinely interesting question."

"It's not interesting," Issy said. Her voice was flat. Everyone looked at her. She had been sitting against the far wall, as she often did — near the door, instinctively, with a sightline to the window. She said very little in these sessions. When she did speak, people tended to stop.

"The children in the compounds weren't the result of an incentive structure," she said. "I was one of them. Whatever is happening in the broader environment — however much of that is design versus drift — what was done to me was not ambiguous. That was deliberate suppression of consciousness." She looked at Marcus steadily. "That we can prove. I'm the proof." A silence. Long enough to be its own kind of statement.

"Yes," Marcus said. "That's where the distinction breaks down. Because whatever's happening in the environment — the broader pattern — the work being done on those children is not accidental. And the Project Clarity document, whatever questions we might have about its provenance, describes an intention that matches what Issy experienced. The intention was there. Whether it scaled to everything we're looking at —" He stopped himself. "We publish what we can demonstrate. The pattern is damning enough without overstating it."

Amélie had been listening and watching and running her hand, every few minutes, along the edge of the table — a habit she'd developed lately, a kind of grounding gesture that kept her tethered to the physical world while her attention drifted toward the data, toward the implications. She thought about what she had felt when she tried to dive twenty minutes ago. The cloudiness. The muffled quality. She had been in this city for less than forty-eight hours and already the Ocean was harder to reach. At the monastery, it had been effortless. The mountain air, the silence, the absence of the city's constant electromagnetic chatter. Rinpoche had said, once, that the practice itself was natural — that what required effort was not the diving but the maintenance of conditions that made diving possible.

"What about the genetics?" she asked. "The Cain and Seth material."

Marcus looked at Issy. A question. Issy considered. Then she nodded.

"The families I was trained by," she said slowly, "have always known they were different. Not better — they would say better, but that's not what they meant. Different. They knew they couldn't do what we could do. And that knowledge —" She paused, finding words for something she had apparently been carrying for a long time. "That knowledge drove everything. Everything. The programming, the trauma work, the breeding programs. They were trying to fix something in themselves. Something they knew was absent and couldn't name."

"The empathy response," Marcus said. "The mirror neuron system. The genetic markers for what we're calling the Ocean-oriented traits — the Seth-line markers. The families show a very different profile." He pulled up the genetic comparison. "Reduced baseline empathy. Enhanced pattern recognition specifically for hierarchical systems — for control structures, not organic ones. Elevated capacity for delayed gratification and long-term systemic planning. All highly advantageous traits for building financial empires across generations. All profoundly disadvantageous for diving."

"They literally feel less," Rachel said. "They feel differently. Whether that's less is — it's complicated. Their orientation is different. Where Seth-line consciousness is drawn toward connection, toward understanding what another person is experiencing, toward cooperation — Cain-line consciousness is drawn toward pattern, toward system, toward control. Neither is pathological in isolation. Together, in a world where one is trying to dominate the other, it produces the history we're looking at."

Marcus closed the genetic files. "But here's what Elena identified years ago and what Issy's testimony confirms: you can breed the genetic markers into a bloodline through intermarriage. The families have been attempting this for centuries. But if the consciousness orientation remains control-based — if what you want the gift for is domination rather than service — the gifts don't function properly. They come out distorted. Fragmented."

"Like someone memorising the words to a song they can't feel the music of," Issy said quietly.

"Yes. Exactly. Which is why the trauma programming. They could breed the genetics into their children — and some of those children would be born with natural empathy, with the diving capacity, with the full Seth-line expression. And those children were useless to them. Worse than useless. Dangerous. So they had to break them."

The room was very quiet. Outside, the sky was beginning to lighten. The city's sounds were changing register: fewer cars, the first birds. Amélie thought about the children in the compounds. About Peter. About the girl who had come to them from the last extraction, who for the first three days had been unable to eat in the same room as other people because she had never learned that shared meals were safe. "We're publishing all of it," she said. "The environmental data — everything Marcus can demonstrate. The genetic comparison. The historical pattern. Issy's testimony." She looked at Marcus. "And we're maKing the case you described — not cartoon villains. Pattern. Because the pattern is its own indictment." She opened a new section of the document.

"And the practices," Elena said. She had been quiet for the last hour, listening from her chair with her eyes slightly unfocused in the way that meant she was half in the Ocean even while present in the room. "We publish the practices. The conditions that support the diving — the silence, the diet, the way you work with the body and the breath, the environment changes that let people begin to feel the Ocean again. The diving techniques. How to do it yourself. Because that's what they're actually afraid of." She looked at Amélie. "Not the history. Not even the genetics. The fact that it's learnable. That anyone can access the Ocean if they know the door exists and how to walk through it."

Amélie nodded. She thought of Argotta wading into the spring at midnight. She thought of Matteu's fifty-two years of held silence. She thought of her grandmother, who had kept this knowledge in a box until the moment she deemed the world ready. Let the swimmer be born who can navigate all the currents. "Let's finish it," she said.

CHAPTER NINETEEN

The Architecture of Emptiness

Paris, April 2025

By the time the grey light came fully through the windows, they had been working for five hours and the document had been downloaded eighty thousand times and Amélie and Marcus were arguing. Not badly. Not the way arguments looked in the families' training programs, where every disagreement was a power struggle with a winner and a loser. More like the way two people argue when they're both trying to get to the same truth and arriving at it from different angles.

Amélie nodded. "That goes in. Everything goes in. The Project Clarity memo," Amélie said. "We can't use it." Marcus had been waiting for this. She could see it in the way he sat — not defensive, but ready.

"It corroborates everything we can demonstrate independently," he said. "It corroborates it perfectly. Too perfectly. A 1962 internal memo from Eisen Chemical that describes, in precise language, exactly what we've just argued happened — and it arrives in our hands after Matteu spent thirty years as a missionary with just enough access to just the right archives."

She held it up between two fingers, the way she had held dubious manuscripts in her years of medieval scholarship, feeling for the weight of something that was either genuine or too convenient. "If I submitted this to an academic journal, the first question would be the chain of custody. The second would be why it hasn't surfaced before."

"Because it was suppressed—"

"That's the answer that can't be verified. And an answer that can't be verified is the answer that gets us dismissed." She set it down. "The pattern makes the case without it. You said so yourself."

Marcus was quiet for a moment. In the quiet, Amélie heard the download counter climbing on Daniel's monitoring screen. Ninety thousand. The Interpol notice was still live. Three major news networks were running pieces on the viral conspiracy theory, and the phrase dangerous medical misinformation was appearing with increasing frequency in the monitoring feeds. Alongside it — this she was watching more carefully — were the other voices. The ones the platforms were flagging and the fact-checkers were dismissing and which were nevertheless multiplying faster than the suppression mechanisms could keep pace with.

"You're right," Marcus said finally. She looked at him. "You're right about the memo," he said. "We include it as a document with a contested provenance and an accurate description of observable outcomes. We don't present it as proof of intent. We present it as one of several things that, taken together, suggest a pattern. The shape of the thing is the proof."

He turned back to his laptop. "That's a more honest argument anyway. I've been too close to this for too long. I've stopped distinguishing between what I know and what I believe."

"That distinction is everything," Amélie said. "It's the only thing that keeps this document credible."

"I know." He looked at the screen. "It's just — I've spent five years looking at this. And the further you go into it, the more it coheres. The more the accidents start to look like design. It becomes very easy to stop asking whether you're pattern-matching."

Sophia, from across the table: "That's the most important thing you've said all night." He almost smiled. "Push back from the sceptic's corner is duly noted."

"I'm not purely a sceptic anymore," she said. "I've watched Amélie dive. I've watched what Isabelle can do with a room full of trauma survivors. I'm not where I was three months ago." She paused. "But I am still the person in this group who asks whether we can demonstrate intent or only observe pattern. Someone needs to be."

"Yes," Marcus agreed. "Someone does." He pulled up the historical analysis he'd been building for weeks — not a slideshow, not a timeline, but a single comparative document. Three cases from three eras, each following the same sequence.

"Let me show you what the pattern looks like. Without the contested documents. Without the genetics. Just history."

Matteu had come down from his rooms an hour ago, unable to sleep. He had been in Paris with them since they'd left the monastery — his choice, unmovable, as everything about him was unmovable once decided. He was sitting in the corner with his tea, listening without speaKing, and when Marcus pulled up the historical analysis, the old priest reached into his coat pocket and placed something on the table. A coin. Bronze, worn almost smooth, the design barely legible. He pushed it to the centre of the table. "Athenian. Fourth century BCE." He looked at Marcus. "Go on. I've been watching this pattern for forty years. I'd like to hear it from someone who arrived at it independently."

Marcus looked at the coin for a moment. Then he began. "Athens, 480 to 404 BCE. Eighty years. The concentrated flourishing of a culture that had, in that period, a particular density of what we'd call Seth-line consciousness — people capable of sustained philosophical inquiry, of art that accessed the Ocean, of political experiments based on something other than pure domination. Socrates, Plato's teacher, describing the philosophical life as a practice of knowing that you don't know — which is, functionally, a description of diving. Aeschylus writing tragedies that moved entire audiences into the kind of collective emotional depth that is, by any description, a shared Ocean experience." He paused. "Then the Peloponnesian War. Twenty-seven years. Financed on both sides by merchant networks that had been building power throughout the golden age. The war destroys the democratic experiment, ushers in two decades of oligarchic rule, and Athens never produces the same density of consciousness culture again."

He moved to the next case. "The Islamic Golden Age. Three centuries. Baghdad, Cordoba, Cairo as centres not just of knowledge — which is how we sanitise it in Western history — but of active consciousness exploration. The Sufi masters teaching diving under a different name. Mathematicians and astronomers working from a cosmology in which the universe was fundamentally alive, fundamentally intelligent, fundamentally available to direct perception. Then — in each city, in sequence — the arrival of a different kind of power. Military rulers who had accumulated authority through the specific Cain-line aptitudes: longterm strategic planning, the willingness to use force without empathy's interference, the ability to accumulate resources without compunction. The libraries burned or dispersed. The Sufi schools suppressed or absorbed into institutional frameworks that removed their essential function. The golden age ends. Within two generations, the culture that produced it is no longer recognisable."

The download counter on Daniel's screen reached one hundred thousand.

Nobody mentioned it.

"The Renaissance," Marcus said. "The most recent iteration. A hundred and fifty years of explosive re-emergence — the recovery of ancient texts, the rediscovery of practices that the Church had been sitting on for a thousand years, art that was simultaneously theology and consciousness technology. And then —" He stopped. "And then the Counter-Reformation. The Wars of Religion. The rise of merchant capitalism that turned everything, methodically, into a commodity. By 1650, the flowering is over. Not gradually. Rapidly. As if something that had been waiting for the right moment moved all at once." He looked around the table.

"The pattern is always the same. Seth consciousness creates. What I'm calling Cain orientation extracts. Creation generates abundance — cultural, spiritual, material. Abundance attracts controllers. Controllers suppress the conditions that made creation possible. Creation stops. Scarcity returns. And the controllers consolidate power over the scarcity they themselves created." Matteu picked up his coin. Turned it over in his hands.

"I was a Jesuit," he said quietly. "Do you know what the Jesuits were, in the beginning? Before the institution fully formed around them? They were the Counter-Reformation's most effective instrument. I was trained in the tradition of Ignatius of Loyola, who designed what is, functionally, the most sophisticated systematic approach to the interior life that European Christianity ever produced — the Spiritual Exercises, which are a guided programme for learning to dive. And the institution that trained me then deployed that tradition primarily as a mechanism for defending doctrine against the very questions it could have answered."

He set the coin down. "I spent twenty years as a living example of that pattern. The practice being used to maintain the structure instead of opening to the depth."

The room was quiet.

"But Rachel asked the right question," Elena said. She had been still for the last hour, and when she spoke everyone turned. "What do they actually win?" She stood, moving to the window. Outside, the mountain was becoming visible in the first real light — enormous, patient, indifferent to what was happening in this room in the way that mountains are always indifferent to what is happening in rooms. "I want to show you something," she said. "Not a reading of the past. A reading of what I can see in the probability streams — the futures that are trying to emerge from the choices being made right now." She looked at Amélie. "I know you've become cautious about visions as evidence. This isn't evidence. This is a map of what I can sense at depth. Take it as such."

Amélie nodded.

Elena closed her eyes. When she began to speak, her voice had the quality that always came in the deep dives — quieter than usual, precisely cadenced, as if she were describing something she was seeing carefully and didn't want to distort.

"I see them. The last families. The scenario where they get everything they're planning for. They live in their secured compounds. The world outside is managed — population reduced to the numbers they decided were sustainable. Most of those remaining are integrated with systems the families control: not science fiction, just the logical extension of current developments, the neural interface made universal, the biological substrate of consciousness mediated through technology they own. The families themselves remain biological. They couldn't bring themselves to integrate. Some instinct warned them not to trust their own technology with their own minds. So they are the last truly biological humans. Living in their beautiful, controlled environments, sustained by the technology their bloodlines spent millennia building. And something is wrong. They have everything they planned for. Everything. Total control. No resistance. No awakening. The Ocean has gone quiet — not because it's gone, but because there is no one left who knows how to listen for it. The world is not destroyed. There are still plants, still animals. But it is creatively dead. Nothing genuinely new is being made. No art that moves anyone. No music that reaches the depth. No innovation that isn't the incremental optimisation of existing systems, going nowhere. Because creation requires the Ocean. It requires someone diving into the depths and bringing something back that didn't exist before. And they have eliminated everyone who could dive. The families are surrounded by wealth beyond measure, power

without limit, lifespans extended by the technology they control. They have their heaven. And it is hell. Not the obvious hell. Not suffering — they've eliminated suffering, more or less, or at least the kinds of suffering they could see and measure. But boredom. A profound, existential, terminal boredom. They have spent three thousand years building toward this moment and it has arrived and there is nothing left to do and nothing being made that matters and no one left who can surprise them. I watch them understand, one by one, what they've done. They built their power in relation to something. Power only means anything in relation to beings who have less. Control only satisfies when something resists being controlled. They built their heaven and installed themselves in it and then discovered that the thing that gave their heaven meaning was the struggle to reach it, and they have won, and the winning is the end of meaning. The worst part — I can See this so clearly — is that they cannot undo it. The consciousness they eliminated is gone. The Ocean hasn't dried up. It never dries up. But the people who could teach others to dive are gone. And the families cannot dive themselves. They have made themselves Kings of a desert they created, and there is nothing left to transform it back into a garden. In some futures I see them fragment. Without external resistance, without shared purpose beyond accumulation in a world where accumulation no longer means anything, the alliances that held for centuries collapse. Families who coordinated across millennia turn on each other over scraps of meaningless power. In one future — the one I look at for only a moment and then have to look away from — I see the last of them finally understanding what they traded away. Understanding that the Ocean they could not access was the only thing that made existence worth experiencing. That they spent three thousand years eliminating the very thing that gave life its meaning because they could not bear that others had it and they didn't. I see them choosing to end themselves. Not from despair, exactly. From

*recognition. From the specific grief of someone who has gotten
everything they wanted and discovered too late what it cost."*

Elena opened her eyes. She was crying. She had not, Amélie
noticed, been aware of it while she was speaKing.

The room was completely still.

Rachel's voice, very small: "That's what they win."

"Yes," Elena said. "That's the victory. Everything they wanted.
And the emptiness that comes with having it." She sat back down.
Sophia reached across and put her hand over Elena's without
speaKing.

It was Isabelle who broke the silence. Her voice was different
than usual — not flat, not the careful control she used when
describing her own history. Something more open. "The Ocean
would have them too," she said. "Even them. Even now." She was
looking at the table, not at anyone in particular. "I spent the first
years after I left the program believing I was broken. That what they
did had closed something in me permanently. That the Ocean wasn't
available for someone who had used those gifts the way I had used
them." She was quiet for a moment. "It took Rinpoche three months
to convince me to even try. And when I finally did —" She stopped.
Started again. "It was there. It had always been there. It doesn't close.
It doesn't hold the things you've done against you. It just — receives
whatever arrives."

"Even them," Amélie said. "Even them. If any of them ever —"
Isabelle looked up. Her eyes were clear. "If any of them ever stopped
controlling long enough to sink, they would find themselves held.
That's not sentimentality. That's the nature of the Ocean. It has no
preferences. It just is."

A notification. The download counter: one hundred and forty
thousand. The Interpol notice, still active. Three new fact-check
flags. And, in a different monitoring feed: a man in Manila posting
that he had been having visions since childhood that he now

understood, and his family thought he was psychotic, and reading this document made him feel, for the first time, that he was not alone.

"We're not just exposing a conspiracy," Amélie said. She was already writing. "We're offering an intervention. We're showing them — and showing everyone — what waits at the end of the path they're on." She thought of Elena's vision. Of the last families in their controlled paradise. Of the recognition that comes too late.

"Maybe some of them, seeing it, will choose differently." "Or maybe they won't," Marcus said. "Maybe they're too far optimised for control to allow surrender."

"Maybe," she said. "But the case has to be made. Because the alternative —" She stopped. She thought of the children. Of Peter, who had finally cried, after weeks, in a room with a window. Of what was at the end of the other path, the one Elena had just described. "The alternative is not acceptable." She kept writing.

We are not going to stop them by fighting the way they fight — through control, through force, through the management of what other people are permitted to know. We are going to stop them by becoming what they cannot be. By diving. By connecting. By swimming in the Ocean they have spent millennia trying to suppress. And by showing everyone — including them — that the Ocean is still here. Still waiting. Still receiving anyone who chooses to arrive. Even now. Even after everything. Because the Ocean doesn't judge. It just is. And anyone who stops controlling long enough to sink will find themselves held. That is not an offer they can take from us. That is the nature of the water.

CHAPTER TWENTY

The Great Turning

Paris, April 2025

"Is this too naive?" Amélie asked the question aloud, staring at her screen. She'd been writing for hours about helping people reconnect to the Ocean, about offering transformation even to those who'd spent millennia suppressing it.

"Is what too naive?" Sophia asked.

"This." Amélie gestured at her work. "I'm writing about offering the path back to everyone. About helping people reconnect to the Ocean. But... should we be extending this to everyone? Including them? Including the families who've spent millennia suppressing consciousness, torturing children, engineering humanity's descent into surface existence?"

The room went quiet. It was Daniel who finally spoke. "I was one of their victims. They took me at twelve. Tried to break me. Tried to split me into pieces they could use. I spent three weeks in hell because of what they do." His voice was steady, but his hands shook slightly. "And I need to tell you something. When I was in the worst of it, when they were trying to fragment my consciousness, when the trauma was so intense I wanted to die... I touched the Ocean deeper than I ever had before." He looked up at Amélie. "And in that depth, I felt something I didn't expect. I felt them. The trainers, the group members orchestrating it, all of them. I felt their consciousness in the Ocean. And they were... empty. Howling. Like black holes that used to be stars. They weren't evil in the way I'd imagined. They were absent. Absent from themselves. Absent from connection. Absent from anything that makes existence bearable."

"I hated them," Daniel continued. "Still do, some days. But I also saw that they're already in hell. The worst hell imaginable— being alive but unable to feel life. Having consciousness but being cut off from the Ocean that gives consciousness meaning. They don't need us to punish them. They're already punishing themselves with every breath, every heartbeat spent in that emptiness."

Elena nodded slowly. "I've seen the same thing in my deepest dives. The Cain-line families... they're not our enemies. They're the most lost parts of ourselves. The parts that chose separation so long ago they've forgotten connection was ever possible."

"But they're still murdering children," Isabelle said, her voice hard. "Still poisoning the water. Still building their digital prisons. Lost or not, they're causing real harm. Present-tense harm. How do we balance compassion for their emptiness with accountability for their actions?"

"We don't balance it," Marcus said. "We hold both truths simultaneously. They're victims of their own disconnection AND they're perpetrators of terrible crimes. They're suffering AND they're causing suffering. Both things are true. Both matter."

The Cain Possibility:

What They Could Become Elena closed her eyes, diving into probability streams again. But this time, she was looking for something different. Not the futures where the families succeeded. Not the futures where they failed. But the futures where they... transformed.

"I'm searching... through possibility... looking for the threads where they choose differently...

There. I found one. It's faint, low probability, but it exists. I see a man. Mid-forties. Descended from one of the primary families. He's been groomed his entire life for control. Educated in the systems, married strategically, positioned to inherit vast wealth and influence. He has three children who are being prepared the same way he was. But something has shifted. He's read the document — Amélie's publication.

At first, he dismissed it. Conspiracy theory. Academic jealousy. The usual narrative his family uses to discredit threats. But something in it haunted him. The description of the Ocean. The idea that there's a depth of consciousness he's never accessed. And so he looks at his life. Really looks. He has everything the world says matters. And he feels... nothing. No joy. No satisfaction. No sense that any of it matters. It's always been hollow. He'd always told himself that was maturity. That his ability to make rational decisions without emotional interference was a strength. His family called it 'clear-sighted.' But reading about the Ocean — about connection, joy, the sense of being held by something infinite — he realises he's not mature. He's empty. And the emptiness isn't wisdom. It's absence. So he tries. Tentatively at first — the practices Amélie outlined. For months, nothing. Just sitting. Just breathing. Just the same empty awareness, except now he's calling it meditation. But he persists. Because the alternative — accepting that this emptiness is all there is — has become unbearable. And then, eight months in, the floor falls out. His consciousness drops — not gradually, suddenly. Like falling through a trapdoor he didn't know was there. And he's in the Ocean. For thirty seconds — maybe less — he experiences what he's been missing his entire life. It's not what he expected. Not transcendent or otherworldly. More like... coming home. Like remembering something he's always known but forgot. The Ocean holds him. Vast, infinite, but also intimate. Personal. And in that holding, he feels something he has never felt before: unconditional acceptance. It doesn't care about his wealth or his power or any of it. It just receives him. Exactly as he is. Empty. Broken. Lost. And doesn't judge any of it. Just says, through its very presence: 'You've always been this. You just forgot. And that's okay. You can remember now.' And then he's back. Back in his body. Back in his meditation room. Tears streaming down his face — the first tears his conditioning allowed. He knows that everything he's built is hollow. Not wrong, exactly. Just beside the point. Compensation for not knowing the Ocean existed. He can't go back. Can't unknow this. He's touched the Ocean, and the Ocean has ruined him for the life he was living. In this probability stream, I see him maKing choices that cost him his position, his inheritance, his carefully constructed life. But he makes them anyway. Because he's tasted something real, and he cannot trade it back for something hollow, no matter how powerful the hollow thing is."

What the Ocean Feels Like

Elena opened her eyes, but her voice carried the depth of someone still partially submerged. "That's what people don't understand until they experience it," she said quietly. "The Ocean isn't a thing you access. It's not a technique you master. It's not a state you achieve. It's what you already are. You're already swimming in it. You've always been swimming in it. You just didn't notice because you were so focused on the surface."

"What does it actually feel like?" Rachel asked. "When you first touch it consciously?"

Elena considered. "It's different for everyone. But there are common elements. Let me try to describe it..." She closed her eyes again, remembering.

"First, there's the sense of vastness. You realise that what you thought of as 'you'—your thoughts, your feelings, your memories, your identity—all of that is just a tiny wave on the surface of something infinite. And you're that infinite thing. You're the wave AND the Ocean. Both simultaneously." "It should be terrifying—realising you're not what you thought you were. But it's not. It's relief. Profound relief. Because the wave is so small and fragile and temporary. It's exhausting being a wave, trying to maintain your form, trying to be separate. But the Ocean is infinite and eternal and effortless. You don't have to maintain it. It maintains you." "Then there's the connection. You feel—not intellectually understand, but actually FEEL—that you're connected to everything. Every other person is another wave on the

same Ocean. Every animal. Every plant. Every atom of existence. All of it is Ocean expressing itself through different forms. When you touch the Ocean, you know this. Not as philosophy. As lived experience."

"And the Ocean doesn't judge,"

Elena continued, her voice becoming more intense.

"This is crucial. The Ocean doesn't care what you've done, what you've thought, what you've become. It doesn't evaluate your worthiness. It doesn't require you to be pure or enlightened or good. It just receives you. Exactly as you are. With all your mistakes and trauma and conditioning and choices. All of it. The Ocean holds all of it without flinching." "That's why," she said, opening her eyes and looking directly at Amélie, "we can offer this to the families. To the Cain line. To those who've done terrible things. Because the Ocean will receive them too. The Ocean doesn't keep score. It doesn't punish. It just is. And anyone who surrenders to it—anyone who stops fighting, stops controlling, stops trying to remain separate—they get held. No exceptions."

"But," Marcus interjected, "there's something else. Something people need to understand. The Ocean is non-judgmental, yes. *But it's not neutral.* There's a... structure to it. A natural law. Elena, tell them what you've seen about the feedback."

Elena's expression grew serious. "Yes. This is important. When you're locked on the surface, disconnected from the Ocean, your actions have consequences—but they're delayed. You might do something harmful and not experience the effects for years, decades, lifetimes. The feedback is slow. This allows evil to compound. Allows people to harm others without immediately experiencing the harm they cause." "But when you dive—when you consciously access the Ocean — everything changes. The feedback becomes immediate. Instantaneous, almost. Because in the Ocean, you feel what others feel. You experience the consequences of your actions directly, not through abstract karma or Divine punishment, but through actual felt experience of connection."

"Show them," Sophia said quietly. "Show them what happens when someone tries to misuse the Ocean."

The Boomerang: Why the Ocean Cannot be Weaponised

Elena dove again, but this time to show them something darker. *"I need to show you a different probability stream. One where someone from the families learns to dive... but tries to use it the way they've used everything else. For control. For manipulation. For harm. "I need to show you a different probability stream. One where someone from the families learns to dive... but tries to use it the way they've used everything else. For control. For manipulation. For harm. I see another man. Also from one of the primary families. He's younger — mid-thirties. Brilliant. Strategic. He reads Amélie's document and recognises something the others miss: if the Ocean gives enhanced perception, enhanced pattern recognition, enhanced ability to sense truth and predict outcomes — then accessing the Ocean could make him an even more effective controller. He doesn't want transformation. He wants power. A new kind of power. So he begins the practices. Not with humility. Not with surrender. But strategically. Treating it like a skill to master, a technology to exploit. And remarkably, it works. After six months, he touches the Ocean. He dives. He experiences the connection, the vastness, the infinite perspective. But unlike the first man I showed you, this man interprets the experience differently. He comes back thinKing: I can use this. The enhanced empathy, the pattern recognition, the ability to read people's real states — these are tools. Better tools than anything he's had before. He begins to deploy them. And for a while, it works. He is more effective than ever — reading people with uncanny accuracy, seeing market movements before they happen, anticipating resistance and neutralising it. But then the feedback starts. It begins small. After a difficult negotiation where he has deliberately deceived someone, he finds he cannot stop feeling that person's confusion and distress. Not as an intellectual observation — as felt experience. In his own body. It grows. He feels the suffering of people harmed by his decisions — not as statistics, but as lived sensation. The child in the programme whose trauma he has authorised: he feels it too. Every moment of it. Because he is swimming in the Ocean, and in the Ocean there is no separation. The child's pain is his pain. He tries to stop diving. To retreat to the surface where he could harm without feeling. But he cannot. Once you have consciously accessed the Ocean, you cannot close the door you have opened. Within three months, he is psychologically shattered. In this probability stream, I see him eventually choosing suicide. Not because the Ocean punishes him. But because he cannot bear the weight of his own choices when he is forced to feel their full impact. The Ocean is a mirror. If you dive with love, you experience love. If you dive with violence, you experience the violence — as both perpetrator and victim, because in the Ocean, there is no difference."*

The Oneness in all Life

Elena emerged from the vision, visibly shaken. "That's what people need to understand. The Ocean isn't a tool. It's not a technique. It's the fundamental nature of reality. It's what you are. And when you consciously realise what you are, you realise what everything else is too. There's no separation. There never was. It was always illusion.

"So when you dive," Sophia said slowly, understanding dawning, "you're not just connecting to some abstract consciousness field. You're recognising that the consciousness looking out of your eyes is the same consciousness looking out of everyone's eyes."

"Exactly," Elena confirmed. "That's what the great traditions mean when they say 'Thou art That' or 'I and the Father are one' or 'Atman equals Brahman.' It's not poetry. It's not metaphor. It's description of direct experience. When you dive deep enough, you recognises that what you thought was your individual consciousness is actually the Ocean temporarily localised in a particular form."

"And once you know that," Daniel added, his voice carrying the weight of lived experience, "you can't unknow it. You can't harm another without harming yourself because there is no other. That businessman who tried to manipulate—he discovered that in the Ocean, the person he was manipulating was himself. The child being tortured was himself. Every being he harmed was himself. Not metaphorically. Actually."

"That's why," Marcus said, "the families are doomed. Not because we're going to defeat them. But because the very thing they're trying to suppress—consciousness awakening, people learning to dive—that awakening makes their control systems obsolete. You can't control people who know they're Ocean. You can't manipulate people who feel you in themselves. You can't exploit people who recognise you as another expression of what they are."

"And if the families themselves dive," Elena continued, "if they try to access the Ocean to use it as they've used everything else—the Ocean will teach them. Through direct experience. Through felt consequence. Through the boomerang. It will show them what they've done. And the knowing will either transform them or destroy them. There's no third option."

"So we're not offering them forgiveness," Amélie said slowly, understanding crystallising. "We're offering them the truth. And the truth either sets you free or it burns you alive. Depending on whether you're willing to see what you've become."

"Yes," Elena confirmed. "And the beauty—the terrible beauty —is that we don't have to judge them. We don't have to punish them. We don't have to be their enemy. The Ocean will show them to themselves. And that showing is both the mercy and the judgment. Both the salvation and the damnation. Depending entirely on whether they can bear to see themselves clearly and choose transformation, or whether they see themselves clearly and choose denial."

The Middle Path: Accountability without Enmity.

"But," Isabelle said, her voice carrying the authority of someone who'd survived their cruelty, "we can't just wait for karma to teach them. Children are being tortured right now. The environment is being poisoned right now. The suppression systems are operating right now. What do we do in the meantime?"

"We stop them," Marcus said firmly. "We expose them. We dismantle their systems. We rescue the children we can rescue. We teach people to dive despite the suppression. We build alternatives to their control structures. We don't wait for them to transform. We actively resist." "But," he continued, "we do it without hatred. Without maKing them into demons. We recognise that they're lost parts of ourselves. We hold them accountable for their actions while recognising that those actions flow from their emptiness. We resist their violence without becoming violent ourselves. We expose their lies without becoming liars. We dismantle their control without trying to control them."

"It's possible," Daniel said, "to stop someone without maKing them your enemy. To recognise they're causing harm without deciding they're evil. To hold both truths: they need to be stopped AND they're suffering. They're perpetrators AND they're victims. Both things are true."

"And we offer the path back," Amélie added, "not because they deserve it, but because the Ocean offers it. We don't decide who's worthy of awakening. We just point everyone toward the depths and let them choose whether to dive."

"Some will," Elena said softly. "The ones who are ready. The ones who can't bear the emptiness anymore. The ones who touch the Ocean and let it transform them. And those few—those few who dive from within the families, who bring their organisational brilliance into alignment with Ocean consciousness—they'll be powerful beyond measure. Because they'll combine both gifts. The Seth-line capacity for connection and the Cain-line capacity for coordination. And together, those gifts can reshape the world."

"But most won't," she continued. "Most will refuse. Most will read this as a threat, as manipulation, as a trap. Most will double down on control. And that's okay. We're not trying to force anyone. We're just showing that the door exists. And the door is always open. Even for them. Even after everything. Even now."

The Invitation

Amélie turned back to her document and wrote: "To everyone reading this—regardless of your bloodline, your conditioning, your past choices: The Ocean is not somewhere else. It's not in the future. It's not reserved for the worthy or the enlightened or the pure. It's here. Now. It's what you are. It's what you've always been. You can access it. Right now, in this moment. You don't need special training or genetic markers or years of practice. Those things help. They make diving easier, more consistent, more stable. But they're not requirements. The Ocean receives anyone who surrenders to it. And when you touch it—when you finally let yourself sink beneath the surface you've been desperately swimming on—you'll discover something that no words can fully capture: You're not alone. You've never been alone. You're held by something infinite and loving. You're connected to everything that exists. You're home. The Ocean doesn't judge what you've done. Doesn't evaluate your worthiness. Doesn't require you to be anything other than what you are. It just receives you. Holds you. Shows you that you're Ocean that temporarily forgot it was Ocean.

But—and this is crucial—the Ocean also shows you the truth of your choices. Not as punishment. As feedback. As natural consequence of connection. If you've caused harm, you'll feel it. Not abstractly. Not as guilt or shame imposed from outside. But as direct experience of what you've created. Because in the Ocean, there's no separation between actor and acted upon. What you do to others, you do to yourself. What you create for the world, you create for you. This is both the terror and the beauty of diving. You can't hide anymore. Can't pretend. Can't separate yourself from consequences. The Ocean shows you everything. Your beauty and your ugliness. Your love and your harm. Your connection and your separation. All of it. Clearly. Without buffer. And then you choose. Transform or retreat. Open or close. Dive deeper or claw your way back to the surface. The Ocean won't force you. Won't chase you. Won't judge your choice. But it will wait. For as long as it takes. Forever, if necessary. Because you're Ocean. And the Ocean can't abandon itself. Can only wait for itself to remember.

This is the invitation. Not just to the Seth line. Not just to those already awake. But to everyone. To the families. To the controllers. To those who've spent millennia running from connection. The door is open. The Ocean is here. The return is possible. Even for you. Even now. Even after everything. The only question is: will you dive?"

She saved the document. Looked up at the group. For people who want the specific steps. But this... this is what matters. Not the technique. The invitation."

"And the warning," Marcus added. "About the boomerang. About what happens if you try to weaponise the Ocean. People need to understand: you can dive, but you can't dive and remain evil. The Ocean won't allow it. It will show you what you're doing. And the showing will either transform you or destroy you."

"Then it's time," Elena said. "Time to publish. Time to extend the invitation to everyone and let them choose. Some will dive. Some will refuse. Some will try to weaponise it and learn why that's impossible. But we'll have done what we can do: shown them the door. What they do with that showing is up to them."

Amélie hit upload. The document spread across the internet. Within hours, responses poured in. Some hostile. Some skeptical. Some curious. And a few—just a handful—from people who worked within the families' systems, who'd felt the emptiness, who were ready to try: "I'm afraid. But I'm more afraid of another forty years feeling nothing. Tell me how to begin."

The transformation had started.

CHAPTER TWENTY-ONE

The Tipping Point

Paris, October 2025 — One Year After Publication

A year after she pressed upload, Amélie posted a single request in every community where people had gathered to practise.

Tell me your story. How did you find diving? What changed? She had not expected what came back. Not the volume — she had understood, in an abstract way, that the numbers were real, that twelve million downloads meant twelve million people, that even a fraction of those becoming practitioners was a fraction of a very large number.

She had understood this the way you understand that the ocean contains a particular quantity of water: accurately, without being moved. What moved her was the weight of a single inbox notification at seven in the morning, three days after she posted the request, which said: 10,000 responses.

She made tea. She sat down at her desk in the apartment she was now, cautiously, living in again — the one in the 11th arrondissement that she had fled eleven months ago in the dark with Elena's journal pressed against her ribs. She opened the first response and began to read.

Sarah, 34, a mother of two in Ohio, had found the document through a friend who sent it with a note that said this might help with your anxiety. She had struggled with panic attacks for ten years. She had tried everything — therapy, medication, CBT, meditation apps — and nothing had lasted. She began the basic diving practice. The first week: nothing. The second week: nothing. She kept going because she had run out of other things to try. Week three, I was sitting in meditation, and suddenly something shifted. Like I fell through a trapdoor I didn't know was there. And I was in this vast

174

space. Infinite space. And I understood — not intellectually but in my body, in my chest — that I WAS that space. Not the anxiety. Not the panic. Not the thoughts. But the space in which all of that occurred.

My kids have noticed. My husband has noticed. My eight-year-old asked me to teach her, because she sees something in me that she wants. So now we practise together every morning.

Amélie read this one three times. Then she got up, refilled her tea, stood at the window looking at the street below — a woman walKing a dog, a delivery driver stacKing boxes — and felt something she couldn't name that was somewhere between joy and vertigo. She sat back down and kept reading.

James, 52, was a police officer in London who had been working for twenty-eight years. He had dealt with what he'd seen through alcohol, anger, and avoidance, and was heading, by his own account, toward divorce, early retirement, and drinKing himself to death. A colleague had forwarded the diving manual. He was not, he wrote, a spiritual person. He was a sceptic by training and desperate by circumstance. It took him six months of daily practice before anything happened. When it did, it changed everything. I saw that all the violence I'd witnessed, all the pain and suffering — it was all happening in consciousness. And that consciousness itself was untouched by it. Like the ocean isn't damaged by the waves on its surface. That didn't erase the trauma. Didn't make the memories go away. But it gave me a place to stand that wasn't destroyed by them. I've started a weekly group for first responders. Twenty officers, firefighters, and paramedics, all with PTSD, learning to dive. It's the best thing I've ever done in my career.

She thought about what Marcus had said during the long nights at the monastery, working through the suppression research: A population of Ocean swimmers can't be controlled through fear.

She thought about James, still doing the same job, still in the same precinct, changed at the level of what he brought to it. She thought about the twenty people he was teaching. Half a million teachers, Marcus had said at the one-year gathering, looking at Elena's survey data. Half a million people actively helping others learn to dive. He had said it with something in his voice she had never heard from him before — a quality very close to awe.

Lai was 26, a software engineer in Singapore who had been raised atheist. He had found the document through a forum post he had clicked on intending to debunk it. They worked. Three months of daily meditation, and I had an experience that shattered my materialist worldview. I dropped into a state where there was no "me" anymore. Just awareness. Just experience happening. And from that place, it was obvious — luminously, undeniably obvious — that consciousness is fundamental. Not produced by brain but received by it. I'm still a scientist. I'm still working in tech. But now I'm working on AI with a completely different framework. Not trying to create consciousness from complexity, but trying to understand what consciousness uses complexity for. It's changing everything I thought I knew.

She sat with this one for a while. A materialist who had tried the practices in order to prove they wouldn't work, and who had then, with the particular intellectual honesty of someone whose training is in evidence rather than belief, gone where the evidence led. She thought of her own first real dive. Of standing in the courtyard in the Paris dawn with two men approaching and the sudden, shocKing arrival of the Ocean — not the careful managed depth of the practice room, but the actual thing, flooding in. She had not been trying to experience anything. She had been trying not to be hurt. The Ocean had not waited for the right conditions.

The last response she shared with the community that week was from Maria, 43, in Madrid. Maria had stage IV pancreatic cancer.

The doctors had given her six months, maybe a year. That had been nine months ago. I found your work through a hospice volunteer who thought it might help me face death. I started practising. Learning to dive. Touching the Ocean daily. And something miraculous happened. Not physical healing — my body is still dying. But I stopped being afraid. I'm keeping a blog — "Dying Consciously" — documenting this process. It's helped thousands of other terminal patients. Because I'm showing it's possible to die awake. To die swimming. To die knowing what you are. Thank you for giving me this gift at the end of my life. Or maybe it's not the end. Maybe it's just a transition. Either way, I'm ready.

Amélie read this one and then stopped reading for a while. She sat with her hands in her lap, not meditating, not doing anything — just being in the room with what Maria had written.

The November light was flat and grey through the window. The delivery driver had finished stacKing boxes and gone inside.

The woman with the dog was long past.

Her grandmother had kept a box with documents in it for decades, waiting for the right moment. Amélie had sometimes wondered, in the months since, what her grandmother had been afraid of. What had made her wait so long. She understood now. Not because she was afraid. Because she understood the weight of what it meant to offer something this large to the world, and the impossibility of knowing whether the world was ready, and the certainty that it didn't matter — that the offering had to be made regardless, because the alternative was to keep the box closed. Let the swimmer be born who can navigate all the currents.

At the one-year gathering, Thomas had brought his laptop. "Twelve million downloads," he said, pulling up tracKing data. "Official count. Translated into sixty-three languages. Shared copies, printed versions, word of mouth — the actual reach is probably three to five times that. And practice numbers: approximately four million people worldwide reporting active diving practice. Of those, roughly two million practicing daily for three months or more." He paused. "Of that two million: sixty-three percent report reliable access to Ocean consciousness. Forty-two percent say it's changed their lives significantly. Twenty-eight percent are now teaching others."

"Half a million teachers," Marcus said. "More," Thomas said.

"Those are the ones we can track." Elena added what she'd been observing in the surveys: the resonance effect. People who hadn't practised, or barely practised, reporting spontaneous diving experiences — sudden drops into depth during ordinary activity, no preparation, no framework. The Ocean arriving uninvited, as it had arrived uninvited in a Paris courtyard on an October morning.

"The field is changing," she said. "It's as if each person who learns to dive makes it slightly easier for the next person. Not metaphorically — I can feel it. The barriers are lower than they were a year ago.

What took months is taking weeks." Thomas looked at his charts. "If current growth continues — exponential rather than linear, accounting for the resonance effect — tipping point is somewhere between two and seven years. That's the mathematical range. But—"

"But consciousness doesn't follow mathematical predictions," Rinpoche said, from the end of the table. He had been listening with his eyes half-closed in the way that meant he was present in two registers simultaneously. He smiled slightly. "Water that has been slowly heating — seems nothing is happening, nothing is happening, still nothing — and then suddenly it boils. The tipping point arrives without announcement." He looked around the table. At Marcus, who had spent five years mapping a system of suppression and was now watching that system scramble and fail in real time. At Isabelle, who had come to them broken and was teaching her own group of survivors. At Elena, who had carried thirty years of diving records in a leather journal and had pressed it into the hands of a woman she barely knew in a flat at dawn, trusting it to survive. "We could spend time with the mathematics," he said. "Or we could practise."

That was how Amélie wrote about it, later — not the numbers but the quality of the year. The way the world had been changing not all at once but in thousands of specific moments, most of them invisible: a nurse in a hospital in Osaka who had started teaching a weekly group for her ward and noticed the patients were healing differently; a pilot scheme in three prisons whose recidivism numbers had come back so surprising that the programme coordinator had written to Amélie asking if she could possibly have made an error; a man in Manila who had been having visions since childhood and had spent thirty years believing he was ill, and who had written to her the morning after the upload to say that for the first time he understood what he was. She could not make those stories into a single coherent shape. She could not stand at a lectern and describe the movement because the movement was ten thousand stories and each one was a universe. She had pressed upload at 3:47 in the morning, in a borrowed kitchen in Paris, because she had run out of other options. She had not known what would happen. She had known only that her grandmother had waited long enough.

Maria in Madrid was dying consciously, and James in London was teaching twenty first responders to find the floor beneath their trauma, and Lai in Singapore was asking entirely different questions of his AI research, and a woman in Ohio was teaching her eight-year-old daughter to dive before school. This is what we're doing, she had said at the gathering. Not changing ideas. Changing lives. Actual human beings, in actual suffering, finding a way through.

The tipping point, if it came, would look like that. Not a number on Thomas's chart. Not a threshold crossed. Just another morning, and another story arriving in her inbox, and someone somewhere finding the trapdoor they didn't know was there, and falling through.

CHAPTER TWENTY-TWO

The Remnant and the Eastern Teachings

Sant Anna de les Abadesses, Spring 2025 — Earlier That Year
They had returned to Sant Anna in February — the surveillance in Paris had intensified after the third publication wave, and the mountains were where they thought most clearly. Matteu had not pretended he wasn't relieved to be home.

The monastery of Sant Anna de les Abadesses had become something its builders never anticipated—a convergence point for scattered seeds finding their way back to each other.

In the three weeks since Amélie's publication spread across the internet, they'd gone from six people hiding in the mountains to thirty-seven. Not all at once. Not in an organised way. But steadily, like water finding its level, people arrived who'd read the document and recognised something in themselves they'd never had words for.

A nurse from Barcelona who'd always known when patients were about to die. A young man raised in a Thai monastery who'd been told he carried "old karma." A former banker whose pattern recognition had made millions but left him hollow. A Jewish scholar who'd spent thirty years studying Kabbalah's suppressed teachings. And on a grey December morning, Sister Catherine. She came alone, carrying years of stolen truth in a weathered leather satchel. Elena met her at the monastery gate, and before either woman spoke, something passed between them—the recognition swimmers give each other when they meet on the shore.

"They excommunicated me," Catherine said simply, following Elena inside. "Twenty years in the Vatican archives. Twenty years finding pieces they thought they'd destroyed. And last week, they finally noticed." She didn't sound bitter. She sounded free.

The Continuity

That evening, they gathered in the library—the original Remnant and the new arrivals, descendants and scholars and survivors all pressed together in the warm space lit by candles and an ancient fireplace.

Catherine spread her documents across the reading table with the careful reverence of someone who knows she's handling something precious. Photocopies, translations, photographs of manuscripts she'd accessed during decades in restricted archives.

"I need to show you something," she said. "The link everyone's been missing, the possibility that the Desert Fathers, the earliest Christians, personally experienced what Yeshua tried to teach us.

She pulled out a page—Greek text with English translation below: *Let the nous descend into the kardia.* When the mind sinks into the heart and remains there unwavering, this is the beginning of true prayer—not words, but presence. One sits in stillness. One counts the breath as the ancient contemplatives taught. One watches thoughts as clouds passing. One descends from the head into the chest, and from the chest into the silence beneath all thought." — From the journals of Father Jean-Baptiste Mercier, a French Monk who spent decades studying the Desert Fathers and their practices. His writings, though never officially published, circulated among certain contemplative communities in the mid-19th century.

"The prayer of the heart requires that we descend from the intellect into the heart. One sits in stillness. One observes the breath. One watches thoughts pass like clouds. One descends from the head into the chest, seeking the silence beneath all thought." — Attributed to the tradition of the Philokalia, as understood by contemplative Monks of 19th-century France. "Evagrius, one of the Desert Fathers went into the Egyptian desert in 345," Catherine explained.

"The official story says he went to pray and fast. But what he actually did was teach a form of meditation. Advanced practices which appear to be similar to what Buddhist Monks taught. And it is said he claimed that these came from Yeshua— from a 'secret tradition' the apostles passed down but never wrote in the Gospels."

She showed them another document. "He described stages of consciousness—watchfulness, inner silence, direct perception of Divine nature—that match exactly what Tibetan texts describe. Same experiences. Same progression. Just different vocabulary."

"The Church declared him a heretic in 553," Catherine continued, her voice carrying decades of quiet anger. "Banned his works. Labeled his practices dangerous. Why? Because if Christians could access Divine consciousness through meditation—through their own practice—they didn't need priests. Didn't need sacraments. Didn't need the Church's mediation. They could dive themselves."

"But the Desert Fathers kept practicing," Father Matteu said quietly. "In Egypt, in Syria, in the wastelands where Rome's control was weak."

Catherine pulled out another page. "Look at this—from the actual Desert Fathers. This is Abba Macarius, mid-fourth century." She read aloud: "Sit in your cell, and your cell will teach you everything. The Monk who flees from his cell is like a fish out of water.' And here's his teaching on prayer: 'There is no need at all to make long speeches; it is enough to stretch out one's hands and say, Lord, as you will, and as you know, have mercy."

"That's it?" Amélie frowned. "That's the contemplative practice everyone talks about?"

"That's the foundation," Catherine said. "But look at this one— from Amma Syncletica, a female Desert Father." She showed them another page: "In the beginning there are a great many battles and a good deal of suffering for those who are advancing towards God and afterwards, ineffable joy. It is like those who wish to light a fire; at first they are choked by the smoke and cry, and by this means obtain what they seek. As it is said: Our God is a consuming fire. So we also must kindle the Divine fire in ourselves through tears and hard work."

"Divine fire," Amélie repeated. "That sounds metaphorical."

"It was," Catherine admitted. "But here's what's fascinating—later Christian mystics, the Hesychasts in the 14th century, developed something called the *Prayer of the Heart*. They taught the 'descent of the nous into the kardia'—literally *bringing the mind down from the head into the heart centre*. They synchronised this with breathing, with the Yeshua Prayer: 'Lord Yeshua Christ, have mercy on me.'"

She pulled up another document. "And they reported the same phenomenon that Buddhist and Hindu meditators describe: inner heat, protection from cold, altered states of consciousness. There's even a recorded incident of a Hesychast Monk surviving a Russian winter in his cell without fire."

"So Christianity did have contemplative practices," Amélie said slowly. "But not in the 4th century when these Desert Fathers lived?"

"That's the official story," Catherine said. "The Desert Fathers practiced stillness, solitude, and simple prayer. The elaborate techniques came six centuries later with the Hesychasts. But..." She paused. "What if that's backwards? What if the Hesychasts were recovering something ancient that had been suppressed?" "Why would it be suppressed?"

"Because it works," Catherine said quietly. "Because if you can teach ordinary people to access altered states of consciousness through their own practice—no priest, no church, no intermediary— then you don't need the institution anymore.

The Desert Fathers fled to the wilderness right when Christianity became the official Roman religion. Right when the church became about power and control instead of direct experience." She tapped the Syncletica quote. "She says we must kindle the Divine fire in ourselves. Not receive it from a priest. Not wait for grace to be administered through sacraments. Kindle it ourselves. That's dangerous theology."

"So what are you saying?" Amélie asked. "That the Church deliberately obscured their own contemplative tradition?"

"I'm saying the evidence suggests they had one, and that it shared remarkable similarities with Eastern practices—stillness, silence, watching the mind, breath awareness, descending attention from head to heart. And I'm saying that by the Middle Ages, when the institutional Church was at the height of its power, those practices had been pushed to the margins. Literally—to desert hermits and isolated monasteries where they couldn't spread."

Elena leaned forward suddenly. "That's tummo. That's exactly what Tibetan Monks practice. I learned it in Thailand—they called it 'inner heat meditation.' You generate fire in the belly through breath and visualisation. Advanced practitioners can sit naked in snow and melt it with body heat."

"Because it's a similar practice," Elena said, understanding crystallising. "What the Desert Fathers called 'inner fire' and what Tibetan Monks call 'tummo'—it's the same technique. Yeshua possibly learnt it in Tibet and taught it to his closest disciples. They practiced it in Palestine. And after his death, the Monks who went into the Egyptian desert preserved it.

The lineage never broke. It just went underground." Catherine nodded, pulling out more documents.

"The Desert Fathers wrote about prayer constantly, but always in devotional language so it would survive Church scrutiny. Look at what they actually said—and what it reveals." She read from the first page: "Arsenius, flee, be silent, pray always, for these are the source of sinlessness." - Abba Arsenius, 4th century. "And this one, from Abba Macarius: 'There is no need at all to make long speeches; it is enough to stretch out one's hands and say, Lord, as you will, and as you know, have mercy.'"

"That's just simple prayer," Amélie said.

"Is it?" Catherine pulled out another quote. "Listen to this— Abba Poemen: 'Teach your heart to keep that which your tongue teaches.'" She leaned forward. "Why the heart? Why not the mind? And look at this one: 'A hermit used to say, Ceaseless prayer soon heals the mind.' And another: 'No one can see his face reflected in muddy water; so the soul cannot pray to God with contemplation unless it is first cleansed of harmful thoughts.'"

"They're talKing about interior practice," Miriam said slowly. "Exactly. And they weren't doing it in their heads."

Catherine showed them more passages. "The Desert Fathers had a word— hesychia. It means stillness, but not just outer silence. Inner tranquility. A calm centredness. And they talked constantly about 'staying in your cell.'" She read: 'Sit in your cell, and your cell will teach you everything.' That's from multiple Desert Fathers. They didn't just mean a physical room. They meant learning to be present, to stay, to not flee from what arises."

"So what are you saying?" Amélie asked. "That they were meditating?"

"I'm saying they developed practices that created the same results that other contemplative traditions report. Look—" Catherine pulled up her final document.

"Later, in the 14th century, the Hesychast Monks made it explicit. They taught what they called the 'Prayer of the Heart'—bringing the mind down from the head into the chest, coordinating prayer with breathing, achieving inner stillness." She tapped the page. "The Hesychasts claimed they were recovering ancient Desert Father practices that had been lost. What if they were right? What if the Desert Fathers discovered these things but couldn't write them down explicitly because it would have been seen as too... pagan? Too similar to Greek philosophy or Eastern practices?"

"But you don't have proof of that," Amélie challenged.

"No," Catherine admitted. "I have suggestive evidence. I have them emphasising the heart over the mind. I have them talKing about ceaseless prayer—not occasional verbal prayer, but a state of being. I have them insisting you must stay in your cell, in your body, in stillness. I have them warning against thoughts that disturb inner tranquility."

She looked at both of them. "And I have Amma Syncletica saying: 'In the beginning there are a great many battles and a good deal of suffering for those who are advancing towards God and afterwards, ineffable joy. It is like those who wish to light a fire; at first they are choked by the smoke and cry, and by this means obtain what they seek. So we also must kindle the Divine fire in ourselves through tears and hard work.'"

"Divine fire," Miriam repeated. "In ourselves. Not received from priests—kindled."

"Right. And look what happened." Catherine's voice hardened. "By the Middle Ages, these practices were pushed to the margins. To isolated hermits. To Monks on Mount Athos where the institutional Church couldn't control them.

The emphasis shifted to sacraments administered by clergy, to intercession through Mary and the saints, to anything except direct experience." She gathered the documents.

"Your grandmother's bloodline— the Cathars—they knew something had been lost. They taught that the Kingdom of God was within, that you could access it directly through practice. Not through priests. Not through sacraments. Through your own work of kindling the Divine fire."

"That's why they were destroyed," Amélie said quietly.

"That's why they had to be destroyed," Catherine corrected. "Because if ordinary people can kindle Divine fire in themselves—if they can achieve hesychia, inner stillness, direct communion with God through their own practice—then what do they need the Church for?"

"But the Desert Fathers were part of the Church," Amélie pointed out.

"They fled into the desert," Catherine reminded her. "They fled from cities, from Church politics, from the newly Christianised Roman Empire. Abba Arsenius literally heard a voice say: 'Flee from men and you will be saved.' They went as far from institutional Christianity as they could get while still calling themselves Christian." She stacked the pages carefully. "I think they knew something. I think they practiced something. And I think by the time the institutional Church consolidated power, that knowledge had become dangerous.

So it was coded, hidden, practiced only in secret—until groups like the Cathars tried to revive it. And we know what happened to them." "They knew," Miriam whispered. "The early Christians knew that Yeshua wasn't teaching them to worship a distant God. He was teaching them to become what he demonstrated. To dive while remaining grounded. To touch infinity while staying functional in the world."

"And for three centuries, that's what they practiced," Catherine said. "In the desert, far from institutional control. Until the Church consolidated power and decided that direct experience was too dangerous. Too uncontrollable. By the seventh century, the mystical practices were almost completely suppressed. Made heretical. Replaced with doctrine, ritual, obedience."

"But some survived," Sister Catherine continued. "In hesychasm in the Eastern Orthodox tradition. In certain Benedictine and Franciscan contemplatives in the West. Hidden. Whispered about.

Practitioners recognising each other in secret. Keeping the actual practices alive while the institution insisted there were no practices, only correct belief." She looked around at the assembled group. "That's what we are. The latest generation of Desert Fathers. Not Monks in Egyptian caves, but descendants scattered across the modern world, finding each other, remembering the practices that were almost lost.

The Remnant isn't new. It's ancient. We're just the current iteration."

Elena's Visio : The Grounded Transcendence

"Show us," Marcus said to Elena. "Show us what Yeshua may have learnt. How the tummo practice worked. How it connects to what the Desert Fathers preserved."

Elena closed her eyes, her breathing already shifting into the rhythm they'd all learned to recognise—the pattern that meant she was dropping into the Ocean to read its depths.

"I'm in Ladakh. Winter. Yeshua is seventeen, in his second year of training. The monastery is brutally cold — stone walls, high altitude, wind that finds every gap. The monks sit for hours in thin robes, apparently unaffected. Yeshua watches them and wants to know the method. The technique. The practice that makes this possible.

Tenzin watches him watching them.

'You want to know how they do it,' he says.

'Yes.'

'I will show you. But I must first show you something else — because without this, the cold will only ever be a problem to be solved. And that is not what we are teaching.'

'Tell me,' Tenzin says. 'Have you ever held a small animal? Or stood before something so beautiful it stopped your thoughts entirely — a flower, a vista, a scent carried on the wind?'

Yeshua nods.

'And in that moment — what did you feel?'

'Something opened. In the chest.'

'Yes. That opening — that warmth — that is not sentiment. That is not emotion in the ordinary sense. That is the Divine, reflected back to you through something beautiful enough to make you forget, for just a moment, to be anywhere other than here. Love and beauty are the simplest doorways. They require no training, no technique, no gift. They work because they are already made of the same thing you are looking for. When you feel them fully — you are already there.'

He tells Yeshua to sit. Just sit. No technique. No instruction except one: become still enough to notice what is already there.

Yeshua sits. His mind immediately begins looking for the method — the breath pattern, the visualisation, the thing to do. Tenzin says nothing. Just waits.

After some time — long enough that Yeshua stops waiting for instruction — something shifts. Not something he does. Something he notices. A warmth in the chest. In the heart. Not generated by effort. Not produced by technique. Simply — there. Quiet and steady, as though it had always been present and he had simply never been still enough to feel it.

'What is that?' he asks.

'That,' Tenzin says, 'is where we begin.'

He explains. Not as doctrine — as fact, the way one points to a mountain. The warmth is not a product of the bloodline. It is not a reward for practice or devotion. It is the nature of what every human being is, underneath the noise of thought and reaction and fear. It is the Divine speaking in the only register available to it — not words, not visions, but warmth. Presence. The quiet certainty of being held.

'Anyone can find it?' Yeshua asks.

'Anyone who becomes still enough. That is the whole of the teaching. Not technique. Stillness. The warmth is always there. It is the person who is usually elsewhere.'

Only now does Tenzin take him outside.

The cold is immediate and shocking. Yeshua's body braces. Every reflex says: resist, tighten, flee inward. But Tenzin says: 'Find it here. The same warmth. It does not leave because the conditions are hard. It does not require comfort or safety. Find it here, in this.'

And Yeshua understands — this is the real teaching. Not how to generate heat against the cold. How to find, in the midst of the cold, the warmth that the cold cannot touch.

He sits in the snow. Breathes. Lets the cold be cold rather than fighting it. And as he stops fighting — as the resistance softens into stillness — the warmth returns. The chest. The heart. The steady, unhurried presence of something that was never disturbed by the cold at all.

His body is still cold. He can feel that. But he is no longer entirely in his body's reaction. He is also somewhere else — somewhere vast, unhurried, holding both the cold and the warmth simultaneously. The cold is real. The warmth is also real. And the warmth is deeper.

This is what the Desert Fathers will later call hesychia. Stillness. Not the absence of difficulty but the presence of something larger than the difficulty. Not the suppression of pain but the discovery that beneath the pain — beneath fear, beneath shock, beneath grief — there is a place that has not been touched by any of it. That cannot be touched. Because it is not made of the same substance as suffering.

When a person is injured. When a person is frightened. When a person has been broken by something. If they can find that stillness — even a thread of it — the pain is still there, the body still registers what has happened, but the emotional storm settles. Not because the wound is healed. Because they have found the part of them that is larger than the wound. The part that is Ocean. The part that holds it all without being destroyed.

Tenzin watches Yeshua open his eyes an hour later.

'The monks,' Yeshua says. 'That is how they do it.'

'Yes. Not technique. Not force. They have simply found — and keep finding — the warmth that is always there. And from that warmth, the cold is just weather. Something happening at the surface. Experienced fully. Not suppressed. But held in something vast enough that it does not become the whole of reality.'

He looks at Yeshua steadily. 'This is not a teaching for the gifted. This is not a teaching for the bloodline or the trained or the specially chosen. This is available to every person who has ever lived. The only requirement is the willingness to stop — fully stop — and feel inward rather than outward. Most people spend an entire lifetime not knowing it is there. Not because it is hidden. Because they are always moving too quickly to notice.'

'Then why don't people know?'

Tenzin's expression holds something old and a little sorrowful. 'Because the world teaches them to look everywhere else.'

Tenzin is quiet for a moment. Then he says something else.

'There is one more thing. And I tell you this carefully, because it can be misunderstood.'

'When a person touches this warmth — finds the stillness, rests in the Ocean — something happens in the body. The nervous system settles. The breath slows. The signals the body sends in fear or pain begin to change. This is available to anyone. Anyone who finds stillness deep enough will feel their body begin to follow it inward. A kind of peace. A settling. The hurt is still there. But the suffering around the hurt — the fear, the resistance, the story the mind tells about what the pain means — that loosens. The body is still affected. But the person is no longer entirely at the mercy of what the body is reporting.'

'And beyond that?' Yeshua asks. Because he can already sense there is more.

'Beyond that,' Tenzin says carefully, 'there are people who can go further. Who can touch this stillness so completely, so deeply, that something moves through them into another person. Not from *themselves — from the Ocean, through them. A transmission. A contact at the level where the body is still fluid, still responsive, still in conversation with the vast consciousness that underlies it. At that depth, healing becomes possible. Not always. Not on demand. Not by will. But as a natural consequence of being deep enough.'*

'Most people find the warmth and are grateful for it. Find that pain softens in stillness, that fear settles, that something in them knows how to hold suffering without being destroyed by it. This is not a small thing. This is everything, for a human life.'

'But a few — very few — can go deep enough that the boundary between their Ocean and another person's Ocean becomes permeable. Can hold someone else in the warmth so completely that the other person's body remembers what it is. What it has always been. And begins, sometimes, to return to it.'

He looks at Yeshua directly.

'Your bloodline carries this capacity, deepened across many generations. But the gift is not the healing. The gift is the depth. The healing is only what becomes possible at that depth. Do not confuse them. Do not make the healing the thing you seek. Seek the depth. Seek the stillness. Seek the warmth. Everything else — if it is meant to flow — will flow on its own.

Fully Divine and fully human. Not metaphor. Actual lived experience. Actual practice."

Elena opened her eyes slowly, and for a long moment the room was silent.

Maria's Teaching: The Skilful Heart

Then Maria, the nurse from Barcelona, stood up. "I need to show you something. Something I learned the hard way. About what Elena was describing—the skilful distance, the empathy that doesn't drown you."

She looked around the circle. "When I first started feeling patients' pain—really feeling it, not just sympathising but experiencing it as if it were in my own body—I thought that was the gift.

I thought that's what being a healer meant. Absorbing their suffering. taking it into myself." "And I got sick. Exhausted. Every shift left me drained. I'd go home and collapse. Started having nightmares about patients. Started feeling pain in parts of my body that weren't injured. I was absorbing everything and it was destroying me." "Then I read Amélie's document. Started practicing. Started learning to dive. And something shifted.

Let me show you." She gestured to a woman named Claire who'd arrived last week, suffering from chronic pain after a car accident.

"May I work with you? So everyone can see what I mean?" Claire nodded, sitting in a chair in the centre of the room. Maria stood behind her. "First, I'm dropping," Maria said quietly. "SinKing from my head into my chest. Into my heart. This is what the Desert Fathers called descending from nous into kardia—from mind into heart.

Watch." Her breathing changed—slower, deeper, belly-centred. The quality of her presence shifted. Everyone in the room could feel it—a deepening, a thickening of the space around her. "Now I'm feeling into Claire. Not with my hands—I'm not touching her yet. With my heart. In the Ocean, we're not separate. So if I'm in the Ocean and Claire's in the Ocean—because everyone's always in the Ocean even if they don't know it—then I can feel what she feels."

Maria's face shifted slightly. "There. I can feel it now. The pain in her lower back. Sharp. Like knives. And underneath it, fear. Old fear from the accident. The body's still holding the trauma." "Now watch what I don't do," Maria said. "I don't take it into myself. I used to do that—feel her pain and make it mine. Absorb it. Carry it. And then I'd need healing myself. But I learned something from practicing what Elena showed us. From what Amélie wrote about Yeshua learning from the Buddhist masters."

She was quiet for a moment, breathing. "I'm feeling Claire's pain completely. Not avoiding it. Not shutting it out. But I'm not clutching it either. It's like—imagine holding water in your cupped hands. If you clutch tight, trying to hold every drop, you crush the bowl of your hands. The water spills. You lose it. But if you hold gently, openly, the water stays. You're containing it but not strangling it." "That's what I'm doing with Claire's pain. Feeling it fully. Letting it into my heart. But not maKing it mine. It flows through me like water through a channel. In through my heart, down through my body, into the earth, into the Ocean. I'm conducting it, not containing it."

She placed her hands lightly on Claire's shoulders now. "And from this place—where I'm feeling everything but grasping nothing —I can perceive clearly what needs to shift. Not with my eyes. With something else. The pain looks like... like static on a radio. Like disruption in a pattern. Claire's body knows how to be healthy. But the pattern got disrupted by the trauma. And it's stuck." The room was completely silent except for their breathing— Maria's deep and slow, Claire's gradually matching it.

"So I'm not healing Claire. I'm just... holding the space. Holding the clear pattern in my heart. Showing her body what 'healthy' looks like. Offering it. But she has to receive it. Her body has to choose to reorganise. I can't force anything. I can only offer. Like holding up a mirror that shows you what you look like when you're well."

Several minutes passed. Then Claire gasped softly. "It's... it's different. The pain. It's still there but it's... softer. Like it's not screaming anymore." Maria stepped back, and her presence seemed to lighten slightly.

"And notice—I'm not depleted. I'm not exhausted. I actually feel more energised because connecting with the Ocean energises me.

But I didn't take anything from Claire, and I didn't give her anything of mine. I was just the channel. The clear space where the Ocean could flow through." She looked at Claire. "You might thank me. People usually do. And I need to tell you—don't. Or rather, thank the Ocean. Thank whatever you call the Divine. Thank your own body for remembering how to heal. But not me. Because if you thank me, if you make me special, if you decide I have power you don't have—then you give away your own power. You stop looking for the Ocean in yourself because you think you found it in me. And that doesn't help either of us."

"This is what the Desert Fathers meant," Elena said softly, "when they wrote about being 'empty vessels.' About letting God work through them without claiming ownership of the miracles. They weren't being falsely humble. They were describing accurate technique. The moment you take credit, you create ego attachment. The ego grows. The channel narrows. Soon you're working from personal power—which depletes—instead of from the Ocean— which never depletes."

Thomas's Question

Thomas, the former banker, had been listening intently. Now he raised his hand hesitantly. "I need to ask something. Something practical. About this 'expecting nothing in return' teaching. Because I understand it spiritually. I understand that the Ocean gives freely. But I need to understand how it works practically. How do you survive? How do you pay rent? How do you feed your family?"

He looked at Maria. "You're a nurse. You get paid for your work. Is that wrong? Are you supposed to work for free because you're channeling the Ocean?"

The room erupted in murmurs—clearly everyone had been wondering the same thing but hadn't wanted to ask.

Maria smiled. "I asked Elena this exact question last week. Because I felt confused. Am I supposed to quit my job? Work only for free? How do I pay my bills? Feed my daughter? I'm a single mother. I can't just 'trust the universe' and hope money appears."

"Tell them what I told you," Elena said. "She said there's a difference between receiving fair exchange and receiving expecting return. Between being compensated for your time and energy, and requiring gratitude or recognition or specific outcomes."

Maria sat down, gathering her thoughts. "Here's what I've learned, what I'm still learning: I work as a nurse. I get paid a salary. This is exchange—my time and skill and presence in return for money I need to live. This isn't wrong. This isn't ego. This is practical reality in a world where we need shelter and food." "But when I'm with patients, I'm not doing it for the money. The money is the exchange that lets me be there, but it's not why I'm there. I'm there to be a channel. To let the Ocean flow through me. Whether patients get better or not—that's not my responsibility. Whether they're grateful or not—that's not my concern. Whether I feel good about myself afterward—that's not the point." "I've learned to separate the exchange from the expectation. I accept payment because I need to live. But I don't heal for payment. I don't require that healing happens as condition of feeling good about myself. I don't need patients to praise me to feel valuable. The payment is for my time. The healing is the Ocean's work. I just show up, stay clear, and let it flow."

"But what about someone who wants to be a healer full-time?" asked a woman named Annette who'd arrived two days ago. "Not as a nurse with a salary, but as... I don't know, a massage therapist? An energy worker? Someone who only gets paid when people come for healing?"

Annette looked uncomfortable asking. "I'm a massage therapist. I've always felt I could do more than just physical massage—I can feel people's energetic patterns, their emotional blocks. After reading Amélie's document, I started understanding what I've been sensing.

But I charge for sessions. I have rent. My son needs to eat. Am I corrupting the gift by charging money?"

198

CHAPTER TWENTY-THREE

The Practical Path

Sant Anna de les Abadesses, Spring 2025 — Earlier That Year
Elena stood and moved to stand near the fireplace, her face illuminated by the flames.

The question about charging money hung in the air. Everyone turned to Elena.

"This is the question everyone faces," she said. "The mystics and Monks who preserved these teachings—they lived in monasteries. They were fed, clothed, housed by the community. They could practice 'expecting nothing' because their material needs were met. But most of us aren't in monasteries. We have rent. Children. Responsibilities. We live in a world that runs on exchange."

"So how do we practice giving freely while also needing to receive? How do we channel the Ocean while also earning a living? This is the tension everyone faces. And there's no simple answer. But there are principles." She held up one finger. "First: Your gift is not your currency. What flows through you when you dive, when you channel the Ocean, when you heal—that's not yours to sell. That's the Ocean's work. You didn't create it. You can't charge for it. That would be like charging people for sunlight." A second finger. "But: Your time, your training, your skill, your presence—these have value in the world of exchange. You spent years learning anatomy, learning massage technique, learning to maintain clear space. This training has worth. Your time has worth. You're allowed to exchange these things for what you need." A third finger. "The distinction is subtle but crucial: You charge for the container, not the content. You charge for the session time, for your trained skill, for the space you create. But not for the healing. Not for the Ocean flowing through. That happens or it doesn't.

It's not conditional on payment." Annette was nodding slowly. "So when someone comes for a massage—I charge them for the massage, for the hour of my time, for my training. But if healing happens beyond the physical work, if something shifts energetically—that's extra. That's the Ocean's gift through me. I don't charge more for that because I didn't do it. It happened through me."

"Exactly," Elena confirmed. "And this changes how you hold the transaction. You're not thinKing 'they paid me, so I have to heal them.' You're thinKing 'they paid for my time and skill. I'll offer my clearest presence. The Ocean will do what the Ocean does. I have no attachment to the outcome.'"

"But what if nothing happens?" Annette asked. "What if I offer the session, I stay clear, and no healing occurs? Am I stealing their money?"

"Did you show up?" Maria asked. "Did you offer your trained skill? Did you stay present? Did you create clear space for healing to occur if it was meant to?" "Yes, but -" "Then you honoured the exchange. The healing isn't guaranteed. You can't control whether the Ocean flows in the way someone wants. You can only offer the conditions. Sometimes healing happens immediately. Sometimes it happens later. Sometimes it doesn't happen at all—not because you failed, but because that person's journey includes their suffering for reasons you can't understand."

Marcus spoke up. "I'm struggling with this too. I was a banker. Made millions by being brilliant at pattern recognition. Now I understand that was an Asher gift, used badly. Used for control and profit instead of service. So I liquidated my assets. Gave most away. Kept just enough to live simply for a few years while I figure out how to use the gift properly." "But I can't live on savings forever. Eventually I'll need income. And the skill I have—seeing patterns, predicting probabilities—it's incredibly valuable in the market. I could easily make money again. Should I? Or would that be falling back into the old trap?"

Father Matteu, who'd been quiet, spoke. "The gift is neutral. Pattern recognition isn't good or evil. What matters is your intention. Why are you using it? For what purpose?"

"Say you work as a financial consultant," Matteu continued. "You help people understand markets, see patterns, make informed decisions. You charge for this service—for your time, your expertise, your analysis. This is fair exchange. But you're not using your gift to manipulate people, to extract more than fair value, to create dependencies. You're offering clarity. Helping people see more clearly. And the seeing you offer comes from your diving, from the Ocean showing you patterns that others miss." "The difference," he said, "is that you're no longer attached to the outcome. You don't need your clients to make money to feel successful. You don't need them to follow your advice to feel validated. You don't need them to praise you to feel worthy. You offer your clearest perception. They use it or don't. They succeed or fail. And you remain unattached. You gave what you could give. The results are beyond your control."

"But I still need them to pay me," Marcus said. "Doesn't that create attachment?"

"Only if you confuse the exchange with your value as a person," Elena said. "Only if you need the money to prove something about yourself. If you can hold it lightly—I offer this service, this is the fair exchange rate, you can accept it or not—then the transaction doesn't corrupt the gift." "Think of it like a plumber," she continued. "A plumber charges for their time and skill. But the water flowing through the pipes? That's not theirs. They didn't create it. They're just maKing sure the channel is clear. You charge for clearing the channel. For your time, your training, your presence. But the water—the insight, the healing, the Ocean flowing through—that's always free. That's given, not sold."

The Practical Examples

A woman named Isabella — a school teacher for twenty years — raised her hand. She wanted to teach children to dive, to reach them before the world trained them out of it. But she had a mortgage. A daughter at university.

"Charge for your time," Sophia said. "Not for the Ocean. For your labour. And use your discernment on the rate — full price for wealthy schools, sliding scale for those who can't. The heart of the thing is why you're doing it. If it's to share what you've found, fair compensation lets you keep sharing."

Isabella nodded slowly, something settling in her expression.

Amélie watched her and thought: this is what the work looks like. Not mystical. Practical. A mortgage and a sliding scale and the intention behind it. Exchange is part of living in form. What matters is your heart. Are you doing it for wealth and recognition? Or are you doing it to share what you've learned, and accepting fair compensation lets you continue doing it?"

A man named Henri raised his hand. "I'm a doctor. Emergency medicine room. I make a good salary. And I've been feeling guilty about it since I started understanding these teachings. Shouldn't I give it all away? Work for free?"

"Do you work extra hours without pay?" Father Matteu asked. "Yes. Often. When people need care, I don't care if they can pay."

"Do you treat patients differently based on their wealth?"

"No. Everyone gets my best care." "Do you perform procedures you know are unnecessary just to bill more?"

"Never." "Then you're already giving freely while accepting fair exchange," Matteu said. "You're not working for money. You're working to serve, and money happens to be how your society compensates that service. You don't refuse payment for emergency surgery—that would be absurd, you need to eat. But you also don't withhold care from people who can't pay. You're already holding the balance."

"The key," Elena added, "is that your sense of worth doesn't come from the payment. You'd do the work even if payment structures were different. The work itself matters to you. The healing matters. Helping people matters. The money is just the practical mechanism that lets you continue."

Henri sat back, and the room held the question for a moment — not unresolved, but deepening. Some things only answered themselves through years of practice.

The Final Teaching: Surrender in the Marketplace

Elena moved back to the centre of the room. "Here's what I've learned, what I'm still learning: We're not Monks in caves. We're swimmers in the marketplace. We have to participate in exchange while not being ruled by it. We have to earn while not maKing earnings our purpose. We have to receive while not requiring return." "This is harder than cave-dwelling. Harder than monastery life. Because we're constantly navigating the tension. Every day, every transaction, every relationship—we're practicing the balance. Giving freely while accepting fair exchange. Opening our hearts while maintaining clear boundaries. Serving without depleting ourselves. Diving while walKing. Being in the Ocean while handling money." "And we'll fail at it constantly.

We'll get attached to outcomes. We'll need validation. We'll feel resentful when people don't appreciate us. We'll slip back into working for reward instead of working from love. This is normal. This is the practice. Not perfecting the balance, but returning to it every time we notice we've lost it." "The test isn't whether you charge money. The test is: Can you do the work just as fully for someone who can't pay? Can you release attachment to their gratitude? Can you feel satisfied even when the healing doesn't happen the way you hoped? Can you dive just as deeply when you're tired, when you're scared, when you haven't been paid in weeks? Can you trust the Ocean even when the rent is due?" "These are the real practices. Not how to breathe, how to meditate, how to generate inner fire—though those matter. But how to bring the Ocean into the marketplace. How to swim while buying groceries. How to dive while paying bills. How to stay clear while feeding your children. How to be fully spiritual and fully practical. Not one or the other. Both."

Sister Catherine was nodding. "The Desert Fathers knew this. They wrote about it constantly—the tension between contemplation and action, between prayer and labor, between detachment and responsibility. They wove baskets to support themselves. They tended gardens. They accepted offerings from visitors. They participated in exchange. But they didn't do it for the exchange. They did it because of bodies need food, roofs need repair, and being spiritual doesn't exempt you from physical reality."

"One of my favourite Desert Father stories," Catherine continued, "is about Abba Moses. A wealthy man came to him for teaching. The wealthy man offered gold. Abba Moses refused it. The man was offended. 'Don't you need to eat?' Abba Moses said, 'I eat. But I don't need your gold to know my worth. I'll teach you because teaching is what I do. Give the gold to the poor if you want to give it. But don't give it to me thinKing you're buying enlightenment. That's not for sale.'"

Catherine looked around the room. "They weren't trying to avoid the world," she said. "They were learning to carry it without being crushed by it. That's all any of us are doing."

❖ ❖ ❖

Maria's Closing

Maria stood again, looking around at everyone. "Here's my practice now. Maybe it helps someone. Every morning, before I go to the hospital, I sit for twenty minutes. I dive. I connect with the Ocean. And I make an offering: 'I'm here. Use me today however serves the whole. Let healing flow through me. I expect nothing. I require nothing. I'm just showing up, staying clear, and offering what I can offer.'" "Then I go to work. I do my job. I care for patients. I accept my salary. But I'm not doing it for the salary. I'm not doing it for gratitude. I'm not even doing it to heal people, because I can't control whether healing happens. I'm just showing up, staying clear, and letting the Ocean flow through me."

"Some days, miraculous healing happens. Patients who should have died survive. Pain that should have been unbearable becomes manageable. And I don't take credit. I say 'Your body knew what to do. You're strong. Keep trusting your healing.'" "Some days, nothing remarkable happens. Just routine care. No miracles. And that's fine too. I still showed up. Still stayed clear. Still offered what I could offer." "Some days, patients are grateful. They thank me, write kind notes, tell my supervisor I'm wonderful. And I let that flow through too. I don't cling to it. Don't need it. Don't make it mean anything about my worth. It's nice. It's sweet. And it passes."

"Some days, patients are awful. Rude, demanding, ungrateful. They treat me like a servant. And I let that flow through too. Their suffering is speaKing. Their fear is acting out. It's not about me. I stay clear. Stay open. Keep offering what I can offer." "And every night, before sleep, I sit again. Twenty minutes. I dive. I release the day. I let go of outcomes. I return anything I might have accidentally absorbed—any pain, any fear, any attachment. I sink back into the Ocean and remember: I'm not the healer. I'm the channel. The Ocean does the work. I just stay clear."

"This is my practice. It's not perfect. I still get attached. Still get depleted. Still need validation some days. But each time I notice, I return. I dive again. I remember again. And slowly—very slowly—I'm learning to live from the Ocean while walKing through the marketplace. To be fully surrendered while fully responsible. To give everything while expecting nothing."

She looked at Annette, at Thomas, at Henri, at everyone struggling with the same questions. "You can do this. You can swim in the Ocean and pay your rent.

You can dive deeply and feed your children. You can be spiritual and practical. You can channel the infinite and accept fair exchange for your time. It's not either-or. It's both. Like Yeshua learned in Tibet. Like the Desert Fathers practiced in their cells. Fully Divine and fully human. Heaven and earth. Ocean and marketplace. Both."

The room was silent. Outside, dawn was breaKing over the mountains. They'd been talKing all night.

Elena spoke softly into the quiet. "This is what we teach. Not just the meditation techniques, not just the breathing practices, not just how to feel and heal. But this. How to live it. How to bring the Ocean into ordinary life. How to swim while doing laundry, paying taxes, arguing with your teenager, sitting in traffic. This is the real practice. The real test. Not how you are in the temple. How you are in the world."

"This is what the Remnant exists for," Elena continued. "Not to escape into monasteries. But to bring the Ocean into the mess. To show that awakening doesn't require renunciation — it requires integration. The Divine and the human. The transcendent and the practical. Wholeness." She paused, and in the quiet Amélie heard the mountain outside — wind through pine, the first birds, the particular hush of a place that had been holding people's questions for eight centuries.

"Not by being perfect," Elena said finally. "But by returning. Every time. That's the whole of it." "And slowly—very slowly—we learn to be what we're teaching. To live what we're offering. To embody the integration we're inviting others into."

"This is the work. This is the way. This is the Remnant."

CHAPTER TWENTY-FOUR

The Awakening

Global, Summer 2025

Six months after Amélie's document spread across the internet, the Remnant had grown in ways none of them had anticipated. Not dramatically. Not like a movement with leaders and manifestos and marching crowds. But quietly, organically, like mycelium spreading beneath the forest floor—invisible until suddenly, everywhere, mushrooms emerged.

Safe houses had opened in twelve countries. Not through planning, but through necessity. Someone in Berlin read the document, recognised themselves, and offered their apartment.

Someone in São Paulo, same thing. Melbourne. Vancouver. Barcelona. Tokyo.

One by one, swimmers finding each other, creating spaces where others could learn to dive.

The gatherings started small. Five people in a living room. Ten people in a rented hall. Twenty people in a park at dawn, sitting together, breathing together, dropping into the Ocean together. And something was happening. Something the rational mind would dismiss but that anyone who'd learned to dive could feel: the more people who touched the Ocean, the easier it became for others to touch it.

As if consciousness itself was shifting.

As if the Ocean was rising to meet those who reached for it.

Elena called it "the resonance effect." When one person dove, they created ripples. When ten people dove in the same space, the ripples amplified each other. When a hundred people across the world were diving simultaneously—whether they knew about each other or not —something in the field itself changed. The barrier between surface and depth thinned. But what surprised everyone most wasn't the numbers or the spread or even the resonance effect.

It was the joy. The Quiet Joy.

Maria sat in the small apartment she shared with her daughter in Barcelona, morning light streaming through the window. She'd been awake since five, sitting in meditation as she did every morning now. Not because she had to. Because she wanted to. Because these twenty minutes had become the most precious part of her day. She'd dropped into the Ocean perhaps ten minutes ago, and now she was just... there. Resting in the depths.

No effort.

No striving.

Just being.

And in her chest—in the physical space where her heart resided— there was a sensation she still struggled to describe to people who asked.

It wasn't excitement. It wasn't the euphoria of drugs or the rush of falling in love or the high of accomplishment. It was quieter than that. Steadier. It was like coming home after a long journey and finding your favourite chair by the fire, exactly as you left it.

It was like being held by someone who loved you unconditionally and never getting tired of that embrace. It was like the deepest contentment amplified by the knowledge that this contentment was not circumstantial—not dependent on anything being right in your life—but fundamental. Built into the fabric of existence itself. Her heart felt... full. But not in the way a balloon is full, stretched and pressured. Full in the way the Ocean is full—vast and spacious and containing everything while somehow having room for infinitely more. And warm. There was actual warmth there, physical warmth that she could feel spreading from her chest through her body.

The Desert Fathers had written about this. The Buddhist texts described it. The Sufi poets sang about it. But until she'd experienced it herself, she'd thought it was metaphor. It wasn't metaphor. It was literal. Her chest was warm. Her heart — the physical organ—felt different. Felt expansive. Felt alive in a way it hadn't before she'd learned to dive.

Sometimes in meditation, the warmth would intensify until it felt like there was actual light in her chest. Golden light. Pulsing gently with each heartbeat. And from this light, from this warmth, from this fullness—everything else flowed. The compassion that no longer exhausted her. The clarity that helped her see what patients needed. The peace that stayed with her even during chaotic shifts. The joy—oh, the joy—that bubbled up at unexpected moments for no reason at all. Just joy. For being alive. For breathing. For existing.

She opened her eyes as the morning meditation timer chimed softly. Her daughter, Sofia, was already awake, maKing coffee in the kitchen. Fourteen years old and going through the typical teenage storms of emotion and identity. But lately, Maria had noticed something changing.

"Mom?" Sofia called. "Can you teach me? What you do in the mornings?"

Maria felt her heart expand even further. "Yes," she said simply. "Sit with me tomorrow. I'll show you." This was how it spread. Not through preaching or convincing or arguing. But through being. Through the quiet joy that others could feel emanating from those who'd learned to dive. Through children noticing that their parents were different—calmer, more present, more alive—and wanting whatever that was.

The Little Miracles

Thomas walked through London's financial district on his way to his new office. Six months ago, he would have been tense, calculating, mentally running through the day's strategies for extracting maximum profit from minimum effort. Now he was just... walKing. Feeling his feet on the pavement. Noticing the light. Aware of the people around him—their hurried energy, their stress, their underwater panic that he recognised because he'd lived in it for forty years.

He'd started a small consulting firm. Nothing dramatic. He helped people understand markets, see patterns, make informed investment decisions. He charged fair rates. He worked reasonable hours. He made enough to live comfortably but not extravagantly.

And something had started happening. Small things. Things he might have called coincidences before he'd learned about the Ocean. Like this morning. He'd been thinKing about a client who needed help understanding renewable energy investments. Just thinKing about it during his morning meditation. Wondering if he knew anyone with expertise in that sector. And then, walKing to work, he'd stopped at his usual coffee shop. The woman in line ahead of him was reading a report titled "Renewable Energy Market Analysis 2025." He'd smiled, said "Excuse me, I couldn't help noticing—are you in the renewable sector?" She'd turned out to be an analyst for a major green energy fund. They'd talked for fifteen minutes. She'd given him her card. Said call me if you need any insights. Happy to help.

Just like that. The exact person he needed, appearing in his coffee shop the morning he was thinKing about it.

Or last week. He'd been working with a young couple trying to figure out how to invest their savings. They were overwhelmed, afraid, certain they'd make wrong choices and lose everything. Thomas had spent an hour with them, explaining options, showing them patterns, helping them see that they didn't need to be afraid. At the end, they'd tried to pay him. He'd said no. "This was just a consultation. If you want ongoing help, we can discuss that. But this conversation—consider it a gift." They'd been stunned. Said no one in finance gives anything for free. He'd shrugged. "I'm learning to live differently."

Two days later, a new client had called. A referral from someone Thomas had never worked with. Wanted help managing a substantial portfolio. When Thomas asked how they'd found him, the client said, "A friend told me you helped them understand investing without trying to sell them anything. That you actually cared whether they made good decisions, not whether you made a commission. In this world, that's rare. I want to work with someone like that."

The new client's business more than made up for the free consultation. But that wasn't the point. Thomas wasn't doing it for reciprocity. He was doing it because it felt right. Because living from the Ocean meant offering what you could offer, expecting nothing, and trusting that somehow, everything would work out. And it did. Not magically. Not without effort. But there was a flow to his life now that hadn't been there before. Things clicked into place. Opportunities appeared. The right people showed up at the right time. Resources materialised when needed.

He'd tried to explain this to his sister last week. She'd been skeptical. "So you're saying if you're spiritual enough, the universe just gives you what you want?" "No," he'd said. "I'm saying when you stop grasping, stop forcing, stop trying to control everything—when you just stay clear and offer what you can offer—life starts to flow. Not because you're manifesting it. But because you're finally moving with the current instead of against it. The opportunities were probably always there. I just couldn't see them because I was too busy trying to create my own opportunities through force and manipulation."

"And you're happier?" his sister had asked. He'd laughed. "I make a tenth of what I used to make. I live in a one bedroom flat instead of a penthouse. I have no prestige, no reputation in the industry, no power. And I'm happier than I've ever been in my life. Because I'm not empty anymore. The joy doesn't come from the success. It comes from the Ocean. And the Ocean is always here."

Annette's Practice

Annette, the massage therapist from Lyon, had gone back home after three weeks in the Pyrenees. Back to her practice, her clients, her ordinary life. But everything was different.

She'd set up her treatment room differently now. Nothing dramatic. Just small changes. A candle that she lit before each session. A small bowl of water she placed near the table—a reminder that she was working with the Ocean, not with her own power. A cushion where she sat for five minutes before the first client arrived, dropping into the depths, connecting with the vastness, reminding herself: I am the channel, not the source.

Her first client after returning was a regular—a woman named Danielle who came monthly for chronic back pain. Danielle had been seeing Annette for three years. Same routine every time. Ninety minutes of deep tissue work, targeting the knots in her shoulders and lower back. Annette was good at it. The pain would ease for a few weeks, then return. But this time, Annette worked differently. She started the same way—warming the muscles, working into the tissue. But about twenty minutes in, she felt it. The invitation to drop deeper. To stop working from technique alone and start working from the Ocean. She paused, hands resting lightly on Danielle's back. Took a breath. Let her consciousness sink from her head to her heart. Felt the warmth bloom in her chest. Dropped into the Ocean. And suddenly she could perceive more. Not with her hands— with something else. She could feel the pain in Danielle's back, yes. But she could also feel what was beneath the pain. Old grief. A loss Danielle had never processed. The grief had lodged in her body, creating chronic tension that no amount of massage could permanently release because the emotional root remained.

Annette didn't say anything. Didn't analyse. Didn't try to fix. She just...held the space. Held Danielle in the Ocean. Kept her hands on the tense muscles but stopped trying to force them to release. Instead, she offered. Offered the possibility of release. Offered the spaciousness of the Ocean. Offered presence, warmth, acceptance of what was. And after a few minutes, she felt it. The muscles under her hands softened. Not because Annette was pushing harder or using better technique. But because something in Danielle had let go. Some permission had been granted. Some old holding had released. When the session ended, Danielle sat up slowly, moving her shoulders experimentally.

"That was... different," she said. "I don't know what you did, but it feels different. Lighter. Like something actually released instead of just getting temporarily worked out."

Annette smiled. "I learned some new things. Started working a bit differently."

"Well, keep doing it," Danielle said. "That's the best I've felt after a session in years."

Annette didn't explain. Didn't try to teach or preach. Just accepted the payment, thanked Danielle for coming, and sat back down on her cushion after Danielle left. She placed her hands over her heart, feeling the warmth there, the fullness, the quiet joy that was becoming her constant companion.

"Thank you," she whispered to the Ocean. "For flowing through me. For letting me be useful. For this gift of service." And she meant it. Every word. The gratitude wasn't forced or performative. It was real. Bubbling up from the depths. Gratitude for being alive. For having hands that could touch and help. For the privilege of being a channel. For the joy—the quiet, steady joy—of living aligned with the Ocean instead of fighting against it.

The Spreading Ripples

In Tokyo, a businessman named Hiroshi sat in his office at 11 PM, staring at his computer screen. He'd been working sixteen-hour days for twenty years. It was normal. Expected. The price of success. But three weeks ago, someone had sent him a link. A document. In Japanese, translated by someone who'd read Amélie's original publication and felt compelled to share it widely. Hiroshi had read it out of boredom. And something in him had cracked open.

He'd started simply. Ten minutes of sitting before work. Just breathing. Just noticing. And slowly, over three weeks, something had shifted. The desperate drive to succeed—it was still there, but quieter. Less urgent. He could feel it as a pattern in his body now. A tightness in his chest. A clenching in his belly. The fear that if he wasn't constantly working, constantly achieving, he would disappear. Would become nothing. But beneath that fear, he'd found something else.

Something vast and steady and peaceful. Something that was there whether he succeeded or failed. Whether he worked or rested. Whether he achieved or didn't.

Tonight, at 11 PM, staring at his computer, he made a decision he never thought he'd make. He shut down the computer. Stood up. Put on his coat. And went home. Not because the work was finished. It wasn't. But because he was finished for today. Because he was learning—just beginning to learn —that his worth wasn't measured in output. That he could rest without disappearing. That the Ocean would still be there whether he worked sixteen hours or eight.

He walked through Tokyo's neon-lit streets, and for the first time in twenty years, he noticed them. Really noticed. The lights. The people. The life moving around him. He'd been so focused on getting ahead that he'd never actually looked at where he was.

When he arrived home, his wife was still awake, reading in bed. She looked up in surprise. "You're early. Are you sick?" "No," he said. "I'm just... trying something different."

She studied his face. "You look different."

"I feel different." He didn't explain. Didn't have words yet. But he sat on the edge of the bed, took her hand, and said, "I want to learn to be here. With you. Not just physically present but actually here. I don't know how yet. But I want to try."

His wife's eyes filled with tears. "I've been waiting for you to come back," she whispered. "For twenty years, I've been waiting for you to come back from wherever you went."

"I'm coming back," he said. And meant it.

Lucia's Peace

In São Paulo, a young woman named Lucia sat with her terminal illness and felt... peaceful.

She'd been given six months. Maybe less. Pancreatic cancer, too advanced for treatment. At twenty-nine, her life was ending before it had really begun.

Three months ago, she would have been destroyed by this. Raging against the injustice. Drowning in fear. But two months ago, a friend had sent her Amélie's document. Lucia had read it thinKing what do I have to lose? Started practicing. Started diving. Not to cure the cancer—though who knew, maybe that would happen. But to meet death consciously. To not spend her last months in panic and denial. And something remarkable had happened.

As she learned to dive, as she touched the Ocean daily, her fear... softened. Didn't disappear. But transformed into something else. Into curiosity. Into acceptance. Into a strange, unexpected gratitude for the time she'd had.

She'd started a blog. "Dying Consciously." Writing about what it felt like to practice diving while watching her body deteriorate.

About the pain and the fear and also the beauty. The unexpected beauty of knowing each day might be your last. The clarity it brought. The way it stripped away everything inessential. Her blog had gone viral. Thousands of people reading her posts. Many of them terminally ill themselves, finding comfort in her words. Finding permission to meet death with curiosity instead of just terror. But what she couldn't quite capture was the feeling in her chest. The warmth that was there even when her body hurt. The fullness that persisted even as her physical form wasted. The joy - actual joy - that bubbled up some mornings when she opened her eyes and thought I'm still here. Still swimming in the Ocean.

She'd tried to explain it to her oncologist last week. "I know this sounds crazy, but I'm happier now than I was before the diagnosis. Not about dying. Obviously I'd prefer to live. But I'm happier as a person. More present. More alive, even while dying." Her doctor had looked uncomfortable. "That's... that's good, I suppose. The meditation is helping with anxiety?"

"It's not about anxiety," Lucia had said. "It's about remembering what I am. I'm not just this body. This body is dying, yes. But I'm also the Ocean. And the Ocean doesn't die. It just changes form. I'm learning to identify more with the Ocean than with the body. And that makes the dying less frightening." The doctor hadn't known what to say to that. But Lucia knew. Lucia understood. And when the time came— and she could feel it coming, could feel the body preparing to release — she wouldn't die in fear. She'd die swimming. Diving. Merging back into the Ocean she'd emerged from.

Going home.

CHAPTER TWENTY-FIVE

The Families' Response

Geneva / Paris, Summer 2025

Marie-Claire had come back quietly — no announcement, just a message through the secure channel and then her car in the courtyard at dawn. She looked older than the first time Amélie had seen her at the château, or perhaps simply more tired. She sat at the kitchen table and accepted coffee and said nothing for a long moment.

"The families are meeting in Geneva this week," she said finally. "I thought you should know what they are planning."

"How do you know this?"

"I still have one person inside. Someone who has been watching for a long time and is not yet ready to leave — but who believes we should know what is being said in those rooms." She wrapped both hands around her cup. "I trust what she tells me. And what she is telling me is serious."

Amélie looked at her across the table. There was nothing to say that wasn't already understood between them — that this information had cost something to bring, that the woman sitting across from her was still paying a price she had chosen with full knowledge of what it would demand.

"Thank you," she said finally. "For coming."

Marie-Claire nodded once. Then she looked toward the courtyard window, and her expression shifted into something quieter.

The children from the rescued compounds were settling slowly into their new lives— some at Sant Anna, some in the safe houses the network had opened across Europe. Their presence was marked in small ways: a drawing on the refectory wall, the sound of a game in the courtyard. Marie-Claire sometimes sat with them. Amélie had noticed that.

In a private estate outside Geneva, the families gathered for an emergency meeting. Wilhelm Eisen stood at the head of the table, his face grim.

"The situation is deteriorating faster than we anticipated. The Rousseau document has been translated into forty-seven languages. Downloaded over ten million times. And worse—people are practicing. Actually practicing the techniques. We're seeing increased electromagnetic signatures consistent with meditative states across populations globally.

"Our traditional methods aren't working. We've tried discrediting Rousseau—called her crazy, planted stories about mental illness, accused her of running a cult. Nothing sticks. The document is too well-researched. The genetics too verifiable. And the people who practice the techniques... they're experiencing real results. You can't debunk someone's direct experience."

"We've tried the usual suppression," another member added. "Compound Veil protocol. The full EMF deployment. Ramped up the entertainment complex — the attention capture systems are running at levels we've never attempted before. But it's like trying to hold back the tide. Once people touch the Ocean, once they feel it—they don't go back. They keep diving. And they teach others."

"How many have awakened?" someone asked. Elena's contact in the Council—the man who'd helped her escape the château—spoke up. He'd been invited to this meeting as an outside observer, knowing the families needed perspectives they weren't getting from their usual circles.

"Our estimates suggest somewhere between five and eight million people worldwide have begun regular practice. Of those, perhaps five hundred thousand have achieved what we'd classify as stable diving capacity. And the numbers are growing exponentially.

The resonance effect Dr. Rousseau described—it's real. The more people dive, the easier it becomes for others. We're approaching a tipping point."

"Can we eliminate her?" someone asked bluntly. "Rousseau. The core group. Take them out, maybe the movement loses momentum."

"We tried," Wilhelm said quietly. "Three times. Each attempt failed. Not because of security—they have almost none. But because..." He hesitated. "Because the attempts fell apart. People we'd hired refused the job after meeting her. Said they couldn't do it. Felt something they couldn't explain. One of our most reliable contractors came back and said he'd quit the business entirely. Said he'd 'seen something' that changed him. He's disappeared into one of their safe houses."

"They're converting our people," Marissa said. "Not through argument. Through presence. Our contractors, our surveillance teams—anyone who spends time around these swimmers starts to... change. Starts questioning. Starts feeling drawn to whatever it is they have. We're losing operatives faster than we can recruit new ones."

"What about the children?" someone asked. "The breeding programs. Can we accelerate them? Create more controlled divers to counter the wild awakening?"

Wilhelm's face darkened. "That's the other problem. The programs are failing. We've lost three facilities in the past two months. Staff refusing to participate. Some actively helping children escape. And the children themselves—once they start diving voluntarily, consciously, without trauma—they can't be controlled. They develop conscience along with ability. They become useless to us."

He pulled up a report on the screen. "This is from our Munich facility. We had a twelve-year-old, third generation, perfect genetic markers. Exceptionally gifted. We'd been conditioning him since age four. He should have been our most successful case. Last month, he somehow accessed Rousseau's document on a smuggled device. Started practicing the voluntary diving techniques. Within three weeks, he'd undone five years of programming. Integrated his fragmented personalities. Woke up."

"He's with the Remnant now," Wilhelm continued. "Teaching other children how to heal from the programming. How to integrate. How to become whole. Every child he reaches is a child we lose." The room was silent.

Then someone spoke—a younger member, perhaps forty. Friedrich, Wilhelm's grandson. The one who'd been "trained properly," who should have been the next generation's success. "Maybe we're approaching this wrong," Friedrich said quietly. Every head turned. "Maybe we can't stop this. Maybe we shouldn't try. I've been... I've been reading the document. Studying it. And I've been trying the practices." He looked at his grandfather. "I'm sorry. I know this isn't what you wanted to hear. But I needed to know. Needed to understand what we're actually fighting."

"And?" Wilhelm's voice was dangerous.

"And they're right. About everything. The Ocean is real. The diving is real. The joy, the connection, the clarity—it's all real. I've felt it. And I understand now what we've been doing. We've been trying to steal fire. Trying to take the gifts without the conscience. Trying to dive without surrendering. And it doesn't work. It can't work. The Ocean won't allow it." "The boomerang effect Rousseau described—I've experienced it. I tried to use the diving to predict markets, to manipulate outcomes. And it backfired. Immediately. Painfully. The Ocean showed me what I was doing. Made me feel the consequences. I couldn't maintain the separation between gift and conscience. They're linked at a fundamental level."

He stood, facing the assembly. "We have two choices. We can keep fighting this, keep trying to suppress what's awakening. We'll lose. Maybe not today, maybe not this year. But we'll lose. Because you can't suppress evolution. You can't stop consciousness from recognising itself."

"Or we can transform. Can learn to dive properly. Can use our resources, our organisational capacity, our long-term thinKing—but oriented through the Ocean instead of against it. Can become what we could have been all along: brilliant coordinators in service to the whole instead of brilliant controllers in service to ourselves."

"That's heresy," someone said.

"No," Friedrich replied. "That's survival. And it's also the truth. We've been living in hell—the hell of separation, of emptiness, of controlling everything and connecting with nothing. I've tasted both now. The control and the connection. And I choose connection. Even if it costs me everything you've given me. Even if you disown me. I choose the Ocean."

Wilhelm stood slowly.

"Get out."

"Grand-Père—" It was Marissa, her voice careful, a hand half-raised. The gesture of someone who had seen this particular storm before and knew its edges.

"I said get out!" Wilhelm's voice cracked. "You've betrayed everything. Everything we've built. Everything we've protected. Get out of this house. You're no longer family."

Friedrich nodded slowly. "I'm sorry you can't see it yet. But I love you anyway. And when you're ready — when the emptiness becomes unbearable — the Remnant will be there. The Ocean will be there. We don't abandon anyone. Not even you."

A silence. Something passed across Wilhelm's face. For less than a second — so briefly that a casual observer might have missed it — the authority dropped.

The architect of control, the man who had not wept in forty years of building and protecting his family's legacy, looked at his grandson and showed, just for that instant, what was underneath all of it. Then it was gone.

"Get out." His voice was flat. Command voice. The voice that ended conversations. "You're no longer family. Get out of this house."

Friedrich held his Grand-Père's gaze for one more moment. He had seen it.

Friedrich nodded. He looked sad, but not broken. He walked out. He walked out.

The room erupted in arguments. Some agreeing with Friedrich. Some demanding his elimination. Some uncertain.

Wilhelm raised his hand for silence. "We take a vote. Do we double down? Increase suppression, eliminate the key figures, accelerate the programs? Or do we..." he couldn't quite say it. "Or do we consider what Friedrich said. Consider that we might need to transform instead of fight."

The vote was close. Closer than Wilhelm had expected. Twelve to continue the suppression. Eight to consider transformation. Five abstaining—unable to decide, trapped between old loyalty and new possibility.

"Twelve is enough," Wilhelm said. "We continue. We fight. We suppress this awakening before it destroys everything we've built."

But as the meeting ended, as members filed out, Wilhelm sat alone in the conference room. And for the first time in forty years, he felt something he'd been trained to never feel. Doubt.

The Heart Opening that night, across the world, thousands of people sat in meditation. Not because they'd been told to. Not because it was doctrine or obligation or path to salvation. But because they'd discovered something that made them want to sit. Something that made twenty minutes of silence the highlight of their day.

In Barcelona, Maria sat with her daughter Sofia, teaching her the breathing, showing her how to drop from head to heart.

In London, Thomas sat in his small flat, feeling the warmth bloom in his chest, marvelling that this simple practice—just sitting, just breathing, just being—could generate such profound contentment.

In São Paulo, Lucia sat with her dying body and felt more alive than she'd ever been, the Ocean holding her so gently she could almost hear it whisper: You've always been me. You're coming home.

In Tokyo, Hiroshi sat with his wife for the first time in years—really sat with her, not just sharing space but sharing presence—and felt something in his chest crack open. Old grief pouring out. Old love pouring in. The heart remembering how to feel.

And in Geneva, alone in his study, Wilhelm Eisen sat in his chair. He didn't know why. Didn't understand the impulse. But something in him needed to be still. He closed his eyes. Not meditating. Just closing them. Just being quiet for a moment in a life that had been all noise, all achievement, all control. And in that moment—just for a heartbeat—he felt something. A warmth. In his chest. Where his heart was. He opened his eyes immediately. Frightened. But the warmth remained. Just barely. Just enough to be noticed. He sat with it. Confused. Curious despite himself. The warmth was...pleasant. Not threatening. Not painful. Just warm. Just there. For forty years, he'd felt nothing in his chest but tension and emptiness. And now there was warmth. Just a flicker. But real. He touched his chest, as if he could feel it through his skin. And in that moment, he understood what Friedrich had been talKing about. What the Rousseau document described. What millions of people were discovering.

This was what he'd been missing. This warmth. This sense of... something. Life? Love? Connection? He didn't have words for it. But it was there. And it was real. He sat for five more minutes. Just feeling the warmth. Just being with it. And when he finally stood and went to bed, something in him had shifted. Not transformed. Not converted. But shifted. The doubt had grown into something else. Into possibility. Into the first tentative wondering: What if they're right? What if there is something else? What if I've been swimming on the surface my whole life, and there are depths I've never touched? What if I don't have to die empty?

The Quiet Miracles Multiply

All over the world, people who'd learned to dive were discovering something they'd never expected. Life became... softer. Easier. Not in the sense that challenges disappeared. But in the sense that they flowed differently. Annette in Lyon noticed it when clients started appearing exactly when she needed them. Not through marketing or networking. Just appearing. Referrals from people she'd never met. Opportunities emerging from unexpected places. Her practice thriving not because she was building it, but because she was allowing it to grow.

Thomas in London noticed it when insights came exactly when needed. Not through analysis or strategy. Just knowing. Seeing patterns before they fully emerged. Understanding clients' needs before they articulated them. Not as manipulation—because the knowing came with compassion, with genuine desire to help—but as clarity. As natural perception that arose from swimming in the Ocean. A woman in Vancouver who'd been struggling with poverty for years started diving. Within two months, she found a job she loved, doing work that felt meaningful. Not through aggressive job hunting. She'd just met someone at a park, started talKing, mentioned her skills, and was offered a position. Right place, right time. But not coincidence. Flow.

A man in Cape Town who'd been estranged from his brother for fifteen years sat in meditation one morning and felt a powerful impulse: Call him. He did. His brother answered, voice shaKing. "I was just sitting here, thinKing about you. ThinKing I should reach out. After all these years. And then you called." They reconciled that day. A teacher in Mumbai who'd been trying unsuccessfully to reach a troubled student for months learned to dive. Started dropping into the Ocean before class each day. Started approaching the student from presence instead of from agenda. Within two weeks, the student opened up. Started trusting. Started learning. The teacher didn't know what she'd done differently. She'd just stopped trying so hard. Had just been present. And that was enough.

These weren't dramatic miracles. They were quiet ones. The kind that rational minds could explain away as coincidence, confirmation bias, selective memory. And maybe they were. Or maybe—when you stopped fighting the current, when you let yourself be carried by the Ocean—you ended up exactly where you needed to be. With exactly who you needed to meet. Receiving exactly what you needed to receive. Not because you manifested it. Not because you controlled reality. But because you stopped creating resistance. Stopped swimming against the current. Let the Ocean carry you. And the Ocean, it turned out, knew where you needed to go.

The Felt Experience Amélie sat in her apartment in Paris—the same apartment she'd fled from six months ago in terror, but had returned to when she realised the families couldn't actually hurt her anymore. Not because she had protection. But because she'd become too visible. Too many people watching. Too many people practicing what she taught. Eliminating her would only amplify her message.

She was writing the final section of her expanded manuscript. The part she'd been avoiding because it was hardest to put into words. The part about how it actually feels to live from the Ocean. Not the theory. Not the technique. But the lived experience. She wrote: "There's a heat behind the sternum that becomes familiar to everyone who dives regularly. It's not metaphorical. It's physical. You can feel it. Actual warmth. Actual presence. As if your heart—the physical organ—has woken up after years of sleep. At first, it comes during meditation. You're sitting, breathing, dropping into the depths, and suddenly there it is. Warmth blooming in your chest. Spreading through your body. It feels like love, but not directed at anyone. Just love as a state. As the fundamental quality of consciousness itself.

The first few times, it's so beautiful you might cry. After years of feeling disconnected, of living from your head, of trying to think your way through life—suddenly you feel. Not emotions. Not thoughts about feelings. But the Ocean itself, flowing through the heart. And as you practice, as you dive daily, this warmth becomes your constant companion. It's always there. Sometimes faint, just a gentle presence. Sometimes strong, filling your entire chest with liquid light. But always there. Reminding you that you're not alone. That you're held. That you're swimming in consciousness itself.

People ask: what does the Ocean feel like? This is what it feels like. Like coming home. Like being held by something infinite that knows you completely and loves you anyway. Like belonging to existence itself. And from this warmth, from this heart-presence, everything else flows. The compassion that lets you feel others' pain without drowning. The clarity that shows you what's needed without analysis. The joy that bubbles up for no reason, just because you're alive. The peace that stays steady even when life is chaos. The knowing—the direct knowing—that everything is fundamentally okay, even when everything is clearly not okay at the surface level. You learn to live from the heart instead of from the head. Not abandoning thinKing—you still need your mind, still use analysis when appropriate. But not leading with it. Not maKing it primary.

The heart leads. The head serves. And this reordering changes everything. When you live from the head, life is a problem to be solved. A challenge to be conquered. A situation to be controlled.

You're always strategising, always planning, always trying to force outcomes. When you live from the heart, life is a dance to be danced. A flow to be joined. A river to be swum. You're still choosing, still acting, still participating. But from presence. From response. From sensing what wants to happen and aligning with it rather than fighting it. And the small miracles start. Not because you're manifesting them. But because you're finally seeing what was always there. The synchronicities that occur constantly but that thinKing-mind dismisses. The help that arrives exactly when needed but that controlling-mind doesn't notice because it's too busy forcing other solutions. The ease that's available when you stop creating resistance. This is what people feel emanating from swimmers. This warmth. This presence. This quality of being that's attractive not because it's trying to attract, but because it's natural. Like the way flowers attract bees without effort. Like the way fire draws people to gather around it. There's something nourishing about being near someone who's swimming. Something that feeds a hunger you didn't know you had. And this is how it spreads. Not through argument or proselytising. But through being. Through the quiet joy that becomes visible to others. Through the peace that remains steady in crisis. Through the love that flows without agenda. Through the fire in the heart that others can sense even if they can't name it.

People ask: how will we know when enough people have awakened? When the tipping point comes? We'll feel it. In our hearts. All of us swimming in the Ocean will feel it simultaneously. Like the moment dawn breaks. Like the instant spring arrives. Like the breath when winter releases its grip. We'll feel the field itself shift. The Ocean rising through consciousness. The collective waking up.

And we'll know: it's time. The age of separation is ending. The age of remembering has begun. Not through force. Not through revolution. But through ten million people—then a hundred million, then a billion—learning to live from the heart instead of from the head. Learning to swim instead of drown. Learning to be what they always were but forgot: Ocean in form. Consciousness awake to itself. The Divine incarnate in flesh. This is the awakening. Not a distant hope. A present reality. Happening now. In your chest. In your heart. In the warmth that's there when you finally stop running and let yourself be held.

Welcome home. The Ocean has been waiting. And it's so, so glad you remembered.

Amélie finished writing and sat back. Her own chest was warm. Full. Overflowing with something that had no name but that she'd learned to trust completely. She saved the document. Uploaded it. And sent it out into the world—one more message in a bottle, one more invitation, one more reminder that the Ocean was real and rising and ready to receive anyone willing to dive. And in her heart, she felt it. The shift that was coming. The tipping point approaching. The critical mass gathering. Not yet. But soon. Very soon. The Ocean was rising. And nothing could stop it now.

The Meeting of Worlds

One month later, something unprecedented happened. Wilhelm Eisen requested a meeting with Amélie. Not to threaten. Not to negotiate. But to talk.

They met at a small café near the Place des Vosges — his choice, which surprised her. She had expected somewhere anonymous. This was the oldest square in Paris, the kind of place a person chose when they wanted, consciously or not, to feel the weight of time.

Elena came with Amélie, not for protection but as witness.

Marcus waited outside at the café across the street with coffee and a clear sightline.

Wilhelm arrived three minutes before the hour. He was, as always, precisely on time. But he arrived alone, without the usual attache-case precision of a man who moved with staff. No phone on the table. No prepared notes. He sat across from Amélie and Elena and ordered coffee and for a long moment simply looked at his hands. He looked older than sixty-eight. Not in his body — he still held himself with the particular uprightness of someone trained to project authority. But his face had the quality Amélie had learned to recognise in people who had recently undergone something that could not be undone. The look of a landscape after weather.

"I came to tell you that you've won," he said finally. "Not because we're surrendering. But because we can't win. The awakening is spreading too fast. The resonance effect is real. In five years, maybe ten, the old systems won't work anymore. Our methods are becoming obsolete."

"I didn't come to gloat," Amélie said. "If that's what you're expecting."

"No." He looked directly at her. "I came because I need to understand. I've been practicing. For six weeks. Just sitting. Just breathing. Just... trying." He paused. "My grandson Friedrich — before I sent him away, he left me a copy of your original document. I found it in my study the following morning, under the paperweight on my desk. He must have placed it there at some point. I don't know if it was deliberate." Elena said nothing. Amélie said nothing. "I read it," Wilhelm said. "Twice. And I recognised things. That is what was disturbing. I recognised the language for something I had assumed was a weakness to be trained out — a tendency I noticed in myself as a young man and systematically suppressed, because in the world I was raised in, it had no use. The warmth you describe. The sense of depth beneath ordinary experience. I recognised it as something I once had, and learned to close."

The coffee arrived. None of them touched it. "So I tried," he continued. "Every morning, for six weeks. Just sitting. Waiting to feel something. For the first three weeks, nothing. Just the noise in my head. The things I've built and the things I've done and the calculations I apparently cannot stop running even in silence." He stopped. "And then. Very faint. Just a flicker. But —" He touched his sternum with two fingers, briefly, unselfconsciously, then caught himself doing it and stopped.

"Is it real? The Ocean? Or am I wanting it so badly that I'm manufacturing it?"

"What do you feel right now?" Elena asked. "In your chest."

Wilhelm closed his eyes. A pause. Then: "Warmth. Faint. But there."

"That's real," Elena said softly. "That's the Ocean recognising itself. Saying: I'm here. I've always been here. You just didn't notice."

Wilhelm opened his eyes. They were wet. "I disowned my grandson," he said. The words came with the weight of a man who had been carrying them for a month. "I cast him out. Because he chose what you're describing over everything I built. And now I understand why he chose it. He found something real. Something I told myself didn't exist. I taught him that the warmth was weakness. That depth was risk. That you controlled your world or your world controlled you." He looked at Amélie. "He said he loved me anyway. When I sent him away. I've spent a month not being able to stop hearing it."

Amélie reached across the table and placed her hand over his. "It's not too late. The Ocean doesn't keep score. You can dive today, this moment, and it will receive you exactly as you are."

"But what I've done —"

"Will have consequences," Elena said. Her voice was clear and warm in equal measure. "The boomerang is real. When you dive deeply, you'll feel what you've created. You'll experience the suffering you've caused. Not as punishment from outside, but as the natural feedback of genuine connection. It will be painful. Possibly unbearable, some of it. But it is also the only path to becoming whole. To using what you carry — the brilliance, the organisational capacity, the extraordinary long-term thinKing — for service instead of control."

Wilhelm sat with this for a moment.

Then: "I want to find Friedrich."

"We can arrange that," Amélie said.

"And I want to learn to dive. Properly. Whatever that means at sixty-eight after forty years of doing everything your document says produces Surface Swimmers." There was something almost wry in the last phrase — the first hint, in this man, of the ability to see himself clearly.

"Is it possible? Or have I cut off the access permanently?"

"You felt the warmth," Elena said simply. "The access was never cut. You just learned to ignore it. The Ocean doesn't close doors."

Wilhelm stood. His shoulders shook, just once, then steadied. The tears ran down his face, and he did not wipe them, which was, Amélie thought, its own kind of beginning.

"Thank you," he said, "for not turning me away." He left money for the coffee and walked out into the Place des Vosges, the oldest square in the city, the afternoon light falling through the arcades the way it had fallen for four centuries.

Amélie and Elena watched him go. "Do you think he'll really transform?" Marcus asked, joining them after Wilhelm left. "I don't know," Elena said. "The pull back to old patterns is strong. The emptiness is familiar. Transformation is terrifying. He might try for a while and give up. Might touch the Ocean and then run from what it shows him."

"But," she continued, "he might not. He might be one of the ones who makes it through. Who faces what he's done, feels it fully, and chooses transformation anyway. And if Wilhelm Eisen can transform —if the head of one of the most powerful families can learn to dive and orient toward service—that changes everything."

"That's what we're doing here," Amélie said softly. "Holding space for transformation. For everyone. Even those who seem irredeemable. Especially those. Because the Ocean redeems everyone who's willing to be redeemed. And we're the ones reminding people that redemption is available." They sat in silence for a moment, feeling the weight of it. The work they'd taken on. The invitation they'd extended. The door they'd opened that could never be closed again. The Ocean was rising. And it would keep rising until everyone remembered they were already swimming in it. Until everyone came home.

The Tipping Point Approaches

Over the following months, reports came in from around the world. Ten million people practicing regularly. A million achieving stable diving capacity. The resonance effect accelerating. New practitioners touching the Ocean within days instead of months. The barrier thinning. The families splitting. Some choosing to fight. Some choosing to transform. Others paralysed between the two, unable to commit. More children escaping programming. More staff refusing to participate. More facilities shutting down. The suppression systems failing. The Compound Veil systems failing. Information spreading too fast to contain. The truth too widespread to suppress. And everywhere—everywhere—the quiet joy spreading. People waking up. Feeling the warmth in their chests. Learning to live from the heart. Discovering the small miracles. Finding the flow. Not perfect. Not everyone. But enough. Growing exponentially. Approaching critical mass.

The Remnant estimated they needed fifteen to twenty percent of the global population diving regularly for the tipping point. For the collective field itself to shift. For the Ocean to rise through consciousness so completely that separation became harder than connection. That control became more difficult than cooperation.

That the old paradigm became literally impossible to maintain. They were at two percent. But growth was exponential. Two percent would become four percent. Then eight. Then sixteen. Within a decade—maybe less—the world would transform. Not through revolution or war or the old paradigm's collapse. But through emergence. Through the new growing within the old until the old simply fell away like a snake's skin. Unnecessary. Obsolete. No longer able to contain what was emerging.

The age of separation was ending. The age of remembering had begun. The Ocean was rising. And in ten million hearts around the world, the warmth grew. The joy bubbled. The peace spread. The miracles multiplied.

Welcome home, the Ocean whispered. Welcome home. I've been waiting. And you've finally remembered. Finally, finally, remembered.

CHAPTER TWENTY-SIX

The Doorway

Paris, Autumn 2025

Paris, three weeks after the café meeting — the surrender, she had started thinKing of it, the morning the man from the families had sat across from her and asked what it felt like to dive.

The strange thing about everything changing was how ordinary it looked. Amélie sat at the wooden table in the corner of her apartment — her own apartment, not the safe house, not the monastery, not Elena's couch — and drank coffee in the morning light and listened to the city doing what Paris always did: existing with perfect indifference to any particular human drama. The moped below her window. The bakery smell from three doors down. The couple arguing on the pavement in the particular French register that could be passion or could be a disagreement about parKing.

Ten million people were practicing. The document had been translated into forty-seven languages. Three members of the families had now formally defected, including Wilhelm's niece, who had contacted Marcus last week asking, with a kind of desperate politeness, if someone could explain to her what diving was and how to begin.

And Amélie was sitting in her kitchen drinKing coffee. She had learned, in the months of work with the Remnant, that this was part of it too. The stillness between actions. The moments of simply being in a body, in a kitchen, in a city, in an ordinary Tuesday morning. The Ocean was not only in the depths of meditation — it was here too, underneath the moped noise and the coffee smell and the ordinary particular weight of being a human being alive in Paris in autumn.

Grand-mère Élise had known this. Had sat at her own kitchen table every Sunday morning writing letters by hand, and Amélie had thought it was just an old woman's habit. Now she understood it differently. It had been a practice. A way of being present in the world without retreating from it. Staying in the Ocean while standing in the kitchen.

She had been afraid, for a long time, of what she would find in that apartment. Not the grief — she had made some peace with that, not because the loss had become smaller but because she had grown larger around it. What she had been afraid of was something else. The weight of what her grandmother had known and waited to tell her. The inheritance waiting in that box on the kitchen table, in that letter in careful script. You carry what I carry. You have always been able to feel it, even if you have been afraid to name it.

She had been afraid that going back to the apartment would feel like an ending. A finalising. The last conversation she would ever have with a woman who was no longer there to have it.

She was still sitting with that when Marcus appeared in the doorway.

He had been working in the other room — he was always working, filling in the next piece of the picture, pulling together evidence for the second wave of publication. He looked at her the way people in the Remnant had learned to look at each other: not asking, but available. "Go," he said. He hadn't even seen what she was thinKing. Or perhaps he had. Either way.

"I'm not sure I'm ready," Amélie said.

He sat down across from her, wrapped his hands around his own coffee. "I've been watching you for months," he said. "You were ready the day you walked into the safe house. You just needed to get here first."

She thought about that. The idea of arrival — not as a place you reached but as a state you grew into. The way the monastery had felt like coming home not because it was her home but because she had finally become the person who could recognise home when she found it. "I'm going to go back to her apartment," she said.

"I know."

"I don't know when I'll be back."

"I know that too." He looked at her over his coffee. "The work will keep. Some things are more important than the work."

She left her coffee half-finished on the table and walked out into the October morning.

The apartment smelled of lavender and old paper and the particular dust of undisturbed rooms. The afternoon light came through the lace curtains and laid its same pattern on the floor it had always laid. Nothing had changed. Nothing had moved. The small wooden table by the kitchen window, where her grandmother had written letters by hand every Sunday morning for as long as Amélie could remember, was exactly where it had always been. She sat down at it. For a long moment she simply sat. Feeling the quietness of the room. The accumulated presence of decades — all the Sunday mornings, all the letters, all the time her grandmother had sat here knowing what she knew and waiting, patiently, for the right moment to pass it on. The box had been on the kitchen table. She could still feel the weight of it in her hands. The letter inside, in Grand-mère's careful script. You carry what I carry. You have always been able to feel it, even if you have been afraid to name it. She laid her hands flat on the wooden surface. The same table. The same light. And in her chest, steady and unmistakeable, the warmth. Not like the first time she had felt it — that half-frightened, half-desperate warmth in the café before everything began, when she had thought she was grieving herself into strangeness. This was different. Full and known. The warmth of the Ocean, familiar now as breathing, as the heartbeat she had learned to lead from.

She understood, sitting here in her grandmother's kitchen, that Élise had felt exactly this. Had sat at this table, on Sunday mornings, writing letters by hand, feeling this same warmth in her chest and living quietly from it. Had known what she carried and carried it with grace for eighty-two years. Had left Amélie the letter because she had known Amélie would need it. Had known, perhaps, that Amélie would sit here one day and feel the warmth and understand. The gifts work across death. The Ocean doesn't end where the body does. It was not exactly a presence. It was not a voice. But sitting in the honey light of the empty apartment, Amélie felt the connection — the same way she could feel other swimmers in the depths of meditation, lights in deep water, lives woven from the same source.

Grand-mère Élise was not in this room. But she was not gone. The warmth in Amélie's chest was partly hers. Had perhaps always been partly hers. She stayed for an hour. Not writing. Not working. Just sitting, as her grandmother had sat, feeling what her grandmother had felt. When she finally stood, she left the key on the table. She would not need to carry it anymore. The door was open now. She had stepped through. The Ocean was rising. And in the rue des Rosiers apartment, in the Sunday-morning light on a Tuesday afternoon, something that had waited eighty-two years to be passed on was finally, fully, received. Finally, finally, remembered.

She walked back through the Marais in the late afternoon light. The city was doing what it always did. A woman arguing on her phone outside the pharmacy. Two men unloading crates from a van, the thud of wood on cobblestone. The smell of coffee and exhaust and the particular cold that comes off the Seine in November, carrying something ancient with it, something the city had never quite lost. She had walked this street a hundred times. More. She had walked it grieving, distracted, afraid, purposeful, numb. She had walked it the morning after the Bibliothèque, unable to feel the ground under her feet. She had walked it three months ago, heading to a café to meet a man who wanted to surrender, carrying the weight of ten million people practicing something her grandmother had known in her bones. She walked it now and it was exactly the same street. And entirely different.

At the corner of rue des Francs-Bourgeois, a girl — fourteen, perhaps fifteen — was sitting on the low wall outside the pharmacy with her eyes closed. Not asleep. The quality of her stillness was unmistakeable. Her hands rested open in her lap. Her face was completely at ease in the particular way that had nothing to do with relaxation and everything to do with depth. Amélie stopped. A woman — her mother, by the resemblance — came out of the pharmacy and touched the girl's shoulder. The girl opened her eyes without startlement. Just opened them, as if she had simply returned from somewhere. "Tu étais là encore," the woman said. You were there again. Not alarmed. Used to it.

"Oui, Maman," the girl said. And then, noticing Amélie standing on the pavement, she held her gaze for one moment. The look of recognition. The look that Amélie had first seen in Sophia's eyes in the safe house above the bakery, that she had seen since in forty-nine rescued children, in a former Vatican archivist, in a Tibetan-trained Catalan Monk, in a man who had spent his life trying to suppress what he could now no longer deny.

The girl smiled. Small and certain. Then she slid off the wall and followed her mother inside. Amélie stood on the pavement for a moment.

Ten million people, the last count had read. A number too large to hold. But this was what it looked like, she understood. Not a movement. Not a revolution. Just a fifteen-year-old girl on a wall in the Marais, going where she had always been able to go, no longer needing to hide it. Just a mother who had learned to say: you were there again. Just that. Ordinary as breathing. Spreading the way breath spreads — not by force, but because it is what living things do.

Her phone buzzed. A text from Marcus. The news was brief: three new translation groups, Swahili, Tagalog, Mandarin. Elena's holding dinner. And Peter won't go to bed until he knows if you're coming.

She stood in the street and felt the warmth in her chest and thought about Peter, eight years old and three years broken and slowly, carefully, becoming something else.

Thought about Elena. Thought about the girl on the wall. Thought about her grandmother, sitting at a kitchen table on Sunday mornings for sixty years, carrying this quietly, alone, waiting. Not alone anymore.

She wrote back: On my way. The street opened before her. The city moved around her. Somewhere under the noise of the mopeds and the vendors and the couple arguing about parKing, she could feel it — the deep current, vast and unhurried, indifferent to urgency in the way that only ancient things can afford to be. It had been here before the city. It would be here after. It was not rising. It had never fallen. It had simply been waiting for enough people to remember it was there. She walked on. The Marais. The river smell. The last of the light going gold above the rooftops. Behind her, in a fourth-floor apartment on the rue des Rosiers, a key lay on a kitchen table. The door was open.

Ahead, somewhere in the gathering dark — two thousand years back, and no distance at all — an old woman stood in a temple doorway in Jerusalem and felt what was coming. Anna, daughter of Phanuel, of the tribe of Asher. She had been waiting eighty-four years. She was almost ready.

End of Book One

THE ETERNAL OCEAN SERIES

One: Bloodline of the Eternal Ocean

Paris, 2024. Dr. Amélie Rousseau is a medieval historian who doesn't believe in coincidences — until a midnight break-in at the Bibliothèque nationale hands her evidence that will upend everything she knows about the Merovingian bloodline, the lost tribe of Asher, and the nature of human consciousness itself.

What begins as a scholarly mystery becomes a race against those who have kept these secrets buried for thirteen centuries — and a journey into the depths of an Ocean that connects all things.

Book Two: Anna the Prophetess

Jerusalem, 4 BCE. Anna, daughter of Phanuel, has lived in the Temple for eighty-four years — a widow and prophetess from the tribe of Asher who sees what others cannot see. Her gifts are not supernatural. They are genetic inheritance, preserved through millennia of careful lineage, waiting for this one moment of recognition.

When a young couple presents their infant son at the Temple, Anna's lifetime of preparation crystallises into a single act of seeing — and sets in motion an awakening that will take two thousand years to complete.

Book Three: The Remnant

Present day. Johanne Smith is nineteen years old, a college dropout, and — according to every doctor she's seen — broken. ADHD. Dyslexia. Synesthesia. Anxiety that makes her feel everything too intensely.

Then she stumbles across a document — Dr. Rousseau's research — and discovers that every trait she's been taught to suppress is actually ancient consciousness architecture, encoded in her DNA by the tribe of Asher over two thousand years ago. She isn't broken. She's built for exactly this.

She has sixty days before everything changes. The question is which side of history she'll be on.

SNEAK PEEK: ANNA THE PROPHETESS

Book Two: The Eternal Ocean Series

The temple was silent except for the whisper of her breath.

Anna stood in the shadows, watching the young couple present their firstborn son to the priests. The child was small, wrapped in simple cloth, yet she felt it immediately—the unmistakable resonance of the bloodline. The same current she'd felt flowing through her own veins for eighty-four years.

This was no ordinary child.

She stepped forward into the lamplight, her ancient feet steady despite her age. The young mother—Mary, she'd learned—looked up with startled eyes as Anna approached.

"Blessed are you among women," Anna whispered, reaching out to touch the child's forehead. The moment her fingers made contact, she gasped.

The Ocean opened. Not as she'd known it—not as whispered promises and distant memory—but as living, breathing presence. The child's eyes met hers, impossibly aware, and in that gaze she saw everything: the bloodline stretching back to Atlantis, the thread of Asher woven through generations, the prophecy that would unfold over two millennia before the awakening could truly begin.

"What do you see?" Mary asked, her voice trembling.

Anna's own eyes filled with tears. "I see the bridge," she said. "The one who will hold the door open between worlds. Between the Ocean and the land. Between what was and what will be."

She looked up at Joseph, then back to Mary. "The bloodline continues through you. The promise made in ancient times is fulfilled in your son. But Mary..." Anna's voice dropped to a whisper. "The path will not be easy. The ones who guard the separation—they will come for him. Just as they came for the others. Just as they've hunted the bloodline since Atlantis fell."

"What do we do?" Joseph asked, his hand protectively on Mary's shoulder.

Anna smiled, though her heart ached with the knowing. "You do what all carriers of the bloodline have always done. You protect the knowledge. You pass on the truth. You teach him to dive. And when the time comes..." She paused, holding the child close one final time.

"When the time comes, you let him fulfil his purpose. Even if it breaks your heart to watch."

She handed the child back to Mary. "His name will be remembered. Not just for what he teaches, but for what he carries. The Ocean consciousness made flesh. The Divine Incarnate. The awakening that will take two thousand years to complete—but which begins today, in this temple, with this child."

Anna turned to leave, then looked back. "Twenty centuries from now, his teaching will be distorted, weaponised, used to control rather than liberate. But the truth will survive. Hidden in the bloodline. Encoded in those who remember. Waiting for the moment when enough people are ready to understand that what he demonstrated wasn't unique—it was the natural state of human consciousness when we finally stop swimming and remember we are the Ocean."

Mary clutched her son tighter. "Will we see you again?"

"I don't know," Anna said softly. "But my part is complete. The bloodline continues through you. And through him. And through all who will come after."

Anna the Prophetess

To be notified when Book Two releases, visit: www.lyndallkai.com.

ACKNOWLEDGMENTS

This book emerged from years of exploration, study, and meditation on the deep questions that have haunted humanity since we first looked up at the stars and wondered who we are. To the researchers, mystic, and scholars who have dedicated their lives to uncovering hidden history and exploring the nature of consciousness - thank you for blazing the trail. To the readers who have taken this journey with Amelie - thank you for your open minds and hearts.

And to everyone who has ever felt the warmth in their chest and wondered if there might be something more - this book is for you.

WHAT IS TRUE

Historical and Factual Notes

This novel is a work of fiction. Amélie Rousseau, Marguerite Valcourt, the Remnant, Unit 14, Director Crale, Father Matteu, and all other characters are invented. The events described did not happen.

The history, however, is real.

What follows maps the major historical and factual claims in this book to their documented sources. Where the novel departs from the evidence — into interpretation, speculation, or the author's own understanding — that departure is clearly marked. The reader is invited to verify everything and to form their own conclusions.

The sources listed are those the author consulted. They are not the only sources. The questions raised here have occupied serious scholars for centuries. What follows is a doorway, not a ceiling.

❖ ❖ ❖

I. THE MEROVINGIAN DYNASTY AND THE COUP OF 751 CE

1 The Merovingian Dynasty

The Merovingians were the ruling dynasty of the Franks from approximately 457 to 751 CE, founded by Merovech (Meroveus), whose origins remain obscure in the historical record. The dynasty produced Clovis I (c.466—511), who united the Frankish tribes and converted to Christianity; Dagobert I (603—639), regarded as the last powerful Merovingian King; and the line of later "do-nothing Kings" (rois fainéants) who held the title while Carolingian mayors of the palace exercised real power.

The royal power associated with long hair is well-documented. Gregory of Tours records that cutting the hair of a Merovingian prince was understood as depriving him of his claim to Kingship. This practice is not disputed by historians.

Source: Wood, Ian. The Merovingian Kingdoms, 450—751.
Longman, 1994.
Gregory of Tours. History of the Franks, trans. Lewis Thorpe. Penguin
Classics, 1974.

2 The Carolingian Coup of 751 CE

Verified historical record. Pepin III sent envoys to Pope Zachary I asking whether the man who held the power of a King should bear the title. The Pope's response — recorded in the Royal Frankish Annals — was that it is better that the man who has the power should be called King. Childeric III, the last Merovingian, was tonsured and sent to a monastery. This was the first papal authorisation of the deposition of a reigning Christian King in European history.

The marriage of Pepin's wife Bertrada of Laon into a line with Merovingian connections is documented in the Annals of Saint Bertin and later sources. Whether the Carolingians understood this as preserving the bloodline, as political legitimacy, or simply as a useful genealogical claim is disputed. The novel takes the first interpretation.

Source: Royal Frankish Annals (Annales Regni Francorum),
749—751 entries, trans. B. Scholz. University of Michigan Press,
1970.

McKitterick, Rosamond. The Frankish Kingdoms under the Carolingians. Longman, 1983.
Nelson, Janet. "Kingship and Empire." Cambridge History of Medieval Political Thought, 1988.

3 The Assassination of Dagobert II

Verified historical record. Dagobert II was murdered while hunting near Stenay in December 679 CE. The Life of Saint Wilfrid (written by Stephen of Ripon in the early eighth century) records that he was killed by treacherous dukes with the consent of the bishops. He was subsequently venerated as a martyr. His exile to Ireland as a child is documented; he spent years in Irish monasteries before returning to claim the Austrasian Kingship in 676.

Source: Stephen of Ripon. Life of Bishop Wilfrid, trans. J.F. Webb.
Penguin Classics, 1983.

Wood, Ian. The Merovingian Kingdoms. Op. cit.

4 The Chronicle of Fredegar

A genuine seventh-century Frankish compilation, c.658—660 CE. The Latin passage connecting Frankish origins to the tribe of Israel (Et dicunt quidam quod gens Francorum de tribu Israel descendit) is authentic. The Merovech passage — describing his conception from a sea-beast of Neptune — is equally authentic. Most historians treat both as legendary. The marginal annotation Non est fabula. Vidi signum. Sanguis recordatur is fictional, but marginal annotations of this character exist throughout medieval manuscript traditions.

Source: Fredegar. Chronicarum libri IV, ed. B. Krusch. MGH SRM
II, 1888.

Wallace-Hadrill, J.M. The Fourth Book of the Chronicle of Fredegar.
Oxford University Press, 1960.

II. THE TRIBE OF ASHER AND THE SCATTERED TRIBES

5 The Tribe of Asher

Asher was the eighth son of Jacob, born of Zilpah (Genesis 30:12—13). The tribe settled in the western Galilee and coastal plain bordering Phoenicia, with territory extending to Tyre and Sidon (Joshua 19:24—31). Jacob's blessing of Asher (Genesis 49:20) and Moses's blessing in Deuteronomy 33:24—25 are among the most expansive blessings given to any tribe. The anointing imagery of oil as Divine presence runs throughout the Hebrew scriptures.

The Testament of the Twelve Patriarchs is a genuine second-century BCE text. The passages regarding Zebulun and mercy are authentic.

Source: Brown, Raymond E. The Birth of the Messiah. Doubleday, 1977, revised 1993.

Charles, R.H. (trans.). The Testaments of the Twelve Patriarchs. Clarendon Press, 1908.

6 The Assyrian Conquest and the Westward Migration

Verified historical record. The Northern Kingdom of Israel fell to Assyria between 734 and 722 BCE. Samaria fell to Sargon II in 722 BCE. The ten tribes of the northern Kingdom were dispersed and lost to subsequent historical record as identifiable entities. The westward migration of some Israelite refugees via Phoenician trade routes is historically plausible — Asher's territory bordered Phoenicia directly, and Phoenician trade networks reached Iberia, Gaul, and beyond. Modern genetic research has documented Levantine markers in Western European populations, though the precise origin of these populations is contested.

Source: Finkelstein, Israel, and Neil Asher Silberman. The Bible Unearthed. Free Press, 2001.

Kuhrt, Amélie. The Ancient Near East c.3000—330 BC. Routledge, 1995.

7 Anna the Prophetess

Luke 2:36—38 is verified scripture. Anna is explicitly identified as from the tribe of Asher. She is described as a prophetess, living in the Temple in fasting and prayer. Upon seeing the infant Yeshua, she immediately recognised him and spoke of him to all who were waiting for the redemption of Jerusalem. Why Luke specifies her tribal identity — a detail omitted for almost every other figure in the nativity account — is a question without a satisfying scholarly explanation. The novel offers one interpretation. It is an interpretation, not established fact.

Source: Brown, Raymond E. The Birth of the Messiah. Op. cit.

Fitzmyer, Joseph A. The Gospel According to Luke I—IX. Anchor Bible, Doubleday, 1981.

III. BEFORE RECORDED HISTORY

8 The Shemsu-Hor and the Turin King List

The Turin King List is a genuine Egyptian document, dating to the reign of Ramesses II (c.1279—1213 BCE). It records pre-dynastic rulers described as the Shemsu-Hor — the Followers of Horus — with reigns totalling over 13,000 years. The document is authentic and damaged; precise readings of the longer reigns are contested. Mainstream Egyptology treats the pre-dynastic sections as mythological. The novel treats them as potentially recording something else.

Source: Gardiner, Alan H. The Royal Canon of Turin. Griffith Institute, 1959.

Quirke, Stephen. Who Were the Pharaohs? British Museum Publications, 1990.

9 The Apkallu: Seven Sages of Sumer

The Apkallu tradition is documented in genuine cuneiform sources — the Uruk King List and Babylonian incantation texts. Seven antediluvian sages served as counsellors to pre-Flood Kings and emerged from the primordial waters (Abzu). They are depicted in Mesopotamian art in fish-human form, understood by scholars as symbolic of their origin from the depths, not as zoology. The tradition that these sages transmitted knowledge of civilisation before the Flood is consistent across Mesopotamian sources.

Source: Reiner, Erica. "The Etiological Myth of the Seven Sages." Orientalia 30 (1961).

Van Dijk, J.J.A. "Le motif cosmique dans la pensée sumérienne." Acta Orientalia 28 (1964—65).

10 Plato, Critias, and Atlantis

The Atlantis accounts appear in Plato's Timaeus and Critias (c.360 BCE). The passage quoted in this novel — concerning the dilution of Divine nature through intermarriage with mortals, and the corruption that followed — is verbatim from the Critias. The scholarly consensus is that Atlantis is Plato's philosophical invention. The novel treats it as potentially encoding a memory of a prior civilisation. That is the author's interpretation.

Source: Plato. Timaeus and Critias, trans. Desmond Lee. Penguin Classics, 1977.

Vidal-Naquet, Pierre. "Atlantis and the Nations." Critical Inquiry 18:2 (1992).

11 Genesis 3:21 — The Garments of Skin

The Kabbalistic reading of the garments of skin as physical bodies — the moment of incarnation into matter — is an established strand of Jewish mystical thought, most fully developed in the Zohar. It is not mainstream Christian theology. The same interpretive strand appears in Gnostic texts including the Gospel of Philip, in Vedic cosmological accounts of consciousness descending through progressively denser ages, and in Plato's language about the dilution of Divine nature. The novel treats the convergence of these accounts as potentially describing the same cosmological event from different cultural vantage points.

Source: Matt, Daniel C. (trans.). The Zohar: Pritzker Edition, Vol. I. Stanford University Press, 2004.
Layton, Bentley (trans.). The Gnostic Scriptures. Doubleday, 1987.
Swami Sri Yukteswar. The Holy Science. Self-Realization Fellowship, 1894.

IV. GENETICS AND THE BLOODLINE
12 The Cohen Modal Haplotype

The Cohen Modal Haplotype (CMH) is a well-documented genetic phenomenon. A specific pattern of Y-chromosome markers appears with significantly higher frequency in Jewish men who identify as Cohanim (claiming descent from Aaron, brother of Moses) than in the general population. The original study by Skorecki et al. (Nature, 1997) attracted wide attention as a demonstration of genetic continuity across three thousand years. Subsequent research has largely confirmed the finding.

The novel hypothesises an equivalent phenomenon transmitted through the maternal mitochondrial line. No equivalent CMH has been established for the tribe of Asher. The hypothesis is the novel's own.

Source: Skorecki, K., et al. "Y Chromosomes of Jewish Priests." Nature 385 (1997).
Hammer, M.F., et al. PNAS 97 (2000).

13 The Shroud of Turin: DNA Research

The Shroud of Turin is a linen cloth approximately 4.4 × 1.1 metres bearing the image of a man whose injuries are consistent with crucifixion. It is housed at the Cathedral of Saint John the Baptist in Turin and venerated by many as the burial cloth of Yeshua. Its age, origin, and the nature of its image remain subjects of intense and unresolved scholarly and scientific debate.

In 2015, a team led by Gianni Barcaccia of the University of Padova published a genetic analysis of DNA extracted from dust particles vacuumed from the Shroud surface, in Scientific Reports. The study identified plant DNA from dozens of species and human mitochondrial DNA from multiple geographic origins. Among the human profiles detected, haplogroup H33 was identified — a mitochondrial haplogroup associated predominantly with the Druze population of present-day Israel, Jordan, Lebanon, and Syria. The researchers also noted that the Shroud's overall DNA profile was broadly consistent with linens of Middle Eastern origin from approximately 55—74 CE.

What the study does not show: no specific tribal identification has been made. The DNA is fragmentary and drawn from surface contamination accumulated over centuries; it cannot be attributed to any single individual. No claim of a connection to any Israelite tribe, including Asher, has been made by the researchers. The study's methodology and conclusions remain contested.

The scene in Chapter 6 in which Dowed speculates about the Shroud's DNA profile and its possible connection to the Ashérite bloodline is presented within the story as his own interpretation — explicitly framed as unproven and going beyond what the evidence demonstrates. Readers are encouraged to consult the study directly.

Source: Barcaccia, G., et al. "Uncovering the Sources of DNA Found on the Turin Shroud." Scientific Reports 5 (2015).

V. THE AHNENERBE AND THE HISTORY OF SUPPRESSION

14 The SS Ahnenerbe Program

The Ahnenerbe (Ancestral Heritage Society) was a genuine SS institution, established in 1935. Officially an archaeological and cultural research organisation, it conducted expeditions to Tibet, Iceland, and the Middle East. Himmler's personal obsession with race, ancestry, and a superior ancient civilisation is extensively documented. The novel's claim that the Nazis specifically sought families with unusual perceptual or consciousness capacities extends documented fact into interpretation.

Source: Pringle, Heather. The Master Plan: Himmler's Scholars and the Holocaust. Hyperion, 2006.

Goodrick-Clarke, Nicholas. The Occult Roots of Nazism. New York University Press, 1992.

15 Ravensbrück

A genuine concentration camp, operating 1939—1945 north of Berlin, primarily for women. Between 50,000 and 90,000 women died there. The camp conducted medical experiments on prisoners (the Rabbit experiments). The character of Céleste is fictional; the historical context is real.

Source: Morrison, Jack G. Ravensbrück: Everyday Life in a Women's Concentration Camp. Markus Wiener Publishers, 2000.

16 A Pattern of Suppression

The following events are verified historical record, not interpretation.

The destruction of the Druidic tradition at Anglesey (Mona) in 60 CE by Suetonius Paulinus is recorded by Tacitus (Annals XIV.29—30). The Druids were specifically targeted and their sacred groves destroyed.

The Council of Nicaea (325 CE), convened under the Emperor Constantine, established the Christian canon — the authoritative list of texts that would constitute the New Testament. Dozens of gospels, epistles, and acts were excluded, among them texts describing direct individual access to the Divine without priestly mediation. Many of these texts were subsequently suppressed or destroyed. The Nag Hammadi library — a collection of Gnostic texts discovered buried in the Egyptian desert in 1945 — is physical evidence of manuscripts that were hidden, almost certainly to protect them from destruction following the canonisation. This is not disputed history.

BLOODLINE OF THE ETERNAL OCEAN

The Edict of Thessalonica (380 CE) made Nicene Christianity the sole legal religion of the Roman Empire. What followed was the systematic closure of temples, oracle sites, and mystery schools — institutions that had for centuries provided direct experiential access to the sacred outside institutional structures. The Oracle at Delphi, active for nearly a thousand years, was silenced. The Eleusinian Mysteries, practiced for approximately two thousand years and attended by initiates including Plato, Aristotle, and Cicero, came to an end. These were not marginal practices; they were among the most significant spiritual institutions of the ancient world.

The Albigensian Crusade (1209—1229) was the first European military campaign directed by the papacy against a Christian population. The Cathar theology of Languedoc taught that the Divine was within, directly accessible, without priestly mediation. Montségur fell March 1244. Approximately 220 perfecti were burned at the Camp dels Cremats.

The European witch trials (c.1450—1750) resulted in between 40,000 and 60,000 executions, the majority of them healers, herbalists, and midwives — practitioners of knowledge existing outside institutional church authority.

The pattern is real. The interpretation of why these suppressions occurred is the author's own.

Source: Tacitus. Annals, trans. Michael Grant. Penguin Classics, 1996.

Pagels, Elaine. The Gnostic Gospels. Random House, 1979.

Robinson, James M. (ed.). The Nag Hammadi Library. Harper & Row, 1978.

Freeman, Charles. The Closing of the Western Mind. Heinemann, 2002.

Pegg, Mark Gregory. A Most Holy War. Oxford University Press, 2008.

Levack, Brian P. The Witch-Hunt in Early Modern Europe. Third edition. Longman, 2006.

VI. Yeshua, THE LOST YEARS, AND THE EASTERN TRADITIONS

17 The Lost Years of Yeshua

The Gospels provide no account of Yeshua's life between approximately ages twelve and thirty. The only exception is Luke 2:41—52 — the Temple at age twelve. The scholarly consensus is that Yeshua remained in Galilee as a craftsman, and that the absence of information reflects the Gospel writers' lack of interest in his pre-ministry life. This consensus does not claim to know where Yeshua was; it claims only that theories of Eastern travel are unsubstantiated.

Source: Ehrman, Bart D. Yeshua: Apocalyptic Prophet. Oxford University Press, 1999.

Crossán, John Dominic. The Historical Yeshua. HarperSanFrancisco, 1991.

18 The Notovitch Controversy

Nicolas Notovitch was a genuine Russian journalist who in 1894 published The Unknown Life of Yeshua Christ, claiming to have discovered manuscripts at Hemis Monastery in Ladakh describing Yeshua—called "Saint Issa"—travelling to India during the lost years. The story was immediately challenged. The Indologist Max Müller corresponded with the head lama at Hemis, who denied that Notovitch had visited or that such manuscripts existed. J. Archibald Douglas visited Hemis in 1895 and obtained sworn depositions denying the claims. The scholarly consensus is that Notovitch fabricated the story.

Nicholas Roerich (1925) and Swami Abhedananda (1922) both claimed to have seen similar manuscripts — both after Notovitch's bestselling publication. Bart Ehrman has stated that no reputable New Testament scholar gives the Issa manuscripts any credence.

Father Matteu's character holds genuine photographs. This is fiction. The Notovitch controversy is real. The novel's suggestion that the manuscripts may be fraudulent while an underlying oral tradition might have roots in historical reality is presented as interpretation, not fact.

Source: Notovitch, Nicolas. The Unknown Life of Yeshua Christ. R.F. Fenno, 1894.

Mueller, Max. "The Alleged Sojourn of Christ in India." Nineteenth Century 36 (1894).

Ehrman, Bart D. Lost Christianities. Oxford University Press, 2003.

19 Hemis Monastery

Hemis Monastery is real — a genuine Buddhist monastery in Ladakh, established in the seventeenth century, housing significant manuscript collections. It does not, to any documented knowledge, contain manuscripts about Yeshua. The fictional documents in this novel are a narrative device.

Source: Snellgrove, David, and Tadeusz Skorupski. The Cultural Heritage of Ladakh. Aris & Phillips, 1977—1980.

20 The Tibetan Recognition of Tulkus

The Tibetan Buddhist system for recognising reincarnated lamas (tulkus) is genuine and has been practiced for centuries. Extended meditation, interpretation of signs, and testing of candidate children with objects belonging to the deceased lama are all documented aspects of the process. The recognition of the 17th Karmapa in 1992 is a documented event. Father Matteu's claim to have witnessed it is fictional; the ceremony itself is real.

Source: Tenzin Gyatso (H.H. the Dalai Lama). Freedom in Exile. HarperCollins, 1990.

VII.   THE   CHRISTIAN   CONTEMPLATIVE TRADITION

21 The Desert Fathers and Hesychasm

The Desert Fathers and Mothers were real historical figures who withdrew to the Egyptian and Syrian deserts from the late third century onwards. Their sayings, collected in the Apophthegmata Patrum, remain among the most important documents of early Christian spirituality. Abba Macarius, Abba Arsenius, Abba Poemen, Amma Syncletica, and Abba Moses are all genuine; the passages attributed to them in this novel are authentic or closely paraphrased.

Hesychasm — from the Greek hesychia (stillness) — is a genuine tradition within Eastern Orthodox Christianity. The fourteenth-century Hesychast movement, associated with Gregory Palamas and the Monks of Mount Athos, taught the descent of the mind (nous) into the heart (kardia), coordinated with breathing, seeKing an experience of uncreated Divine light. The Hesychast controversy was one of the most significant theological disputes in Eastern Church history.

Source: Ward, Benedicta (trans.). The Sayings of the Desert Fathers. Cistercian Publications, 1975.

Palamas, Gregory. The Triads, trans. John Meyendorff. Paulist Press, 1983.

22 Evagrius Ponticus

Evagrius Ponticus (345—399 CE) was a genuine and significant Desert Father, whose systematic writings on the contemplative life were foundational for later Western developments. His theology was condemned at the Fifth Ecumenical Council of Constantinople in 553 CE, and his works were suppressed or circulated under other names for centuries. Structural similarities between Evagrian contemplative practice and Indian meditation traditions have been noted by some researchers; whether these reflect shared origin, cultural contact, or independent convergence is a genuine scholarly question without consensus.

Source: Evagrius Ponticus. The Praktikos and Chapters on Prayer, trans. John Eudes Bamberger. Cistercian Publications, 1981.

23 Tummo: Tibetan Inner Heat Practice

Tummo (gtum mo) is a genuine Tibetan Buddhist practice, classified among the Six Yogas of Naropa. Practitioners develop the capacity to generate intense body heat through breathing and visualisation. Herbert Benson and colleagues at Harvard Medical School published a documented study in Nature (1982) verifying that practitioners could generate measurable body heat and survive sub-zero temperatures in thin cotton robes.

The parallel drawn in this novel between tummo and the Hesychast "prayer of the heart" is the author's interpretation. It is not an established scholarly position, though it has been explored in comparative religious studies.

Source: Benson, Herbert, et al. "Body Temperature Changes During the Practice of g Tum-mo Yoga." Nature 295 (1982).
Evans-Wentz, W.Y. Tibetan Yoga and Secret Doctrines. Oxford University Press, 1935.

VIII. CONSCIOUSNESS, ENVIRONMENT, AND THE PINEAL GLAND

24 Pineal Gland Calcification

Calcification of the pineal gland is a genuine and documented physiological phenomenon. Calcium deposits accumulate in pineal tissue with age; differences in calcification rates between pre-industrial and contemporary populations have been observed in radiological research. The pineal gland produces melatonin and has been proposed as a site of DMT (dimethyltryptamine) synthesis in mammals, though evidence for significant DMT production in the human pineal gland remains contested.

The claim that deliberate environmental manipulation has been used to accelerate pineal calcification as population-level consciousness suppression is not established fact. The environmental suppression mechanism depicted in the novel — referred to as Compound Veil — is entirely fictional. The broader observation Marcus makes about modern environments being measurably less conducive to contemplative states is the author's interpretation of real but contested research; it is presented as such within the story, with Sophia explicitly pushing back and Marcus consistently declining to claim more than the evidence supports.

Source: Strassman, Rick. DMT: The Spirit Molecule. Park Street Press, 2001.

Benson, Herbert, et al. "Body Temperature Changes During the Practice of g Tum-mo Yoga." Nature 295 (1982).

IX. THE CONVERGENCE OF TRADITIONS
25 The Ocean: Common Ground

The observation that mystical and contemplative traditions across separated cultures describe structurally similar experiences has been the subject of serious scholarship since William James. The Perennial Philosophy — the argument that the world's great spiritual traditions share a common metaphysical core — has its proponents and its critics in comparative religious studies. No scholarly consensus exists on whether these convergences reflect a common underlying reality or independent human responses to the interior life.

The specific traditions drawn on in this novel include:

The Vedantic concept of Brahman — the universal consciousness underlying all phenomena, expressed in the Upanishads through Tat tvam asi (That thou art) — is one of the most developed philosophical articulations of the idea that individual and universal consciousness are ultimately one. The Upanishads date to approximately 800—200 BCE.

The Buddhist teaching of Buddha-nature (tathagatagarbha) holds that all sentient beings possess an innate capacity for awakening. Dzogchen teachings describe rigpa — the natural state of awareness — as primordially pure, timelessly present, and oceanic in scope.

Kabbalistic thought describes Ein Sof (literally Without End) as the infinite Divine ground from which all existence emanates. The Zohar's commentary on Genesis is a primary source for the garments-as-bodies interpretation noted above.

The Sufi teaching of fana — annihilation of the separate self — and baqa — subsistence in God — as articulated by Ibn 'Arabi (1165—1240) parallels the diving and integration described throughout this novel.

The convergences are real. The interpretation — that they point to a single underlying reality — is the author's own.

Source: James, William. The Varieties of Religious Experience. Longmans, Green, 1902.

Huxley, Aldous. The Perennial Philosophy. Harper & Brothers, 1945.

Corbin, Henry. Alone with the Alone: Creative Imagination in the Sūfism of Ibn Arabi. Princeton University Press, 1969.

A NOTE ON METHOD

This novel began as personal research — an attempt to confirm through documented sources what the author already sensed to be true. Every historical claim was verified before inclusion. Where the evidence was ambiguous, that ambiguity is noted. Where scholars disagree, the disagreement is acknowledged.

The fiction is a container. The history is the cargo.

The ocean-consciousness at the centre of this story is neither fiction nor provable academic fact. It is the direct perception of the author, corroborated by the testimony of every contemplative tradition encountered — and by the reports of the millions of ordinary people who have, throughout history, quietly and without institutional permission, found their way to the depths.

If you have found your way to these depths through your own experience — not through this novel's fictional world, but through your own life — these notes were written with you in mind. The history documented here is real and can be independently verified. The lineages described are drawn from genuine scholarship. The pattern of suppression — the Albigensian Crusade, the witch trials, the silencing of the Druidic tradition, the destruction of the Gnostic gospels, the closing of the mystery schools — is documented in the historical record and detailed in the notes above. What you make of it, and whether any of it illuminates something you already know, belongs entirely to you.

The sources above are a beginning. The ocean is deeper than any bibliography.

— Lyndall Kai

ABOUT THE AUTHOR

Lyndall Kai is an Australian writer whose work sits at the crossing point of history, consciousness, and the stories we inherit without knowing it. The Eternal Ocean Series grew from years of historical research into the Merovingian bloodlines, the scattered tribes of Israel, and the contemplative traditions that appear independently across cultures — and from a longer, more personal investigation into her own lineage and the spiritual experiences she could never quite explain away.

She has spent many years exploring the nature of consciousness, and the question at the heart of this series — what if the gifts described in ancient traditions are real, and what if they run in families — is not, for her, purely a fictional one.

She lives in Australia and is currently writing more books on the themes of The Eternal Ocean. The second book in this Series is, *Anna the Prophetess.*

You can find her at www.lyndallkai.com[1]

Did This Book Find You at the Right Moment?

If Bloodline of the Eternal Ocean stirred something in you — a memory, a question, a feeling you couldn't quite name — then it found exactly who it was meant to find.

Readers like you are how books like this survive and reach the people who need them most.

If you enjoyed the journey, I would be truly grateful if you could take a few moments to leave a review at the store where you purchased this book. It doesn't need to be long — even a sentence or two makes an enormous difference.

Reviews help other seekers find their way to this story.

The Ocean is vast. Help me send out the ripples.

With gratitude, Lyndall Kai

---

1. http://www.lyndallkai.com/

www.ingramcontent.com/pod-product-compliance
Lightning Source LLC
Chambersburg PA
CBHW032222050726
47591CB00001B/224